
★

What might have sent an apparently healthy man into a coma?

Joe returned to the house and knelt down again near the table. He wanted to see Vic Rabelard's medical crisis as an accident in an otherwise ordinary life, but his instincts told him that was wrong. Vic had lain on the floor in a coma for perhaps ten hours or more. The previous night he had been in a senseless fight in a bar, where he went in search of his wife, whom he did not want to declare missing but sought hopelessly on his own. There had been another fight not too many hours earlier, before the fight in the bar.

Now his wife was missing and Vic was in a coma.

★

D0733717

FRIENDS AND ENEMIES

SUSAN OLEKSIW

WORLDWIDE®

TORONTO • NEW YORK • LONDON
AMSTERDAM • PARIS • SYDNEY • HAMBURG
STOCKHOLM • ATHENS • TOKYO • MILAN
MADRID • WARSAW • BUDAPEST • AUCKLAND

FRIENDS AND ENEMIES

A Worldwide Mystery/May 2003

First published by Five Star.

ISBN 0-373-26457-7

Printed in U.S.A.

Cast of Characters

Eliot Keogh—paper salesman

Vic Rabelard—part owner of Laspac

Mindy Rabelard—his wife

Hugh Chase—executive of the Tveshter Paper Company

Becka Chase—his wife

Tony Ostell—her son

Richard Ostell—Tony's father, and partner in Laspac

Polly Jarman—chair of the high school reunion

Chief of Police Joe Silva, Sergeant Ken Dupoulis, and the men and women of the town of Mellingham.

ONE

A Friday Afternoon in June

ELIOT KEOGH pressed down the left-hand turn signal and veered into the passing lane, then sped past a black Cadillac going a sedate sixty miles an hour on what was left of the original Route 128 embracing Boston, from Braintree to Gloucester. He had only a few miles left to go to Mellingham, but he was in a hurry.

Chased by the lies he told his wife about this weekend—he'd been concentrating on telling the same story twice ever since he received the first announcement of the twenty-fifth reunion of the class of 1969—he hardly seemed able to get there fast enough. For the truth was, he'd been waiting ever since he was sixteen and his father had precipitously moved the family at the beginning of his senior year, after the best summer of his life, plunking him down into a school whose definition of cool, or awesome as his own teenage daughter said, was anathema to him. It took him weeks to get over the change and adapt but in the end it all went for nothing; he never really fit in. He told himself it was because he'd never abandoned his first school; he'd remained in his own heart a loyal member of the class of 1969 of Mellingham High School. There was some truth to this.

In the last year he had given up trying to share any of this with his daughter. Most of her friends had brand new cars as soon as they learned to drive, so she had looked with undisguised amusement and disbelief at his fond reminiscences of the days when his only friend with wheels had managed to get the old DeSoto moving and taken everyone down to the beach in the evening. She couldn't understand the sense of excitement they had felt; he came to wonder about it too, but the excitement never lessened no matter how much his daughter rolled her eyes.

The memories came back, richer and warmer, every time he drove through a New England town, to which he inevitably compared Mellingham. This one wasn't as pretty; it had no harbor, no village green. That one had a parking lot in the middle of town, something that would never happen in Mellingham. That other one had an old mill decaying right next to the new library; that would never happen in his hometown. In Mellingham the old furniture factories had been small, wooden buildings that were either torn down or converted to other uses, leaving little or no sign of their passing place in local history. And no town had the rocky ways of Mellingham, no quarries blasted for a new driveway, no massive boulders jutting out of an otherwise level backyard, no back roads rising and falling like a rollercoaster, no cliffs tumbling down to the crashing maws of a rapacious sea.

Eliot glanced down at the speedometer and tried to convert 147 kilometers into miles per hour. He knew he was over the speed limit, but he'd forgotten the formula he'd tried to memorize earlier. Even the state cop who had stopped him for speeding less than half an hour ago on Route 1 hadn't known how to convert kilometers to miles, and didn't care. Eliot had been so keyed up by that encounter that he almost lost his temper. Almost.

He had learned the hard way over the years to control his temper, which his wife once called a flash of lightning indoors. It only seemed odd to her that he never lost his temper at work and never turned his temper against her or their children. It wasn't odd to him. His anger had a specific trigger, and he rested his finger on it until the day when he could use it.

Eliot would never lose his temper at work. A salesman for a paper mill in northern New Hampshire, Eliot enjoyed listening to his customers' problems, eliciting long, detailed answers to tactful, probing questions. He was eager to satisfy his customers in any way he could—by speeding up a delivery, untangling billing errors, carrying suggestions for modifications or improvements of the product back to the mill, to the lab, where others would be quick to seize on a customer's wishes. It was a matter of pride to him that he worked well with his customers and in turn could point to his product almost anywhere. Whenever anyone asked him what he did, he got a kick out of saying, "I get the paper into your shirt collar so you can look like a pro after six hours of meetings in a non-air-conditioned room." Sometimes he said, "There's paper you can't see everywhere in this room, and most likely I got it here. Or someone like me." Eliot sold tech paper and loved every ounce of it.

When the cop rebuffed his gentle query about kilometers and miles, assuming that Eliot was looking for a way out of his ticket, Eliot clenched his teeth and said nothing.

"Let's see those rental papers," the officer said.

"Tourists love it around here. But we got lower speed limits." He passed Eliot the ticket.

"Thank you," Eliot managed to reply; he declined to point out the obvious, that only the car was from Quebec, not the driver.

"Well, enjoy it down here in the South." The trooper returned to his car and sped away, still laughing at his own witticism. Eliot remained determined to ignore him and his ignorant barbs. If it weren't for his dogged persistence at the rental office an hour ago, he might have no car at all. The Volvo with the Quebec license plate was the last car on the lot, reserved for a return trip to Canada in the middle of the week, but Eliot did, after all, have a reservation, which he reminded the agent of in no uncertain terms.

The houses through the trees fluttered in his peripheral vision as he lifted his foot from the gas pedal; the gregarious, all-ears salesman shrank aside to make room for the long dormant teenager thrilled that his old friends had not forgotten him. He could see their faces looming in the mackerel sky. The clouds drew him onward as he recognized and named first one face and then another. The final invitation had included a list of names and addresses of alumnae whether they were attending or not, and Eliot had been unable to move his eyes from the names with Mellingham addresses. He remembered every one of them, describing them over the years in detail to his wife while ignoring her comments that at least some of them might have lost a little hair, gained a little weight, grown a little coarse. It didn't matter; this time he would get what he wanted.

The first signs for Mellingham appeared and he slowed to sixty kilometers per hour. Surprised to see this part of the highway untouched by the stripping that had pursued him along Route 1 and then Route 128, he thought it might be a dream brought on by a fanciful longing for another time.

"No more Dr. Seuss for us," he said, imagining his young son just getting up from his nap. "Time to move on to adventure stories with real people. Keep our feet on the ground. Stay in the present." He took a deep breath to calm himself, a man who had reached adulthood abruptly, regretfully, bitterly.

The light blue Volvo turned off onto the first exit to Mellingham and drew up at the stop sign. Eliot looked left, then right, but not a single other vehicle broke the afternoon quiet. To the right the outlying homes of Mellingham beckoned him, to the left the country road that led through the woods to other towns. He had one more phone call to make this afternoon, but he didn't have to make it now. He had until five o'clock at least and it was barely three. He looked right again. What harm could it do, he thought, if I deviate from my schedule just this once?

He pulled the steering wheel to the left and moved onto Pickering Street, driving away from the coastal village of Mellingham and toward the woods, thick in this part of Massachusetts. For less than a mile he drove at barely thirty kilometers an hour, peering at one side of the densely wooded road, then the other. Suddenly, he jammed on his brakes, sending his open briefcase lurching to the floor, scattering papers and notebooks onto the carpet. He barely seemed to notice this as he turned off the road onto a dirt track, declared by a gray sign with black lettering to be the Pickering Preserve. Within a few feet the track widened onto a dirt lot close to the road and Eliot parked. His was the only car there.

With barely a thought to the customer whose order that very morning for paper to use in a new credit card would lift the company immediately from the B accounts to the A accounts, Eliot stuffed his papers, calendar, and address book into his briefcase, locked it, and threw it into the back seat. A million-dollar commitment might get him a promotion, a raise, a heart-stopping handshake from the boss, but a parking space in the old Pickering Preserve was a ticket to heaven. He climbed out of the Volvo, folded his jacket and left it on the front seat, and walked the few feet to the sign, the only part of the scene he had not recalled from his early years.

Across the street the same umbrella pines lined an old path, their branches rising high above long straight trunks, like skirts delicately lifted by ballerinas ready to step forward and dance. Farther down the road came the unmistakable whine of a car entering the tunnel of pines, where the road narrowed and boulders and trees conspired to distort sound, and the state transportation engineers and local conservationists did battle every four years over whether to keep or widen the road. A white pickup advanced, carrying a man and a woman, whose surprise-widened eyes locked onto his own, her expression reprising every look he had met there as a teenager walking out of the woods with a rifle resting in his arms after a day of hunting. It was eerie that so much should be the same.

Eliot locked his car and followed a narrow track into the woods, assessing the changes, hoarding what was unchanged. After a few moments he emerged into a clearing near a small pond. A picnic table marked the center. The sounds of the woods whistled around him. He found a hard dry patch of ground beneath a tree and sat down. For the first time that afternoon he admitted how tired he was.

For weeks he had suppressed all feelings of excitement for his reunion weekend, but they had percolated into his work, stimulating ideas and enthusiasms that had captured the imagination of his regular clients. They had responded to him as they never had before. He had won new business that was larger than anything he had dreamed of. And it was all legitimate, earned legally and ethically, out in the open for all to see. And now he was tired, far more tired than he had ever thought he could be. Not until this moment could he admit what a strain the last twenty-six years had been. Only now did he believe he could settle the score and lay it all to rest.

Eliot pushed his hand through his light brown hair, disarranging the strands neatly combed to conceal a widening bald spot at the back of his head. He folded his glasses and put them in his shirt pocket. His stomach strained against his belt, but this time he didn't think of the canvas in his waistband made by his company or one like it. Instead he thought how everything seemed familiar—the quality of daylight, the clouds in the sky, the trees along the road, the clearing where he met his friends for a hike, the anger fermenting within, even the faces of strangers in a car just passing by. He fell asleep then, the surprise of strangers reflecting his own.

THE TWO STUCCO HOMES at the end of Basker Court once stood politely aloof from the homes on nearby streets, associating only with each other. The building boom of the 1950s, such as it was in Mellingham, changed all that, but the psychological distance remained. Perhaps it was a matter of styles. The new homes on Basker Court were two-story or one-story clapboard houses, with tiny backyards and occasionally a tool shed. The stucco homes were different, duplicates of each other and a vision lost in 1929.

The differences between the two homes themselves were both more obvious and more subtle. On the left, the white stucco was occupied by Vic and Mindy Rabelard and his two teenage daughters; on the right the pink one was occupied by Becka and Hugh Chase and her son, Tony Ostell. They were all good friends and used to each other's ways. For instance, the Rabelards tended a meticulously manicured lawn, every inch of grass trimmed once a week whether it needed it or not. The only break in the even surface of the back lawn was a cobblestone barbecue built sixty years ago. By contrast, the Chases enjoyed a yard of naturally sprawling yew bushes and gleefully shedding flowering trees surrounding a picnic table. A number of wind chimes, of bamboo, metal, and glass, in various states of disrepair, hung among the branches. It was testimony to the solid friendship between the families that Vic Rabelard had never complained about the yew branches that seemed to extrude farther and farther into his property every spring, or that Hugh Chase never questioned the cause of a shrub suddenly dying from what seemed like an overdose of herbicide.

The garages showed similar disparities. For if the Rabelards' garage was a marvel of neatness, the Chases' was a wonder of disarray. This thought kept recurring to Becka Chase a few minutes after three o'clock on Friday afternoon as she tried to find one more spot in the garage to store another donation for the alumnae auction tomorrow night.

It wasn't that the pile was so large or the box on her hip so heavy; it was that there was so little vacant space to begin with and there always seemed to be one more container. Becka tossed a sticky light brown curl away from her eyes and set the box down on a stack of two. She listened to the sound of cardboard creaking. It was not music to her ears, but she dared not admit that. If Hugh knew how little she remembered of everything he told her about paper and paper products, he would be genuinely hurt. He had once told her he could identify how a paper product was made just by listening to it rustle or tear or crunch. It was no wonder he didn't want these stacks in the living room.

When Polly Jarman had first persuaded Becka to take charge of the alumnae auction, she had promised Becka that the auction would consist of nothing more than a few odds and ends to raise a little money for a scholarship fund. That seemed reasonable, so Becka had agreed, mentioning to Hugh a few days later that she might be storing some things in the living room for a month or so before the reunion weekend. But Hugh, placid, devoted Hugh, had been less than enthusiastic, insisting that she store the donations in the garage. This seemed unreasonable to Becka, but Hugh was adamant, so Becka gave in. Now, as she surveyed the piles, she wondered how she could have been so wrong.

It made her uneasy, for the fact was she seemed to be wrong a lot lately. That was about all she was willing to admit to herself—going any further was too painful and too frightening, too demanding of a woman who was ill-equipped to look the truth in the eye. So she blamed other people—Polly for talking her into something without fair warning of its size, Hugh for being non-supportive, the women who cooked and served the meals at the small school cafeteria where she worked for being slovenly and careless and making her look bad.

Every five years her class held a reunion and she went dutifully to each event. She had remained friends with most of her classmates, at least on the surface, and she could usually come up with an excuse to avoid the others. But this reunion seemed to be different, so different that she forgot how she felt and wondered what it was that was stirring people up. Polly, elected class secretary in 1969 and the self-chosen chair of the event, was positively fey, buzzing around town spreading sweetness and light. Becka had a barely controllable urge to strangle her.

Becka balanced a paper bag atop another pile, waited for it to fall; when it didn't, she quickly closed the garage door, and headed to the street, to close up her car. She plucked the mail from the box and entered the house. It was a nice day so she left the front door open. At a small table by the stairs in the hall she arranged the mail, bills and letters in one pile, circulars and catalogues in another, and her son's, Tony's, mail in a third. Though it was hot, she liked the warmth of the sun as it filled the hallway. The house was cozy in winter and airy in summer with large windows and three rooms set in a line, each with a fireplace. Anyone could look from the front door to the back of the house in a single glance, and after many years it had come to feel like a refuge. She walked through to the kitchen just as the back door opened.

"Oh, it's you, Vic. I was just going to call Mindy," Becka said. "You taking the afternoon off?"

"Good timing, is it?" Tall and stocky with black

hair combed straight back, Vic Rabelard had soft, still features that concealed his feelings. Considered shy, he sometimes surprised his friends with a gregariousness that disappeared as suddenly as it had appeared. Becka turned from the refrigerator, where she had gone for something cool to drink.

"You're looking kind of red. Sunburn already?" she asked. "I thought only women wanted to go to reunions either with a tan or ultra thin. There's an antiseptic there for burns if you want it."

"And plying me with gifts yet," he said, grinning at her as he hitched up his pants.

"What's with you?" She turned away. At once his large hands grabbed her and turned her to him. He wrapped his arms around her, bending her back as he pushed his face close to hers. He smelled like motor oil and talcum powder.

"Yeah. Clever. But I wonder about you, Becka. You've got the body of a twenty-year-old. You know it, too, running around in shorts and tank tops like a kid." He spoke without looking at her face, his eyes roving over her body, then focusing on nothing in particular.

"Knock it off, Vic. What's wrong with you?" More irritated than alarmed, Becka crossed her arms across Vic's chest and pushed. It had no effect. He nuzzled her ear. "I told you, it's over."

He pressed her tighter to him.

"If you don't stop this minute, your family tree is going to end with you today." He grunted. "I mean it." She drew her knee up and Vic shoved her away. He looked beaten and angry, with his hair disheveled and shirt askew.

"You women are all alike." He stumbled backward

and leaned against the sink. A dark patch of sweat spread from his armpit across the front of his shirt.

"What the hell is wrong with you, Vic? It's over, remember? That was years ago. We're not going back. Your wife is my best friend and you're over here trying to get my pants down. This is the fifth time you've done this this month. Are you going crazy?" Becka heard the words flying out of her mouth, wondering if she were shouting, if anyone outside could hear her. She hated herself when she got angry; she turned into a vulgar, common person she didn't want to know. She tried to slow her breathing, get a grip on herself. "Clean it up, Vic. We've all been friends for years. Stop hitting on me."

"You don't understand. I got problems." He ran a large hand over his face, staring at the floor.

"I'll say." Becka walked to the other end of the room, wishing she'd had the presence of mind to make a joke about it instead of turning it into a fight. She thought she heard someone coming to the door, but when she stopped to listen, she heard nothing. This was a nice neighborhood; she had a nice marriage. She didn't want anyone getting the wrong idea and ruining everything for her. She looked over at Vic, still wary of him, but he was staring at the floor, mumbling something she couldn't understand.

The afternoon was quiet. The neighborhood was not home to very young children whose laughter and cries crinkled in the bright sunshine, nor was there a gang of teenage boys who walked the short street with boomboxes and rode motorcycles back and forth. Sometimes the loudest noise was the scraping of in-line skates coming to a stop. Most people worked all day, or like Becka, at least part-time.

"Aren't you going to ask me if I'm going to tell Mindy?" Becka asked, struggling weakly against her need to get back at him. "Or Hugh?" Ever since he'd married Mindy, about twelve years ago, his attitude toward women had changed—he didn't seem to notice them anymore. He no longer joked about other men's wives or put women down in general. It was Mindy; she changed him. Once a widower with two girls to raise and no idea how to go about it, now he was rigid about his family life, refusing to let anything get in the way of his time with Mindy and the girls. And now, all of a sudden, in the last month he had returned to his earlier, vulgar self.

"Maybe I'll tell him myself," Vic said.

"Hey, let's just forget it," Becka said. "You're probably not feeling well. Right?" Vic didn't seem to hear her. "You always were one for a joke, Vic."

"I gotta go. There's something I gotta do." Vic lunged out the back door. A car started up somewhere on Basker Court.

AT TEN MINUTES before four o'clock the sleek red coupe crossed the old bridge over a trickling river, descended a hill, then crossed another, smaller bridge over a canal that looked like it was about to overflow its channel, and pulled into a parking lot across from an old mill building. Less than a half-hour drive from Mellingham, the Tveshter Paper Company was only one of over two hundred small mills dotting the Commonwealth of Massachusetts, carrying on a tradition, spanning in the case of Tveshter at least one hundred years, of turning out the finest paper in the world, as anyone in the industry will assert. For many, including Tveshter, the worst parts of the industry were gone: the harsh working conditions, the water churning with chemicals, and the air thick with the smell of sulfur. And even now, despite all the noise of the dryers, the cost to the landscape in earlier times, the mechanization of more and more of the industry, making paper is still an art form that commands the devotion of generations. Tony Ostell was only the most recent in a long line of sons to follow father and grandfather into an industry that is effectively closed to outsiders, a world of men with dark suits and cigars conducting business in the 1990s as though it were the 1930s.

The water in the canal churned and rushed headlong to its old bed a few yards away. Tony Ostell barely noticed it. This afternoon it meant nothing to him—he heard no echo of the songs sung by French Canadians imported in the 1840s to cut the canal, he saw no flashing whitecaps kissing the air as gently as the flutter of tissue paper. He pushed open the glass door, marked only with the word OPEN, and climbed to the second floor. There he passed a young woman sitting at one end of a large room used for reception.

"The old man in?" he asked, raising his left hand in a concealed wave.

"Your stepfather's in a meeting but his office is open if you want to wait in there," the receptionist replied. She and Tony were almost the same age; she kept her eyes on her typing while she spoke.

"Nah, I'll head up to the lab. Talk to Gerry." He slung his small canvas backpack over his shoulder and turned down an oak-paneled hallway; he stopped at an open door, brushed his hand across a darkened nameplate that read Hugh Chase, and tossed his cap onto a chair before moving on. Above him bells rang out—

two short, four long, one short. Czerpak, he thought to himself.

From the very first day he came to work at his step-father's mill, when he was only fourteen and needed a summer job, he had loved the bells. He learned the code during the first week and listened longingly for his own, assigned to him by his stepfather, more out of kindness than necessity, just in case he was needed somewhere else. The bells rang for him just twice— once when his mother came to pick him up early for a dental appointment, and again when he had forgotten to punch out and the night supervisor thought he might still be somewhere in the building. Tony never heard them the second time, and he learned to be careful about his time card after that.

He pushed the door open into the stairwell but in-stead of going up to the lab, he skipped down to the storage area. Immediately he felt restored, as though his real self rested among the bales of rags and pulp. When he was about twelve years old and his parents were recently divorced, Tony developed a fear of being left alone, when he always seemed to get a stiff neck or bloody nose, though he later denied it. But to keep his ex-wife happy and his son calm, Tony's father had taken to bringing him to his office in the Lawrence Superior Paper Company on Saturday afternoons, showing him the different kinds of papers he stocked, the grades of one company compared to those of an-other. Over the years he showed Tony how to test paper with tools he had at home. Then, when he needed a part-time job one summer and his stepfather took him on at the employee-owned Tveshter mill, the world of paper changed him again.

The rag room was a long, low-ceilinged room in

gray light, at the moment empty of people; the walls were painted in two tones of green, which Tony liked to think of as an unconscious allusion to the forest birthplace of its contents. Tony plucked a remnant of white dotted swiss from a bale. It seemed to him there must be a factory hidden in an alley in Boston where little old women spent all day cutting up bolts of white cloth to sell to rag brokers. He couldn't imagine that anyone actually made enough things from dotted swiss to account for all these bales.

He passed the bales of high alpha pulp from the state of Washington, cotton linter from North Carolina, sulfite pulp and eucalyptus pulp, and soft wood pulps, each bale composed of thick pressed white sheets wrapped in a sheet of the same, all waiting to be torn apart and funneled into one of two huge globular vats for cooking.

No one was working around the conveyer belt and ceiling-high funnels that sent the reduced rags to the cookers below, so he headed down the circular metal staircase. A man in his thirties, his long hair tied into a ponytail with earphones on his head, waved to Tony as he emerged into the noise of the mill. To Tony's left were the gigantic globes in which the rags were cooked, but no one was there either. The man with the ponytail had moved on to the first of five large whirlpools, which looked like gigantic halved snail shells, checking the flow of cooked pulp and water. It was noisy here and for the first time in his experience, Tony didn't feel jolted by it. Beyond were the refiners and the Fourdrinier, what he thought of as the real papermaking machine, and the dryers, the source of most of the noise.

Ever since his first summer job here he'd been free

to hang around and help, to come and go like a regular employee. He savored the sense of belonging and studied the industry the way his friends studied the Red Sox. He gave papers in high school on the average life cycle of a fiber (now seventeen in Australia and one in the United States), the trends in recycling (new research into stickies removal), and the introduction of the world sheeter machine (which can cut a twenty-foot sheet of paper but put one hundred people out of work). During his senior year in college he studied the rising cost of production and the ensuing sale of the product in both pulp form and set form overseas. His academic adviser suggested he branch out a little, investigate other industries of the future, such as computers or health care. Tony put him down as a philistine.

A man in overalls and heavy boots came by, showed him the case of a CD he was listening to, signed its excellence, and went on. Tony looked around for someone else to talk to, then shrugged and went back to the stairs. He ran up to the third floor, listening to the bells. It occurred to him it was break time; that was probably why he hadn't run into many of his pals.

The testing lab was empty. A long row of windows in the hallway wall looked on to a brightly lit room with no exterior windows butting against the wide shelf holding numerous testing instruments. The door was closed, ensuring no variation in the carefully controlled humidity and temperature. Tony turned into the office next door. It too was empty, but he could hear a voice speaking intermittently nearby. He leaned through the doorway of another office, waved to the man talking on the telephone, and wandered back down the hall to still another small lab. A workman in heavy boots, his

Walkman dangling around his neck, approached from the other end of the hall.

"Take a look," the man said, showing him a large sheet of paper.

"The new product Hugh was talking about?" Tony asked.

"The very same." He pushed open the door to the lab and left the sheet on a desk, wrote his signature in an open book, and left. "Drop by the break room," he called over his shoulder as he raised the Walkman to his ears.

"I'll do that," Tony promised, though he knew the man couldn't hear him. He watched him pass through swinging doors, then entered the lab, kicking the door shut with the heel of his shoe. Beneath the new sheet of paper lay a stack of magazines, a few unopened letters, and a pile of invoices. Tony knew what they were for; it was Friday, a day to check and reorder, receive and store. He pulled out the swivel chair and drew out the first magazine that met his fingers. It was an issue of the glossy *Tappi Journal,* a monthly dedicated to the paper industry. He flipped the journal open and a cowlick of pages rose up to offer him an article entitled "Characterization of proteins in coated papers by SDS-polyacrylamide gel electrophoresis" by James R. Paulson and Robert E. Moore. Tony tried to settle down to read until someone returned to the lab.

He was still reading ten minutes later when a man in jeans and a plaid shirt loped into the room. "Hey, kid. I didn't know you were here." He gave Tony a gentle punch on his shoulder and crossed the room to the closet. "Got tied up with your stepfather. He's free if you want him now."

"Yeah?" Tony replied, flipping through a copy of

Paper Age, a glossy about the size of a tabloid newspaper. He slouched down into his chair, his worn jeans bunching across his narrow hips. Gerry began to whistle as he pulled on a short white coat. "I blew another interview this week," Tony said. He had meant to tell his mother as soon as he got back this afternoon but he just couldn't face it, so he was telling Gerry instead.

Gerry paused, waiting for Tony to add details; when he didn't, the researcher moved to rearrange his lab equipment so he could more easily view the computer screen. "That's too bad," Gerry replied, drawing up a stool.

"I took the whole day off from work to go up to New Hampshire." Tony shook his head. His hair was neatly cropped on the sides, almost shaved, rising to a fine brown tuft on top. He was a clean, personable looking young man, the kind people took to easily. "I really blew it."

"What was the job?"

"Doesn't matter." Tony flipped the pages roughly now, skimming the headlines, then closed the magazine, and slipped it back in among the others on the desk. Gerry fiddled with his computer.

"Worried about telling your stepfather?"

"No." Tony had a good relationship with his stepfather, nurtured in large part by his father, who only once commented on his ex-wife's choice of a second husband, though the two men had been friends all their lives. "Hugh Chase," Richard Ostell said once when Tony was in junior high, "is a good man. He's in the industry too."

Gerry turned to look at the back of Tony's head; he seemed to be speculating on what exactly it was. "Do you know about that program up in Orono?"

"At the University of Maine?" Tony asked.

"Yeah. Up there. They have that program in paper sciences and the Pulp and Paper Foundation," Gerry said, again staring at the monitor as though it were a shining crystal ball.

"So?"

"So maybe you could go there," Gerry said. "Get some courses under your belt, the kind of thing prospective employers like to see."

"I have a degree. Economics." Tony swiveled aimlessly in his chair. Gerry opened a notebook and began reading a column of figures.

"How long since you graduated from college?"

"I got my degree in December. Six months ago."

"That's not so long," Gerry commented. "You could go back to school for a year or two. I was thinking of something to help you get a foot in the door."

"I have a foot in the door," Tony said. "Right here."

"Then I don't get what the problem is. Why not just settle down here?"

Tony stopped swiveling, hunched his shoulders, and rested his hands on his thighs. "Because my dad thinks I should start out on my own someplace else—get experience, you know? Before joining his company. It's part of his philosophy as a parent, I guess, even though no one around here does anything like that. I mean, Hugh started out here, with his father, and everyone else we know did the same kind of thing. It's just my dad trying to do the right thing, or what he thinks is the right thing. And Hugh thinks he shouldn't interfere in what my old man thinks is best for me. And Mr. Rabelard thinks it's not financially the right time." He grimaced.

"That's a tough one." Gerry started tapping away at his computer. "Everyone trying to do what's right for you, and you get caught in the middle. Got you between a rock and a hard place," he said, without looking up.

"And when I go for an interview at another mill everyone wants to know why my old man doesn't hire me at his place or why Hugh doesn't take me on here. I've got two strong ins and I can't get a job in either place. Try explaining that to an interviewer." He pushed himself away from the desk and stood up, a wry smile softening his words.

"Just a temporary setback," Gerry said, smiling in return.

"Yeah. That's the way I look at it too." He gave Gerry a thumbs-up sign and sauntered out the door with a confident, jaunty smile.

THE LAWRENCE Superior Paper Company occupied a long, modern warehouse on the edge of Mellingham, not far from the highway but tastefully hidden from the sight of passing traffic by a grove of hemlocks. Founded in 1883 as purveyor of papers to traders and printers, Laspac, as it was affectionately known, relocated in Mellingham in 1968 and employed only members of the Lawrence family until the early 1980s. In 1983, for the very first time, the Lawrence Superior Paper Company brought in an outsider. Richard Ostell, an old friend from high school and a sales rep for a small paper mill, was looking for a better job without leaving the industry. With a modest inheritance from his parents, Richard was the answer to a cash shortage that could wreck Laspac's relationship with two mills and a half-dozen end users. The owner, Vic Rabelard, eased him into the business, the mill owners sized him up, and Laspac went on, its centenary becoming a source of celebration after all.

It was not entirely without precedence, therefore, that Richard Ostell contemplated the terms of a shipment due in that afternoon and the order forms for end users. Laspac had purchased a truckload of copying paper from the St. Pierre Mill for $14,557, and had agreed to sell it to four end users (two insurance companies, one lab, and one school) for almost the same price. That meant Laspac was working off their discount—a two-percent discount of the cost charged by the mill if payment was made within twenty days; otherwise, cost was net and no discount.

Richard tapped the metal desk in an office that was serviceable, cleaned once a week, and would make a mother cry for its utility. He picked up the invoice from the mill and reread it. This was ludicrous, he thought. We're going to make three hundred dollars, and for what? He checked his watch. It was almost four o'clock. The truck was already an hour late. There had to be more to this.

Richard put the bill back into the file, and went out into the hall—the unofficial reception area and secretary's office—for a cup of coffee. He gave Mary, their all-purpose office worker, a grunt and a nod and poured twice as much sugar into his coffee as he normally took.

"You're driving me crazy with desire, Mary," he said when his spoon felt the sugar in a lump at the bottom of his cup. "Can't even pour a cup of coffee without being overcome." He winked at her, and she gave him a bored look. He was jumpy and she knew it.

When Richard first bought into the company, he knew there was a good chance the mill owners would take one look at this stranger and pull out, taking one hundred years of business and Richard's stake with them. They had that right, understood with or without a contract, but Richard talked Vic into taking the risk. It was the gamble of a lifetime, and it paid off—for both of them. Richard had no regrets, but he realized only later that Vic was uncomfortable with this kind of uncertainty. He preferred a more conservative approach. Richard was not sure he liked this; he preferred to take the risk and live with the consequences. In what felt to many like a seat-of-the-pants business, Richard saw no reason to sit safely in a corner. So Richard soared and Vic had vertigo. And after all their years in business together, neither one had been able to change the other. Working the discount was a sign that Vic was feeling the pressure and looking for a safe route— or he was losing his judgment.

Richard moved over to Vic Rabelard's desk and began to check the account files Vic had been working on before he left early for the day. His notes were scribbles that Richard had learned to decipher, but today he wasn't sure he'd gotten it right. The phone rang, Mary buzzed him, and he spent the next ten minutes working out the kinks in an order for a small printer in Connecticut. When he was finished, he went back to his own desk, resigned to working through most of the weekend.

Business wasn't bad exactly, he kept explaining to Mary; it was hard. International Paper had cut back their normal supply to sixty percent. It was the same all over. Big and small mills were selling less to their US paper merchants and more overseas. Either in pulp form or set form (finished product), paper was heading overseas where the devaluation of the dollar was making US products especially attractive. When he read in the newspapers ten or fifteen years ago that the Pacific Rim countries were offering top dollar for US wood products—plywood, press board, and other basic building materials—leaving only the lower grades of wood for the local market, he knew it wouldn't be long before the US felt the same crunch in paper.

But knowing this didn't make it any easier.

Richard settled down to work the phone. For all his worries about Vic's moves, he had to give his partner credit. Vic had kept his long-term customers happy and his mills happy when others were chasing new customers and new suppliers. Richard figured it had to come from being in a family business, from looking back on a history in which your ancestors appeared at every turning point, from knowing that your family had survived through all the hard times the industry had ever known, from having some special understanding about the business in your blood. But Vic wouldn't take a risk. Richard shook his head. Even now, knowing he could lose everything because of his partner, Richard envied the history in Vic's life.

The buzzer announcing a delivery rang, and Richard swore in relief. He went out to the loading dock, where two men were just raising the rear door of a trailer. Inside he glimpsed the familiar Tveshter logo. "Holy Mother of," Richard began. He hadn't thought it could get any worse.

BECKA CHASE LOOKED at herself in the mirror, then tore off the print over-blouse that hung well below her denim shorts.

"To hell with it," she mumbled, reaching for her hairbrush. "Men are pigs." She gave her curly hair three vicious swipes and threw the brush down on the bureau. Then she grabbed a paper bag and headed down to the kitchen and the back door. She wasn't sure how she should feel about Vic's behavior, his casual assumption that he could pick up where they left off because he felt like it. Well, that was over twelve years ago and it had cost her her marriage to Richard. And he was the one she was really mad at—Richard, who had spent the better part of their ten-year marriage razzing her, as he called it, all in good fun, and then agreed with alacrity to a divorce so that she could marry her unnamed lover, all the time being so reasonable through it all that she actually came to miss him when it was all over.

And then Vic met Mindy and treated Becka like a woman he barely knew. It still made her furious to think about it. And now, here was Vic, stirring things up again. She let the back door slam behind her, and was bucked by the noise.

"Becka!" a voice called as she descended the back steps.

Becka stopped on the bottom step and waved to Mindy Rabelard.

"Got time for a cup of tea?" Mindy called.

Becka signaled to Mindy to wait a moment, and deposited her bag in the garage. She emerged, brushing dust from her hands. "I'll be glad when this weekend is over," she began, walking toward the other house. "I'm sick to death of junk." Mindy cocked her head to one side and smiled, her black hair shining in the sun. When she did so, it suddenly occurred to Becka that everything about Mindy was precise and brilliant—coal black hair, shiny red lips, crystal white teeth. It was one of many moments when Becka understood why Vic had been drawn to her, and then had to swallow her bitterness. "I'm sounding sort of whiny, aren't I?"

Mindy just smiled at her, slipping her hands into the pockets of her cotton print skirt as she looked down the driveway to the narrow street, studying it. Then she turned back to Becka. "Come in for a cup of tea. Once in a while friends have to stop and listen and breathe."

"Isn't it a little warm for tea?" Becka suggested.

"It's cool inside. Besides, I'm making iced tea for Vic too. It's sort of a ritual with me." She smiled languidly. This was the essence of Mindy, in Becka's opinion. She could do the one thing most unsuited to the day or time or situation and make it seem the perfect choice. She could make hot tea when the temperature was nudging ninety or iced tea when it was falling below zero, steal a woman's boyfriend, and it seemed perfectly right.

Becka looked at her watch. "I'm supposed to be over at Polly's house at four o'clock, that's ten minutes ago." She started to rise on her toes, preliminary to racing to her car.

"It's blueberry twig tea. The last of it, so the last time I'm going to make it." Mindy waited, not moving toward the house, as though her tea-making plans were cut in stone, scheduled for far into the future. Becka cursed her own weakness; she hated herbal tea.

"Oh, hell. Polly's been driving me crazy all year over this reunion. Let her wait." Mindy followed Becka into the house. When Becka first married Hugh she wondered how she'd feel living so close to the man she left her husband for and who then left her.

Hugh didn't give her any choice in where they would live, having bought the house before he proposed, which always made her wonder how important she was to his life. When she moved in, her intended strategy had been to remain aloof, but Mindy forestalled her, and thereafter for some time Becka wondered if Vic had told Mindy about their affair.

Becka couldn't imagine such a conversation. She thought she could, but the one and only time she had tried to broach the subject with Hugh, intending to talk about a mutual friend who was getting in pretty deep with a married man, Hugh had misinterpreted her hesitant lunges at revelation, and said, "I don't care what your so-called friend Stacey has done. Their infidelities mean nothing to me. Have them over as often as you like. But understand this, Becka, that's one thing I won't live with. Stacey's husband may be an asshole, but not me. If you ever have an affair, that's it. You're out. Our marriage is over." They'd been sitting up in bed one Sunday morning, and Becka never got to reply because Tony came in then, wanting Hugh to take him to the park for a ball game.

Hugh's vehemence warned Becka away from any confessions, and she just got used to a layer of alienation separating her from Mindy and Hugh and Vic, and turned her heart to living the life her marriage made possible. Tony became the center of her world, and she didn't really care what Vic and Mindy thought of her after that. After a while, the pretense became the reality.

Mindy went about making tea—boiling water, tempering the pot, filling it with dried leaves and twigs picked from her own blueberry bush—while Becka sat at the kitchen table and chatted idly to Mindy's back, wondering what it would be like to spill it all—her affair with Vic years ago, his coming on to her this afternoon; instead she said absolutely nothing worth repeating. Mindy listened, said nothing until the tea was ready, then turned to set the table.

"I hate to waste the last of it on just me," Mindy said when she had laid out teacups and saucers, spoons, cream and sugar, and a plate of cookies.

"Lordy, I feel like a kid," Becka said, looking at the table as she took the bright plaid cloth napkin Mindy handed her. "Do you remember tea parties like this when you were a kid?"

"Sure, doesn't everyone?" Mindy replied. Becka glanced up at her.

"For all I know about your childhood, you might have grown up without ever hearing the word tea." Becka immediately felt uncomfortable at her thrust into Mindy's private past, for much as she liked to think she had made her peace with Mindy, there was something about the other woman that called for discretion.

Mindy smiled her languid smile. "Did you? Grow up without hearing the word?"

"Not likely," Becka replied, trying to recover her poise. "I remember one time—" She launched into a detailed reverie of her childhood in Mellingham while Mindy poured the tea. Becka took the cup and sipped.

"Is there something bothering you?" Mindy asked after a period of silence. Becka's hand paused above the plate in the center of the table.

"Well, no, not really," Becka said. "Why do you ask?"

"You don't usually reminisce," Mindy said. "And you always take cream and sugar."

"Oh," Becka said. "Well, you never reminisce."

"That's not the point," Mindy reminded her.

"Sometimes I think it is," Becka said, surprised at her own challenge. It had become one of their tacit articles of friendship that Becka never confronted Mindy, nor did Mindy confront Becka, on any matter. "You live more in the present than any person I've ever known. Everyone else who has that philosophy talks about it, but you never do. It's just the here and now and that's enough."

"There is something bothering you," Mindy said, unruffled by Becka's observation. "You're not philosophical either."

"All right. Actually, yes. Something is bothering me." Becka ignored the warning voice in the back of her mind. "Actually, I was wondering about Vic. He seems kind of edgy. Is anything wrong with you two?"

Mindy dropped her eyes as she stirred her tea. It was late afternoon and the sounds of summer were starting to filter through the house—children home from the park, radios playing in upstairs bedrooms, screen doors slamming.

"Is it the business?" Becka asked, pushing on. Mindy glanced at her. "I only wondered because I know he was home this afternoon."

"It's the reunion." She started to laugh. "He sees most of his old classmates every week of the year, but for this weekend I guess he wanted to look spiffy for some of the ones he hasn't seen for a while. He wanted to go shopping and get something better looking than his usual jacket and pants. We went to the mall. Took a drive around the back roads on the way home."

"I only wondered because you know what Richard's like. Since he stopped having to pay child support for Tony, I have no idea if he's broke or a multimillionaire.

As far as I know, Richard and Vic could have sold the business and gambled all the money away at Atlantic City.''

Mindy laughed outright, opening her mouth in one of her wide, warm smiles, shaking her head. ''They haven't done that, I can assure you.''

''It doesn't matter to me anymore. That chaos is out of my life.'' Becka sipped her tea. ''So there's nothing bothering him?''

Mindy took a cookie. ''He's a man. There's always something bothering him. Business, the passing of time, the girls, the cost of living. You know how it is.''

''Actually, I don't know how it is. Not anymore, anyway. Hugh has this Zen thing about life. He sort of stands back, looks at all the chaos, and sees some sort of divine plan.'' Becka hunched over the table. ''I don't really get it, but it makes him easy to live with.''

''Different from Richard, I'll bet,'' Mindy said.

''You don't know how different,'' she said, shaking her head. ''Hugh has never made a sarcastic comment in his life. But Richard?''

Mindy chuckled. ''I can imagine.'' She pushed her cup and saucer to the side. ''He makes a joke out of everything.''

''Yeah, that was the best part about him. He was always up. I miss that,'' Becka said, not looking at Mindy. A fly zigzagged through the air above them, bumped into a door jamb, and changed directions, heading into the dining room. ''It used to really get to me so bad that once—'' She stopped, flushed, and picked up her teacup.

''That once what?'' Mindy said.

''Something you would never do. How did you get to be so settled and happy while the rest of us trip up here and fall down there? Is it because you got what you wanted?'' Becka leaned forward on her arms crossed in front of her.

"I guess so,'' Mindy said. "What about you? You told me once you wanted to go back to school. You said when Tony was grown you were going to get the education you always wanted. Are you going to do it? Now's the time.''

Becka stared at her friend in astonishment. A heavy lace curtain billowed toward them, pregnant with excitement, then deflated. "You remember that? That was years ago.''

"Twelve years ago. Right after you moved in next door,'' Mindy said matter-of-factly. "Tony was ten. Vic and I were just married, already living here.''

"I was just talking. You know how it is. Don't you ever feel like that? When you have a small child, you have to have some kind of dream for yourself or you think you'll go crazy. That's all it was,'' Becka said. "I work in a cafeteria, for God's sakes.''

"I thought you meant it,'' Mindy said. "I wish you had. I'd like to think of you going after something you really wanted and getting it.''

"Mindy,'' Becka said, sitting up and putting both hands on the table. "I'm forty-two years old.''

"So what? I'm forty. You can't be afraid of change just because you're over forty.''

"Of course not, but, it's just that—'' Becka looked around the red and white kitchen as though the reason lay hidden among the canisters and spices. "Did you go to college?''

"I'm not the one who had the dream about going. You are.'' Mindy rose to put the cups and saucers in the sink, a clear signal that she had said all she had to say on the topic, but she had awakened something in Becka.

"What was your dream?" Becka asked.

"To pass the time, raise a family," Mindy said, not breaking her step toward the sink.

"Even if it's not your own?"

Mindy turned and gave her a quizzical look. "You mean my stepdaughters? Yeah. They're enough."

"That's probably the most personal thing I know about you," Becka said. Mindy poured the remaining tea into a pitcher and put the pitcher in the refrigerator.

"If you know how a person feels about things, you know the true person. The rest is just costumes and party manners," Mindy said.

FOR MOST PEOPLE Friday afternoon is a time of winding down, putting aside the worries of work, the stress we promise ourselves or our doctors we will do something about. Vic Rabelard never considered this, and would not have been able to comprehend any of it if taken aside and reminded. His mind was on a time cut away from the regular span of days and weeks and years. With his two hands gripping the steering wheel, he turned his dusty white pickup into the gravel driveway of the Agawam Inn. Vic jammed on his brakes, and the truck skidded to a halt in front of the broad, wooden stairs of the Victorian inn. He clambered up the steps, passing through the main entrance without a backward glance, and hurried to the registration desk, breathing heavily from both excitement and exertion. "Where is he?" he demanded of the first person he saw.

Mr. Campbell, owner of the Agawam Inn and known to have a temper himself, raised and lowered his red eyebrows three times before deciding on a course of action. "May I help you?"

"The Canadian. Where is he?" Vic repeated, leaning over the desk. His face was red with anger and his lips trembled under the effort to control himself.

"What Canadian?" Mr. Campbell replied, bewildered.

"He's here, I know it. Where else would he stay?" He stepped away from the desk and looked up and down the lobby, which was really no more than a formal entry hall of the sort found in dozens of older homes in the area.

"Mr. Rabelard, isn't it?" Mr. Campbell said with a conspicuous effort to be pleasant.

"I asked you a question. Where is he?" Vic moved one step away, one step back.

"I'm afraid I really can't tell you who's staying here and who isn't." Mr. Campbell was about to continue in this vein when Vic barreled back to the registration desk, nearly knocking it off its moorings. "But to put your mind at ease," Mr. Campbell said, hurrying on, "no one from Canada has checked in."

"I don't believe you," Vic said, pushing the desk another inch.

"Take a look," Mr. Campbell said, reaching for the old book register.

"No one?" Vic asked.

"No one," Mr. Campbell reassured him.

Vic was at a loss. His arms dropped to his sides, his mouth fell slack; he gazed around the lobby again, then stumbled out the door. On the bottom step he paused, seemed to recover his sense of purpose, and bolted for his truck, speeding away down the drive and onto the street without a glance for oncoming cars. He drove straight into the center of Mellingham, across the tracks, through the stop sign, up the hill and along through town, past the village green and on to Pickering Street, where he turned and sped past modest homes carefully maintained, past the old apple orchard and the new cemetery, and on until the road passed over the highway.

The white pickup slowed as the road narrowed. Vic peered right and left, trying to see into the woods through the trees and thick underbrush. He jammed on his brakes at the sign for the Pickering Preserve, shocking the motorist behind him, who swung out into the center of the road, honking his horn and yelling curses Vic couldn't hear. Vic turned sharply to make the turn into the preserve and drove up to the light blue Volvo.

There was no one in it. He looked behind him, in front, all around. Finally, he got out of the truck, letting it block the Volvo, and started walking toward the woods, searching for the break in the trees that signaled a path. He knew this had been a favorite hunting area for his friends when they were growing up, but he had come to Mellingham with his family only at the beginning of his senior year, and his father didn't hunt. Vic found the path and hurried along until his foot flattened a branch. It snapped. He halted, listened, moved on more cautiously. After several minutes he came to a clearing and a man leaning against a tree, asleep. There was no one else in sight.

The sounds of Vic's shoes crushing the moss, the stubbly grass, scraping across a granite outcropping, had no effect on the sleeping man. Not even when Vic stood in front of him, blocking the afternoon sunlight, did he stir. The birds, quiescent at Vic's arrival, grew confident during his still watching, chattering and darting about in the tree limbs above his head. He glanced up, then down.

"Hey," Vic said, kicking the sole of the other man's shoe.

"Huh?" Eliot's hands flicked up, his knees jerked; he sat up, looking at the dark figure looming above him.

"That your car?"

Eliot looked around at the clearing, trying to get his bearings, then turned on his hip and leaned on both hands to raise himself up. He was stiff from sitting on the ground for so long.

"Hey. I asked you a question. That your car?"

Eliot stood up, leaning against the tree, pinching the bridge of his nose with his right hand.

"Answer me," Vic demanded.

"What's wrong? What's happening?" Eliot said, still dazed from sleep.

"Nothing's happening. You hear me? Nothing." Vic pushed Eliot's left shoulder to force him to turn toward him. "Nothing. Got that?"

Eliot straightened up and tried to step away from the tree.

"I'm not through," Vic said, pushing Eliot back against the tree trunk. "Answer me."

"I don't know what you want," Eliot said. He was not a small man, but he had not faced a physical challenge since college. For all his fantasies of a return to his youth and his dreams of athletic prowess, he was woefully far from his healthier, brasher, earlier self.

"Don't get smart with me. You think I can't stop you. Well, I can." Vic drew back his right fist and drove it straight into Eliot's right jaw. Eliot's head snapped back against the tree trunk, pushing a sharp edge of bark into his skull. His eyes unfocused, his body limp, he tried to make sense of what was happening. Was it a dream? His tongue tasted something not quite sweet where his tooth had cut the inside of his lip. He touched the spot with his hand and saw blood on his fingertips. It wasn't a dream.

"You hit me," Eliot said, looking from his fingers to Vic and back again. "I don't even know you."

"Yeah, well, I know you. You're here to make trouble for Mindy, but I'm going to stop you." He jabbed his left fist at Eliot's stomach, but by now Eliot was alert to the danger of this man, despite the absurdity of the situation, and slid to his left, dodging Vic's fist and tripping over the tree roots that had so recently cradled him. He stumbled toward the pond trying to regain his balance, did so, and turned to see Vic ready to throw himself upon him. Eliot raised his hands to block him, jumped away, and drew up his fists. Vic ran at him, knocking him over. They landed on a sturdy laurel bush whose twigs and branches drove between the two men wherever possible, cutting hands and gashing fingers, gouging necks and forearms, tearing shirts and scraping pants. The two men rolled along the ground, flattening a clump of star-of-Bethlehem flowers.

Eliot was losing, a fact that did not surprise him. The occasional bouts of boxing he and his fraternity brothers had engaged in had been conducted with goodwill, humor, and enough beer to ensure that no one was ever seriously hurt. But today, there was no good will, no humor, and no beer. And this man was a stranger. What's more, he was serious. Eliot panicked.

With a strength and a will that amazed him in retrospect, Eliot blocked Vic's throbbing blows and grabbed at his throat. Vic began to choke and cough and Eliot smashed his fist into Vic's nose, closing his eyes tight as he did so. Vic pulled back and covered his face with both hands, then rolled over onto one side. Eliot jumped up onto his feet. His shirt was torn open, its buttons scattered among the undergrowth; his tie hung down onto his bare chest; his pants were torn and stained with dirt. He noticed none of this. With adrenaline finally pumping through his arms and legs, he was ready for Vic now, let him try his worst. The salesman jumped around Vic, urging him to get up, taunting him with promises to match him blow for blow. Eliot Keogh could lick anyone.

But Vic didn't move. He held both hands over his nose, drew up a leg, let his foot slide down, and stretched out again. He moved an elbow here, a foot there, with no purpose, no awareness of Eliot Keogh dancing gingerly around him.

"Get up," Eliot said, as nervous as a child afraid the strange kid will take up his dare.

"Why'd you have to come here? Why couldn't you leave her alone?" Vic pushed himself up into a sitting position. Eliot dodged with alacrity, less brave now and confused by the large man's transformation. He lowered his fists and slowly backed away. When he was confident the large man was paying no attention to him, he turned and ran for the dirt lot and his car. Eliot barely glanced at the white truck parked perpendicularly behind him. Instead, he put the Volvo in gear and drove straight ahead, smashing shrubs, flattening tulips, scraping the undercarriage on rocks and bushes, ignoring anything that could make him stop.

TWO

Friday Evening

OVER THE YEARS the Chases and the Rabelards amassed a casual but thorough knowledge of each other's comings and goings. The Rabelards knew that the Chases cooked inside on Friday evenings and then brought their plates out to their picnic table. The Chases knew that Vic Rabelard barbecued hamburgers every Friday night on the old stone barbecue for the entire family or for himself and his wife after she took the girls to whatever sleepover was on the calendar for that weekend.

On this particular Friday, the Chases, like actors in the wings awaiting their cue, stepped through the back door as soon as the sun dropped at five-thirty. Vic Rabelard emerged from his back door carrying a tray, and two teenage girls with black hair followed him down the steps. Both girls had backpacks, but Mindy, right behind them and a practical woman, wielded a small canvas bag. She waved to Becka while the two girls darted across the yard to give Uncle Hugh a hug and a kiss goodbye.

"Vic? We're off. I'm taking the girls over," Mindy said. She followed her daughters to the car, and the others resumed their tasks. Her words had been so predictable that they barely counted as an interruption to the murmurings of other voices of the afternoon—birds, people, televisions, dogs, radios—that no one listened to very closely anymore. The Chases ate and joked and talked about the future, the summer and even the next decade. Vic walked across his driveway to join them, a long fork in his left hand. This too was normal, but the rest was not.

Becka gasped.

"Jesus, Man. What happened to you?" Hugh said when he got a look at the bruises and cuts on his friend's face and arms. Vic looked startled for a moment, then abashed.

"Nothing," he replied. "I'm okay."

"Let me get you something to put on that," Becka said. She signaled to Tony to go on her errand. Hugh glanced at him, and Tony settled back into his seat.

"No, I'm okay," Vic repeated. "Just making sure you're all going down to the reunion tonight." He managed to sound hearty and cheerful.

"Tonight, tomorrow night, and Sunday," Hugh replied.

Vic nodded, said, "Good." He slapped Tony on the back. "How's my pal? Got some interviews coming up?" Tony mumbled a reply, then lunged at his hamburger. Vic wandered back to his barbecue.

"What on earth do you think happened to him?" Becka said.

"It looks like he was in a fight," Tony said.

"He's been awful strange lately," Becka said.

"Maybe I'll just get that first aid cream, the stuff he was always borrowing last summer," Tony said as he rose from the table. "He looks like he's going to want it eventually."

"I'm sure Mindy has taken care of him," Hugh replied, then shrugged. "But go ahead. Can't hurt. He does look pretty miserable. There's some in the garage."

"Yup, saw it." Tony went to the garage, ducking under a broken bamboo wind chime dangling from a low-hanging branch as he entered through a small side door; his parents could hear him rummaging through piles of odds and ends. Beyond the trailing yews they could hear Vic alternately whistling and humming as he tended his coals.

"Do you think if he were neater, he'd have less trouble getting a better job?" Becka asked with one eye on the garage. Hugh laughed. Becka snorted, then calmed herself. She was not as sanguine as her husband was; she sometimes wished he would notice how frustrated she was over Tony's job search.

"He'll be all right, honey. He's just got a fixation on working for me or his father right away," Hugh replied. "His time will come."

Becka sighed, but not with agreement, and started eating again. She sometimes found her husband's platitudes hard to swallow. He was probably right, but that didn't make it any easier. In fact it made it harder. Just once she wanted him to listen to her, agree with her, tell her she was definitely right, and set off to do whatever it was she was right about. It was a fantasy she had—sort of like moving to Hawaii—and she certainly didn't expect it to come true, but she could imagine how good it would feel. That only added to her disappointment. Consequently, resentment sat like a thick lump at her waist, preventing her from feeling optimism or wonder or hope within hours after talking about her son. She and Hugh fell into silence, in which they could hear Vic slapping at mosquitoes and cursing roundly.

"Hey," Vic called out as he approached them a second time. "Maybe I will take that cream. It's good for bug bites, isn't it?"

"Tony went to get some," Becka replied as her son emerged from the garage carrying a small white tube with red lettering. He passed it to Vic and returned to his seat. Vic signed his gratitude and ambled back to his barbecue, smearing the cream on the back of his neck as he did so, dabbing gently on his cuts and bruises.

"What about you, Tony? What've you got on for this evening?" Hugh asked. Tony mumbled something about meeting his friends.

Vic came back into view, this time wiping the sweat from his face. When he saw Becka looking at him, he shook his head, laughed, and said, "The heat's getting to me. Guess I'll get something more to drink." He moved to the back door, glass in hand. "Mindy'll be back any minute now. I've got the coals just about right. Don't want to waste them." He entered the house and emerged a moment later with a full glass.

"Maybe you should go ask him flat out?" Becka said, watching her neighbor. "He really has been awful strange lately." She glanced quickly at Tony, but he seemed to be absorbed in his potato salad.

"It's not our business unless he wants us to know," Hugh replied. "Leave the guy alone. Tony, ready for some coffee?" Tony nodded and Hugh rose, giving Becka a stern but kindly look.

THE LOBLOLLY BAR slouched against the sidewalk across from the village green, its shiny gray paint and gray tiled roof modestly concealing a tidy two-room bar within. Were it not for the small wooden sign hanging over the front door, tourists might easily pass it by as one more colonial home, which it had been at one time, long before it was a bakery, insurance office, tailor, and gift shop. Each new owner added a layer of paint or a new roof or a remodeled front window, ever hopeful that this one change would finally bring in the customers. Not until the Syzyckys bought the building did expectations meet reality, largely because of the character of the Syzyckys.

This is not something Polly Jarman would have understood. Elected class secretary during her senior year—a post she had declined to relinquish ever since—Polly had chosen the Loblolly Bar as the location for the first night's festivities because the site was lodged in her brain. Her father had repeatedly referred to the building throughout her childhood, waxing especially eloquent over the customs practiced therein right after he picked up a mended suit. The head tailor was Master Tony, addressed thus by his chief assistant, a man at least twenty years older than Master Tony and a head shorter. It was, her father said when he drove her to school or to Girl Scouts on Saturdays, a practice that was guaranteed to remind those who needed reminding that respect was earned. Polly stifled a yawn.

Despite her early disdain, years later she thought first of the Loblolly Bar whenever she needed a small .venue. This time it suited her plans perfectly. It was large enough to accommodate all thirty-seven graduates and their spouses (or others, as she delicately phrased it), should all choose to attend, was easy to find, and offered an evening's entertainment at reasonable prices. (The last consideration was also lodged in her brain after years of listening to her father's complaints about the gift shop.)

The only scratch in her perfect record of spiraling plans was the inexplicable failure to consult Theodore Syzycky, the owner of the Loblolly Bar. This could have been a disaster, for Theodore, as he preferred to be called, was an impulsive sort of guy and didn't always show up after a day on the water to open the bar on time. Fortunately, his wife, Patricia, was plugged into the Internet, and received a query on the meaning of the word *loblolly* from a woman in Saudi Arabia via a green bulletin board in the Middle East after she had read another user's declaration that if it were at all possible—short of going AWOL in Berlin—he would be at the Loblolly on the second Friday in June. When Patricia Syzycky got this all sorted out, she prepared Theodore. In short, the bar was open late Friday afternoon when Polly Jarman billowed through the front door, asking about signs and balloons and party foods, none of which was evident anywhere.

"They must have forgot," she mumbled.

"Who's they?" Theodore asked, coming out from behind the bar where he was counting bottles at his wife's insistence, trying to recall just why she had sent him over so early in the evening.

"You know perfectly well who they are," Polly replied as she moved peripatetically around the bar, trying to devise a plan she could implement in the next five minutes. "I've been talking about this reunion all year." This was perfectly true; Polly had been discussing the reunion weekend all year to everyone she met—including Theodore Syzycky. The trouble was that she rarely discussed with Theodore or anyone else the portion of the weekend relevant to that person. And not being an opportunist, Theodore let the business possibilities pass him by, which was why he was now regarding Polly with a mixture of mystification and annoyance. He had a sneaking suspicion that she was the reason his wife had forced him to open the bar earlier than he had intended.

"What's in your back room?" She pushed through the swinging doors to the kitchen, where Patricia prepared the hearty sandwiches that were the only food the bar provided. No one was there.

"Who?" repeated Theodore, who was still wondering who had forgotten what. He had not grown up in Mellingham and thus had numerous blanks in his social vocabulary, which were inevitably revealed when he tried to converse with a native in his or her own terms. He was short and wiry and muscular—he rarely drank himself—and found the hours of the bar wearying, but he loved people, all sorts. Well, almost all. Polly Jarman irritated him.

"Don't you keep any balloons in stock?" Polly asked after opening and closing a random selection of cupboard doors. She had the high cheekbones and light coloring of the old Yankee families; she moved gracefully, even fastidiously, wherever she went, especially in a strange kitchen.

"What's up?" Patricia Syzycky asked as she came through the back door even though she had a pretty good idea. "What're you doing in here?"

"My dear," Polly said, beaming at her. "Just the person I wanted to see." She gave Theodore a dismissive look and headed for his wife. Patricia was a taller, female version of her husband, but that was the only way in which they were similar. She was never stalled, confused, or intimidated by the likes of Polly Jarman. "Who's out serving drinks?" she asked her husband.

"Drinks?" Theodore repeated. "But it's not even six o'clock." He hadn't considered that the bar was open; just because the front door was unlocked didn't mean patrons would be coming in and out, would they? He hurried to the swinging kitchen door, glimpsed at least a dozen men and women milling about, and cast a frantic look at his wife. "She wants balloons," he said over his shoulder as he disappeared into the bar.

"We don't have any balloons." Since passing fifty, Patricia had lost her gift for instant comradeship; she looked on the enthusiasms, the passions and missions of other women with a dry eye and a composed heart.

"I guess I'll just have to ask my committee," she said, looking somewhat lost. Patricia waited. "I suppose it depends on who I can get in touch with who has the time to rush off and do an errand to make this a super, super party." She glanced back at Patricia, then opened the door into the bar. Strains of the song "Aquarius" flowed in. Patricia perked up at the sounds of the music and almost forgot about Polly.

"Maybe I could ask—" Polly paused, then chose a name from among the women in the class. "She's always such a good sport, always willing to help."

"She's got small children. She can't leave them to do errands," Patricia said, then went on humming. Polly frowned; she didn't like being thwarted.

"I'll call Mindy Rabelard. I know she and Vic are coming," Polly countered.

"Mindy has other plans for tonight," Patricia replied, waiting for the other woman's next suggestion. She knew she should be making sandwiches, but she so rarely got to talk back to a customer that she didn't want to stop.

Polly studied the other woman, seemed to come to a decision, and turned to the door. "I'll find someone." She departed to the strains of "Honky Tonk Women."

Sometime later Patricia followed with two large platters of sandwiches, depositing one in the center of a table where Becka and Hugh Chase sat with friends, to the strains of "Oh Happy Day." By now the front room of the bar was filling up with members of the class of 1969 of Mellingham High School, a group of casually dressed teachers, nurses, managers, bureaucrats, and the occasional unreconstructed hippie.

With the second platter raised above her head, Patricia made her way into the smaller, second room where half a dozen couples were talking among themselves. In a far corner a man played a few chords on a guitar, sang a verse, then played some more. He had hung his list of songs for the evening on the edge of one of several bulletin boards that covered the walls of this room, offering the patrons photographs of events celebrated in the bar, postcards from friends on vacation, and programs from sports events whose participants chose the Loblolly for their victory party. It was a neighborhood photo album. Patricia deposited the platter in the center of a large table occupied by Gwen MacDuffy and Joe Silva and some of their friends.

"I didn't know you liked folk music, Chief," Patricia said to Joe Silva. He was tall with black, wavy hair, closer to Patricia's age than Gwen's, and the pragmatic, no-nonsense Mrs. Syzycky had actually felt a pang of remorse for her married state when she first saw him ten years ago. It wasn't so much his looks as his manner; she liked a man with a sense of humor. She admitted to herself that if she had been a woman who would, he would have been the one with whom she might have. The thought lasted a day, and that was that. Patricia liked her life uncomplicated.

"How could I stay away?" Joe replied, turning to her. "You advertise a singer of Latin American music. Music with passion and humor and wit. I had to come." He turned to the table of friends. "Romance and ribaldry no one can pass up."

"Well, I don't know about that," Gwen interjected. Kind, likable, dedicated, Joe Silva kept his playfulness and sense of humor under restraint. He was, after all, chief of police in a staid New England town.

A few more members of the class of 1969 drifted into the room to the sounds of "Crystal Blue Persuasion." Patricia threw up her hands and sighed. "I didn't think they would be bringing their own entertainment for everyone," she said, and left for the other room.

The folksinger announced the end of his break with a few chords and pulled his stool closer to the crowd. He was somewhere in his twenties, traveling around New England on the intricate web of churches, bars, and bookstores that constitute the folk music circuit while he worked during the day in computers or insurance or retail. He began his next set with a song from Guatemala.

The audience, a mix of townspeople who dropped in every Friday evening and alumnae, applauded his efforts to traverse South America in song even if he sometimes didn't know what the words meant or offered creative translations. He was moving clockwise across the shoulder of South America, heading for Brazil, with an enthusiasm that deflected criticism. After a children's song from French Guyana, he rested his guitar on his knee during the applause.

"Now it's your turn," he said with a timid glance at Silva's table. "There's a custom in Brazil," he said. "Two singers make up verses, either freestanding or in reply to each other. The contest can go on for days. They do the same thing in Portugal. Isn't that right, Chief Silva?"

"Oh hey, holding out on us, Joe."

"Hey, you never told me that."

"Put him on the spot."

"Okay, okay," Joe said when the calls didn't die down. He glanced at Gwen MacDuffy. Since she had put her own personal life in order about a year ago, she had become receptive to his attentions, and they saw each other at least once a week. The loneliness that seemed about to overtake his middle years was forgotten. "Yes, we do it all over Portugal. It's called O Desafio."

"Which means absolutely nothing to us," Gwen pointed out.

"It means The Challenge. It's just what he said," Joe explained, nodding to the singer. "It's a contest between two singers, who match each other verse for verse, usually a man and a woman."

"Don't look at me," Gwen said, holding up her hands, but everyone did anyway. His friends urged him on, calling for Joe to give a sample of a true Portuguese song while others clapped in unison. It was a moment he could have passed through gracefully, but he was a man who loved good fun of the sort little available now, and when he did meet it, he rarely had the opportunity to indulge. The singer struck a few chords while Joe studied him, polishing a few lines in his head. His friends urged him on, one man calling for a risqué tale.

"You must take this seriously now. This calls for heart and wit and courage," Joe insisted, only half-joking. It occurred to him that music in America had become a passive experience for most people, probably for almost everyone in this room. It was a sad way to know music, in his view. "All right, I'm ready." He cleared his throat. "We are serious now."

"Portuguese, if you please, for the total experience," one of the women demanded. "Let's do it right."

Joe nodded, paused, then began again.

O Senhora, escute para este senhor
Quanto eu falo triste, real canto,
Eu amo a irma dela unico
Com vida e riqueza a dividar.

O Lady, listen to me
While I tell you a sad, true tale.
I love your daughter only
With life and wealth to share.

Joe's friends cheered and laughed, which he acknowledged with a slight bow and a wave of his hand. He wouldn't dare admit it, but he was inordinately pleased with this sort of fun.

"Now, Sir," he said to the singer. "You must reply."

The young man frowned, chewed his lower lip for a few seconds, then said, "But you have to put it into Portuguese."

"Agreed." Joe laughed.

"Okay, here goes." The young man strummed and sang.

O Sir, I hear your story.
O Senhor, eu ouco o canto dele
And the sorrow in your heart.
E a tristeza no coracao dele

The folksinger paused; everyone waited. A deep, gentle voice flowing from behind them concluded the verse.

But that beauty is too wily
To linger in these parts.
Mas aquela beleza esta mais destro
Para persistir neste distrito.

The audience cheered before Joe had even begun his final translation; they clapped, delighted with the wry sentiment interjected into a seemingly tragic, lovelorn verse. Everyone turned to honor the winner of the contest. Behind them stood Vic Rabelard, his fingers laced around a beer bottle, with Band-Aids on both hands and across one eyebrow. He gave no sign he heard the applause, or intended the wry, humorous tone in his words.

TONY OSTELL HAD NOT been lying when he told his mother and stepfather he was planning on meeting some of his friends later that evening. A quick phone call to a friend's house told him where he could find them when he was ready, but he was not ready yet and he wasn't sure when he would be. He'd been staring at his computer for at least ten minutes, since right after he saw Vic Rabelard's car drive down Basker Court and turn onto Trask Street a little after seven o'clock.

The computer blinked at him, as though it were spitting an electrical charge at his mind, stimulating him to get to work, to pull up the list of qualifications and arguments he had been developing and polishing for the last year as he went from interview to interview, searching for the one opening that would be his beginning. With the optimism of youth, he was convinced he would need it soon. He had listened to his father's story about joining Vic Rabelard's business, but he had no inheritance (since both parents were still living) to smooth his way; then came Hugh's story about beginning in the rag room as a teenager, but he had less than zero chance of getting a job on the floor with his degree, since interviewers considered that a guarantee that he would want to move into sales or management as soon as possible.

Frustrated, he shut off the computer and headed out to the garage. Across the street neighbors on Basker Court were gathering in a backyard, ready to cook steaks on a grill. For no apparent reason, they burst into laughter. The bug lights that buzzed erratically all night long were quiet.

It seemed to Tony that he had never noticed his neighbors before. He knew them by name and that seemed enough. Some of them had children he had known through school or Scouts or Little League, but none was ever more to him than another family who lived on the Court. Of course, that was probably how they felt about him and his family. Flames started leaping from the grill and Tony headed for the garage; he had promised he would clean it up so his stepfather could use it over the next weekend, and this time Tony had to keep his word. He cut across the lawn and went into the garage through the narrow side door, letting it bounce and slam behind him. Outside the neighbors brought out a radio, turning it loud enough for Tony to hear.

Tony moved to the workbench and started putting away small tools, throwing glass bottles into the recycling bucket, and putting away odds and ends he no longer needed. The strains of an old Beatles song drifted in; he sorely wished he'd gone to the beach with his friends instead of lingering to work on his resume just one more hour. All his efforts seemed wasted, whatever he did, however much effort he gave it.

Tony's thoughts ran around and around, skidding along the land of dreams and over the bumpy terrain of reality, but no matter where he started out, he ended up in the same place. A man had to love his work to be happy, and he had to do the work that he loved. He had to hold on to what he wanted and not let anyone rip it away from him. He wiped down the workbench, pleased that his stepfather would at least have room in part of the garage, thanks to him. He couldn't do anything about the hole in the roof that let in the squirrels in winter and summer, but he was satisfied with the rest of it. A car that needed a new exhaust system cut off the neighbor's music; Tony looked out to see a taxi delivering Vic Rabelard to his back door.

It was five after eight. Time to head for the beach.

"I'M TELLING YOU these guys are still out there." The words were those of a man in his early forties dressed in carefully pressed khaki slacks, a Brooks Brothers oxford cloth shirt, tie, and navy blazer, a uniform often worn by Yankee men despite its uncanny similarity to the uniforms of young boys in England's most exclusive public schools. The man in question had tipped his head back and to the side after he spoke, as though he expected an especially violent response.

"Really, Mark, you're too much," a woman said. All four in the small circle were wearing campaign buttons with a blue background and the letters MHS and the number 69 printed in green. All four were also holding what was not the first drink of the evening, but like the rest of their generation, their drinks were beer or wine or non-alcoholic. For the most part, hard liquor belonged to an older generation, along with the Depression, World War Two, the Korean War, and life before television.

"Would I make that up?" Mark protested, shrugging his shoulders in a gesture of bewildered innocence. "They're still using the laundromat in town and outfitting their kids at the local thrift shops. It's a hoot." He took a sip of his lite beer.

"Maybe the band of renegade Green Berets shouldn't be thinking about going into Vietnam to search for remnants of the 82d Airborne," the other man said. "We should be sending them into the Sierras and the Green Mountains and the White Mountains to look for leftover hippies." They chuckled to the strains of "Bad Moon Rising." No one seemed to be able to think of anything else to say, perhaps from the discomfort of recalling long forgotten years of limited financial resources.

"Maybe they want to be left alone," one of the women essayed tentatively. "Just to be at peace. Some people don't like the way the rest of us live. It makes them unhappy."

"Aw, hell," Mark said, waving away her comment.

As teenagers in the 1960s, the members of the class of 1969 watched much of the turmoil of the era from the sidelines; as a result they wavered between envy and admiration, between contempt and loyalty for the principles of their youthful days and older siblings. Some regarded themselves as too sophisticated to be caught up in an altruistic, utopian movement; others longed to be part of something trendy, new, larger than their ordinary lives.

"Who's unhappy?" Polly Jarman said, sidling into the group after hearing the woman's remark.

"No one," the other man replied.

"Good," Polly replied. "We have such a lovely weekend worked out for everyone that I couldn't bear the thought of anyone not having a good time. Particularly since you've all come so far." She put a hand through an arm of each man and drew them close to her. "You fellas only came from Bar Harbor but some have come from as far away as Minneapolis and California." She nodded superciliously, pleased with the results of her yearlong planning efforts.

"And you're going to give them an award," Mark said, looking irritated.

"Eat your heart out, Mark," the woman across from him said. "One class award you didn't win."

Mark raised his hands in mock surrender, saying, "I had no idea you felt this way," and moved toward the bar. Convinced that no guest at any function could possibly be happy wandering around on his or her own, Polly quickly followed him.

"I was so sorry that I couldn't get Mrs. Claflin to come, but she's retired now, in the South, and the trip was just too much for her," Polly said, trying to erase any lingering unpleasantness. "And of course, dear old Manny Fanny has transcended."

Mark turned to study her. "What are you going on about? I thought the principal died."

"He did," Polly said, miffed that Mark didn't appreciate her stylish expression. "Well, never mind that. I want to meet your wife," she said. "Didn't I see you come in with her?" She tried to sound cheery again; Mark sighed, gave her an exasperated look, and nodded to a man and a woman who were talking desultorily.

"Who's the man?" Mark asked.

"Don't you recognize him? That's Vic Rabelard," Polly said. Mark thought for a minute.

"The kid who came in in his senior year?"

"That's him," Polly said, delighted that Mark remembered. "He stayed. Settled down. He and his wife have two girls. Just lovely. They look like her, even though they're not blood."

"What happened to him?" Mark asked. "He looks like he was hit by a truck." Polly was annoyed by this comment; it seemed to her to be in bad taste. She had been hoping the evening would take off into a loud, rousing band of reminiscences and laughter, but instead those who had remained in Mellingham talked to each other about local politics (mostly schools, sewer rates, and where new sidewalks were needed compared to where they were going to go); the out-of-towners caught up on the details of their lives and then drifted into general discussions of national issues. She had been struggling all evening with various techniques for melding the two groups—with little success.

"Oh, Eliot. How are you?" She threw her arms around Eliot Keogh, nattily attired in a lightweight summer suit, yellow shirt, and yellow and blue silk tie,

looking rested and relaxed except for a certain anxiety
in his eyes, a cut on his lip, and a Band-Aid near his
left ear. Polly didn't seem to notice. "You remember
Mark?"

The two men shook hands, mumbled greetings, and
tried to recall what they had thought of each other as
teenagers. Neither one had the inclination to try to im-
press the other, since the bar was filled with men and
women in a state of juvenescence, and all the good-
natured puncturing of pretensions that implied. Both
men opted for courtesy.

"Good to see you after all these years," Mark said,
then paused. "I can't say I remember you well."

"I left after my junior year," Eliot explained.

"And this is Mark's wife," Polly said, beginning the
second round of introductions. "And Vic Rabelard."

"You!" Vic said, turning toward Eliot and cutting
off Polly, who stood dumbly between Eliot and Mark
wondering what was happening to Vic. He stumbled
toward them, knocked viciously at a yellow balloon,
which bobbed and darted from its anchor on the ban-
quette, and wobbled on his feet. His face was red, and
he ran his palms down the front of his jacket as though
to wipe away the sweat. He shook his head jerkily as
he leaned toward Eliot, who jumped back a foot, then
bent his knees and clenched his fists.

"What did you do to her?" Vic asked in a low
growl. "Where is she?" Only Eliot was close enough
to hear him, and he was too keyed up by meeting this
unknown foe again to listen carefully to what he was
saying. Eliot looked desperately around him.

By now the other alumnae had figured out that something was happening and were gathering around to
watch, some with the childish glee of boys at a fight

in the middle of a hockey game and others with the hypnotic stare of those who wished they were elsewhere but couldn't pull themselves away. Still others were convinced they should stop the fight and were ashamed they lacked the courage. A few cheered on Vic, since most of his classmates who remained in Mellingham knew and liked him, and others crowded forward asking questions.

Even Theodore Syzycky pressed close, an energetic man ever appreciative of the sporting event. Not for a moment did it distress him that this affray occurring in his place of business might affect his license or reputation or livelihood. The moment was all, and right now the moment was grand. He jabbed with his left and thrust with his right, bouncing on toes tight with excitement; he jumped forward and danced back, and was nearly knocked off his pins by Patricia pushing her way through the crowd. In her zeal she spun him around, leaving him jabbing dazedly at three green balloons. Chief Silva was right behind Patricia in a second, but soon got ahead of her; he stepped between the two men just in time to intercept a fist in the kidneys and another in the shoulder, neither of which was strong enough to knock him off balance. Vic recognized him and recoiled, bumping into the crowd behind him. Joe thrust his badge in front of Eliot's face. The sales rep slowly unfolded his limbs from the fighting stance and backed away from Silva.

"He attacked me," Eliot said, pointing at Vic.

"Get him a seat and some coffee," Joe told Patricia, indicating Vic.

"He attacked me," Eliot repeated for the fifth time as Joe pushed him into a chair in the other room. "Out in the Preserve. This afternoon. He did." Eliot pleaded with Joe to believe him, but his eyes were flickering around the room as he spoke and Joe was dragging a chair across the floor to sit opposite Eliot.

"Now what was all that about?" Joe began as he sat down. "An old grudge?" He spoke kindly, trying to calm down the other man. Fights could break out anywhere, but Joe hardly expected one to break out among this crowd; their age as well as their reason for gathering militated against it.

"I never saw him before in my life. Honest!" Eliot still had the wild eyes of a man who has just endured an unexpected, frightening assault and does not yet believe it has ended. "He just attacked me. He sees me and he attacks me. He's crazy."

"You're a member of the class of 1969, aren't you?" Joe asked, inspecting the man's cuts and bruises. With his thinning brown hair and expanding paunch, Eliot Keogh didn't look like the type of man to get into fights and Silva was not inclined at this point to make something out of the marks if the other man didn't raise the matter himself. To Joe's eye, the man was a completely ordinary middle-aged, middle-class, middle manager, the kind of citizen every police chief liked to have in his town—someone who never went to excess in anything. This made the current situation all the more puzzling. "You're here for the reunion."

"Yeah, yeah, that's right. Eliot Keogh. I came in today. Flew in from New Orleans." Eliot started to calm down with the change in subject; his breathing grew deeper, slower, though his fingers still dug into his thighs.

"You live in New Orleans?" Joe asked.

"No. New Hampshire. I work for a paper mill. Sales

rep.'' Eliot reached into his pocket for a business card, which he handed to Silva.

''I believe Mr. Rabelard—that's the man you were fighting with—he's also in the paper industry. He owns a paper distributorship with Richard Ostell,'' Joe said, watching for Eliot's response. It was unusual for him to have to break up fights in Mellingham. The tidy homes and narrow streets urged dignity on its modern-day residents, just as its rocky shore and poor soil urged perseverance on those of an earlier era. ''Do you know Richard Ostell?'' Silva asked.

''Richard?'' Eliot said, looking up. For the first time in their conversation, Eliot looked directly at Joe. ''Him and me and Hugh Chase were pals, we were always hanging around together. I came back really to see them.''

''Hugh Chase is here,'' Joe said. ''I think he's been here for a while.''

''He is? I didn't have time to talk to anyone, except Polly. I just came in the door. I'm late, I know, but I had to take a rest.'' He glanced up at Joe, and then apparently thought better of what he was going to say. ''I was heading for the bar when Polly grabbed me,'' Eliot said. ''Then that man came at me. Out of no-where.''

''Is it possible you've met him before, Mr. Keogh?'' Joe asked.

Eliot shook his head.

''Maybe he mixed you up with someone else,'' Joe said. Eliot Keogh was tense, but he seemed to be sober and, except for his fear of being attacked, which was understandable under the circumstances, he seemed sane. ''It's probably just a misunderstanding,'' Joe said. Eliot was about to protest when Joe rose, told

Eliot to wait there, and returned to the front room, where Vic was sitting morosely by himself in a booth, staring down at a cup of coffee.

"Smells good," Joe said. Vic grunted. "Do you want to tell me what happened?"

"I tried calling but no one answered. So I came by to ask Polly." He nodded to the familiar figure barely visible in the crowd at the far end of the room. When the fight was over, the other guests spun off into smaller groups where they tried to talk normally about other things. "I thought maybe she came on without me," Vic said, looking around at the crowd. No one nodded or waved to him; he was a stranger now, or worse, a pariah. Vic had entertained his friends and classmates for a few minutes but in the end he had embarrassed them by revealing that the fight was personal. It wasn't friendly banter; it was a grudge match.

"She's leaving me," Vic said in a whisper. "Because of him." The tears rolled down his cheeks, both repelling and pricking Joe's sympathy. Vic repeated his lament while Joe wondered who was confused here—Eliot or Vic. Or perhaps it was Joe, perhaps both men were drunk and had peculiar ways of manifesting it. Whatever it was, a wife had a right to leave her husband but he didn't have a right to pick fights because of that. Joe tried to assuage Vic's grief by listening and sympathizing, but there was very little he could say; he hadn't even known Vic Rabelard and his wife were having difficulties. He idly wondered if Eliot's bewilderment was from not having heard Vic's name and not understanding who he is.

"Maybe if you go home and talk to her," Joe suggested. More than anything else he wanted both men to drop their argument and go their separate ways. Two men fighting over a woman was a good way of ruining three lives. "Let's get you a cab." Vic gave no sign he heard Joe, who signaled to Patricia. She had been standing nearby, worrying just how much worse the evening could get, and now moved swiftly to the booth.

"Cab, right," she replied, and almost ran to the telephone. Five minutes later, Theodore and Patricia were helping a sweating, stumbling, barely coherent Vic Rabelard into the back of the local taxi, promising him that his truck would be perfectly safe on the streets of Mellingham for the rest of the night, that the police wouldn't ticket it on Saturday morning (Chief Silva would see to it personally), and Mindy was probably at home wondering why Vic hadn't waited for her. After all, it was only 8:00. And, finally, tomorrow was another day, another party, another chance to get together with old friends. Theodore slammed the cab door shut and stepped back onto the sidewalk. In seconds Vic was gone.

"You did that real nicely," Patricia said, putting her arm around her husband and resting her cheek on the top of his head. His eyes glinted in the moonlight and he nuzzled her neck with a cold nose to the sounds of "Hot Fun in the Summertime."

"I UNDERSTAND SOMEONE'S looking for me." The man standing in the doorway between the two rooms of the Loblolly Bar was wearing the blue and green button that identified him as an alumnus, pinned to a seersucker jacket worn over dark blue denims. He was tall, taut in waist and limb with a mild gaze that remained unaltered wherever it landed. Joe Silva turned, recognized Hugh Chase, and indicated with a nod a table nearby.

In the few minutes it had taken the Syzyckys to remove Vic Rabelard from the bar, at least one of the two rooms had returned to normal. Eliot Keogh sat alone at a table trying to figure out how things had gotten so out of hand. For a brief second he had the shocking idea that maybe he had come back after all, all the way back, to the real past, to the last year before he left when people he knew—friends of his parents and parents of his friends—were unable to conceal a cool disapproval beneath their courteous words.

"Eliot Keogh," Hugh Chase called out as he approached the table. Eliot looked up warily.

"So you really made it," Hugh said with genuine warmth, shaking the other man's hand. All Eliot managed to say in reply was yeah, but he said it two or three times depending on whether one interpreted the sound as a sigh or a word.

"Polly said you were here. Good to see you, Eliot. Bring me up to date." The two men sat down, Hugh easily and fluidly, Eliot with the measured movements of a man preparing to bolt at any second. As he settled back into his chair, he noted somewhat enviously that Hugh's hairline might have been receding, like his own, but at least the process was uniform, leaving him with a thinning blond thatch rather than what he, Eliot, had. Unconsciously, Eliot raised his hand to his bald spot and began to talk about his wife. Hugh listened, then mentioned Becka.

"Becka Melonte?" Eliot asked, looking confused.

"The very same," Hugh replied, amused at Eliot's surprise. "And we're very happy."

"I thought she married Richard," Eliot said.

"She did," Hugh said. "They got married right after

graduation and they were divorced by the time I got back from Nam.''

"Oh.'' Eliot's mind was blank. He couldn't think of a single thing to say. All these people were strangers to him, living lives of unpredicted and unpredictable trajectories.

"How about you?'' Hugh asked.

"Me? Fort Knox,'' Eliot replied absently.

"What?''

"After graduation I was drafted but they sent me to Fort Knox. I guarded gold. At least I think that's what it was,'' he said, sighing. "It's all a haze now.''

"Just like it was then.'' Hugh chuckled. The gentle thrust at the memory of their military service woke Eliot up, and they lobbed memories back and forth like unarmed grenades.

"Where is Rich?'' Eliot asked after a while. "I was hoping he'd be here too.''

"He's around. He'll show up,'' Hugh said. Across the room Joe Silva and his friends were making up songs and jokes, keeping the guitar player busy. In the other room a woman was singing along with "Leaving on a Jet Plane'' while someone else hooted at her. "So you're happily married—same wife all this time.'' Hugh spoke off-handedly, but his voice was tight, even.

"Yeah,'' Eliot replied, apparently not noticing the change in his friend, and launched into another story about his wife, whom he unashamedly loved in the same way he had as a twenty-two-year-old. She had encouraged him to do the one thing that mattered to him almost as much as paper did, and then stood by him as he faced the inevitable hurdles. He loved talking about her; it reminded him of whatever in his life was worthwhile. He concluded his rambling tale with a reference to his daughter's latest award in basketball; she played forward.

"My congratulations to her," Hugh said at the end, looking relieved. "I heard about what happened with Vic." Eliot's eyes widened.

"He's crazy," Eliot said.

"Maybe," Hugh said. "He's been odd the last few days. He seems to be under some kind of strain but he hasn't wanted to talk about it."

"He's a crazy man," Eliot repeated.

"I've known him for years. He's always been a decent man who loves his family," Hugh explained. "If you think he's crazy, then something's gone terribly wrong in his life." Hugh ordered another drink. "Anyway, I'm glad to hear you have nothing to do with it." Eliot seemed unable to relax, and Hugh cast around for another topic. In the end, he repeated himself. "It's okay. Vic'll work it out. What about you? Let's get back to your life." In the next room Elvis Presley was singing "Suspicious Minds."

"So, it's true. You came. You actually made it." The brash voice could disrupt any conversation, break up any group; Eliot and Hugh turned at once. Richard Ostell strolled up to the table, hands on his hips, a wry smile lifting his salt and pepper moustache. He was taller than the two other men, and could easily have stood with his hands resting on their shoulders where they sat without putting much of a bend in his elbows.

"You old bastard," Rich said, grinning hugely. "Not even here a day and already you got my partner going wild. Good for you. He deserves it." Eliot stumbled to his feet to embrace his old friend. It was testimony to Richard Ostell's stentorian personality, in contrast to Hugh's irenic one, that Eliot forgot his despondency. It was evident within seconds, however, that Rich was as acidulous as ever. He pulled out a chair and sat down. "You always knew how to make an entrance."

Eliot Keogh was in heaven; he barely knew what he was saying now. The years dissolved, and the first of the darkest ones disappeared entirely. The friends he sat with tonight knew only the boy he had wanted to remain, held no judgment over him; they accepted him totally. The three men bantered as though they were still fifteen.

"I got to hand it to you, Eliot," Richard said, not yet tired of laughing at his own jokes. "You sure know how to make an entrance. The best two I've ever seen in my life. First you blow up the school, and then twenty-five years later you beat up the first classmate you see. A class act," Rich said, in high good humor.

"I tripped," Eliot said, grinning. "You're never going to let me forget it, are you?"

"How many people can set a science lab on fire just by walking into the room on the first day of classes?" Rich laughed and jabbed Hugh, who managed a tolerant smile. "Pay no attention to him," Rich said to Eliot, indicating Hugh. "He's just pissed because he had to raise my son. All I had to do was pay for it."

"Have you guys been riding each other all these years?" Eliot asked, wishing heartily he had been here through it all.

"It gives him something to do," Hugh said, "since he lets Vic do all the work in the business."

"He's just jealous because he was too stupid to take my advice and avoid the draft," Rich countered.

"How did you avoid the draft?" Eliot asked.

"Flat feet," Rich said proudly.

"And how was Hugh supposed to avoid the draft?" Eliot asked.

"He offered to break my arches for me," Hugh replied.

"What!"

"Hey, what are friends for?"

IT IS CUSTOMARY to assume that all high school and college reunions pursue the same path, a predictable curve of awkwardness punctuated by curiosity and probing, followed by ebullience and mellowness, even after allowing for the variety of hues in the greenery along the wayside. The problem is perhaps that alumnae revelers recall their adolescence, and adolescents are notoriously, even avidly, sequacious. Middle-aged alumnae are, therefore, doomed before they even lift their first can of beer.

Patricia Syzycky had reached this point in her ruminations by thirteen minutes before midnight, almost an hour after her husband, Theodore, had cha-cha-cha-ed away from the bar, only to collapse into a dark mass reminiscent of seaweed in the last booth at the back. He was, as he had once opined many years ago, a morning person at heart. Patricia pulled two more beers and set them on the counter.

The few patrons not members of the class of 1969 had departed some time ago, the guitar player had collected his pay and gone off to scribble down verses from the evening's marathon singing contest, and the oldies but goodies in musical history from the glorious year of 1969 had been replaced, at the mischievous instigation of Richard Ostell, with the singing, swaying, sashaying, hip-hop-hopping heptad, which was, just then, making its way down the center aisle to the tune of "Sugar, Sugar," of which they seemed to be able to recall only the first two words. "Great fun. You're a great lady and you throw a great party." Eliot Keogh leaned across the bar on both arms, sweat and joy glistening from every pore.

"Thank you, sir. Why don't you let me call you a cab," Patricia replied, moving toward the telephone.

"He's not drunk," Rich said, slapping his old friend on the back. "He blubbers. All through high school he did exactly the same thing. Like an old woman."

"You know, Mr. Ostell," Patricia began, marveling that she and Theodore managed to remain in business, "one of these days someone's going to do you in and put all of us who know you out of our misery."

Rich put his elbow on the bar and roared with laughter. "You're a pinchable broad, you know that?" He slapped Hugh in the chest with the back of his hand.

"Stop working so hard at it," Hugh said.

"Rich, one of these days I'm going to get even with you," Eliot said, turning to him. He tried to look angry, but his face collapsed into a stupid grin. "I'm okay," he said, turning to Patricia with a woozy, dazed smile. "Just really happy." Still skeptical, Patricia looked at Rich, who shrugged in a show of ignorance, then at Hugh, who nodded confidently.

"In that case, good night, sir." She bowed slightly and Eliot turned to the crowd and yelled out good night to all, but no one paid him the least attention. Rich slapped Eliot on the back again and pushed him to the door. Hugh slid into a booth beside his wife, Becka, and joined another conversation about sewer rates. Behind the people sitting opposite him he could see Polly Jarman watching the revelers, her old classmates, with a look of amazement giving way to dismay. When Patricia announced it was midnight, for some inexplicable reason, everyone cheered.

NONE OF THE *joie de vivre* of his classmates reached Vic Rabelard. At midnight he sat at the dining room table in an otherwise empty house, right where he had settled just after eight o'clock when the taxi driver had helped him up the back steps and left him after Vic's repeated assurances that he was all right. He'd had enough energy left to pour himself a glass of iced tea and excavate a leftover tuna fish sandwich from the refrigerator. At first he nibbled the sandwich while standing in front of the open refrigerator, then made his way to the dining room, where he continued to nibble and sip, but since sitting down he'd felt progressively weaker, and he knew it wasn't entirely physical.

He pushed away the sandwich crust. A sheet of paper-white moonlight fell over his hand, turning the red, raw spots from his earlier fight into gray patches. He reached into his pocket and smeared antiseptic cream on his hands and neck, gently working the cream into his skin. It was a wonder to him that he hadn't noticed before the direction of his life. Mindy was everything to him, had always been everything to him, and probably would always be everything to him, but the little things that helped get him through life—and sometimes the big things too—came from other people. Becka always loaned him her antiseptic cream—every summer, after his first bad burn, she was right there with a tube or a jar or a bottle—never accusing him, reminding him, cutting him down. Hugh gave him a line of paper to distribute when it looked like he was skating on ice that was cracking beneath his blades. And he was going to pay that debt, for sure. And Richard. Richard saved everything so Vic could go on worshipping Mindy. And where did it all lead?

Vic drew his hands down his shirt front, wiping away the sweat, wishing he'd installed an air-conditioner downstairs instead of just one, in their bedroom, upstairs. The girls didn't complain, but the older he got, the more the summer heat bothered him. He stretched out his legs, kicked off his shoes, wiggled his left foot, which had gone to sleep, and pushed his chair back from the table. He could think only of Mindy, of her black, sleek hair curling forward to cup a pink ear, her bangs tickling her eyebrows, short black waves swinging against her smooth white neck like heavy satin tassels as he followed her up the stairs to bed, and of her promise in the beginning—the one thing he couldn't get out of his head. He reached for the iced tea.

That was the one thing about Mindy that no one else could ever come close to. She always kept her promise. You only had to ask her once, never mention it a second time if she agreed, and later, when the time was right, she did what she said she would. Mindy, with her dark eyes of promise, always kept her word.

Desperate, Vic pushed himself upright, stood, swayed forward, then back, and collapsed on the floor. His left arm twisted awkwardly beneath him; the flesh of his cheek pressed upward against his eye. All he could see were the gray strands of the rug and the tiny grains of dirt settled among them. He seemed to have entered another environment, but he wasn't sure where it was or how he'd gotten here. The gray threads turned into bare shrubbery in winter. This must be how Gulliver felt when he first woke up among the Lilliputians.

THREE

Saturday Morning

THE MORNING AFTER the first night of the reunion weekend took its expected course. Those who had come from afar, even if afar was only fifty miles, studied their consciousness of self as they lay in bed in the Agawam Inn or in a guestroom in a friend's home, wondering how they were different, trying to sense in one moment of sublime perception the vast growth that separated their current selves from their adolescent outlines, striving for a panoramic view of their true identity, as though one could actually emerge to watch the self be. The quest was instigated not by profound insights but by excitement, plain old excess stimulation that for want of a better subject was turned back onto the thinker.

Becka Chase was not an exception. Unfortunately, she already knew all about this sensation, which skewed the direction of her thoughts. Her divorce almost twelve years ago, followed by Vic's subsequent abrupt end to their clandestine affair, had triggered an overwhelming anxiety and urgent self-assessment, such as she allowed herself then. She drew out and studied like entrails her bad habits of impatience, sarcasm, and selfishness, vowed to remake her character, and snapped all morning at her mother when she dropped by the card shop where she was working then. A few months of this unrelenting misery led her to desire only peace and security. The disruption of her ideal conception of herself thus had not led to any deeper understanding of her identity, and she put aside the quest to know herself as a journey highly overrated. The one truth to emerge from this time was her admission that she felt naked after her divorce. So her period of discontent came to an end only after she settled into another marriage, with Hugh Chase, and felt free to devote herself to raising her child. She was happy.

Becka turned her thoughts to her son, Tony. What she saw amazed her—she measured her life by him. If Tony was doing well—in school, in sports, at home—it had to be because she was doing well. Even her work supervising a cafeteria in a small, private day school held no special place in her life; it was a job. Nothing more. She neither wanted nor needed anything other than Tony's life to appreciate her own. For him she was ready to sacrifice everything—even Hugh. If he came home from school in a larky mood, her own mood instantly improved. Over time she ceased to understand the connection between them and viewed him as her talisman. He made her feel good, so she did everything she could to make him happy. Her needs melded with his, were sublimated in his, without her even being aware of it.

Every once in a while she sensed a tickling in the back of her head. She thought it might have something to do with her son but she couldn't quite get at it, which was why Becka sometimes thought she was going around in circles, wearing a track in the ground of her life. With the resistance typical of her intellectual life,

Becka attached the feeling to whatever was bothering her at the moment. This Saturday morning that meant Tony's job-hunting woes.

"Don't worry so much about it," Hugh said, trying to sound unconcerned from his side of the breakfast table. "He'll get something better. The right job will open up." Becka tried to smile; she wanted to believe him. She had promised Tony she would talk to Hugh and Richard just one more time, but it was a promise made without thinking, an emotional blank check written by a mother who had long ago forgotten the reasons for saying no. Now as she watched her husband drink his morning coffee and fill in the last of the crossword puzzle, she wondered what it was costing her. She knew she was paying with pieces of her marriage, but which pieces? Would the rising tension between them erode a vacation? Still the murmuring of a confidence? Dampen a joke? Open a rift?

"Hugh," Becka began again, leaning across the breakfast table. For a second she recalled Vic's description of her body and was confused, flattered. "Tony—"

"Have you seen Mindy this morning?" Hugh asked, interrupting her. Becka shook her head and leaned back; she was not within earshot of success. "Hmmph. I'm a little worried about Vic, after last night."

Becka reached for the coffeepot sitting on the warmer between them on the kitchen table. Hugh was a generous man; he had taken Tony to his heart, helping him with summer jobs, college tuition, advice about his future. Becka had been free to raise him as she saw fit unless Tony went too far and became defiant. Whenever something like that happened, whenever Tony transgressed one of the boundaries that lay invisible between them, Hugh spoke to Becka and Becka spoke to Tony. And when Hugh decided he didn't want to talk about Tony anymore, Becka knew she had crossed one of those boundaries.

"That was rather bizarre, wasn't it?" Becka said, pouring herself another cup of coffee; she would have to approach her husband another time. "It isn't like him to lose his cool like that." When she thought about it, she was torn between fascination with the spectacle of two old friends fighting in public and revulsion at knowing anyone who would make such a mess out of his life for all to see. "I feel sorry for Polly. She must have been appalled."

"Don't worry about Polly. She'll recover," Hugh said. "The Hindu god of thunder. Five letters." His pen rested on the crossword puzzle.

"You're not asking me that, are you?" she replied in better humor. "So, do you think we'll survive the weekend?"

Hugh chuckled. "Maybe that's why Mindy decided not to come. Too much of a good thing." The reunion party at the Loblolly Bar had seemed to Hugh just another evening in a long line of parties that had little meaning for him. He liked his old classmates, willingly saw them regularly, but had no lurking desire to resurrect the past or a buried part of himself. He knew what he had buried and why, and nothing had ever persuaded him to reconsider that decision.

"I can't believe she didn't tell me," Becka said as she rose to answer the telephone. "I was sure she meant to go last night."

"It was probably just a last minute thing," Hugh said. "Sarah or Angelina. Six letters." He pondered the clue for 23 down while Becka chatted on the phone for a minute. When she replaced the receiver in its cradle, she looked puzzled.

"That was Mindy's girls," Becka said. "They were on a sleepover last night and someone was supposed to pick them up for their swim class at the pool this morning." Becka paused. "No one came. And the girls said no one was home to answer the phone when they called just now."

"She's probably just late," Hugh said now working on 27 down.

"Mindy's never late," Becka said, going to the window.

"Is her car there?" he asked without looking up.

"No, neither is Vic's," Becka said. "It was still parked downtown when we left last night, wasn't it?" Hugh nodded as he filled in 17 across.

"Maybe you should go over and see if he heard the phone," Hugh said, tossing the newspaper onto the table. "I've got things to do. What time do we have to be there tonight?"

"Cocktails at six, dinner at seven-thirty, auction at nine. Dancing from ten till midnight," Becka said as she put the breakfast dishes in the sink. "And if you're feeling really jolly, there's a tour of the new high school—for those who haven't seen it—and an exhibit at the library on the last twenty-five years in Mellingham."

"How exciting," Hugh drawled.

"Show some respect."

"I'm going to the office. I'll be back around three." He gave her a quick peck on the cheek and headed out the front door. She could see him driving down Basker Court as she crossed the grass strip dividing the two properties. It occurred to her she had let him go without getting his help to move the donations for the auction over to the Agawam Inn. She'd have to cajole Vic into helping her, as risky as that might be. She knocked on the back door, trying out different phrases. She knocked a second time, then used her key and pushed the door open.

"Vic?" Becka called out as she entered the back hall. The lights were on in the kitchen, a radio announcer promised the news in five minutes in a distant room, the refrigerator hummed. In that second she could not have told anyone what day or year it was, so mundane were the sounds and sights and smells that greeted her.

"Vic?" she called out again as she crossed to the dining room. She leaned into the room, ready to call out again, even louder, then reached out with her right hand to grab the door jamb. Her knees buckled. She gasped, stepped back. Before her lay Vic Rabelard crumpled on the floor.

"Vic?" Becka called out, standing frozen in the doorway. She moved swiftly to his side, feeling for a pulse, raising his eyelids. She wasn't sure why she did this; it seemed the right thing to do. But now she didn't know what these motions had told her. He seemed to be alive but certainly not awake and not asleep.

"Mindy?" she called out. No answer. Becka stood up and moved away from Vic, then ran into the living room. It was empty. She ran upstairs, looking into each of the four bedrooms and the bathroom, and hurried down the back stairs. She and Vic were the only ones in the house. She ran to the telephone and called for an ambulance, then went back into the dining room, crouched down a few feet from him, and waited. The impulse to run through the house again to find some-

one, anyone, was still strong, making her bounce up on
her bended knees, then settle back, once again laying
her hand on Vic's shoulder. The radio announcer promised two free tickets to a Red Sox game to the tenth
caller who identified the composer of the next song he
played.

"They're on their way," Becka said. It seemed a
stupid thing to do, to talk to a man who had to be
unconscious or near death, but she felt she had to say
something, anything to reassure him. She knew her
mindless talk also had something to do with a need to
hold onto reality, the ordinary sequence of events that
could comfort and make order out of chaos. She knew
this the way people know the truth about their lives in
moments of shock or great stress, and then wait for the
ordinariness of days to cover it up again. This was
going to be one of those moments—and it was going
to last a long time. She could tell.

"Do you happen to know what's happened to
Mindy?" she asked, comforted by the sound of her
own voice.

"I looked upstairs just now," she said. "No one's
up there." She tried to hear the approaching siren.
"I'm sorry, Vic. I'm getting stupid, I know." She
dropped her head onto her arms folded on her knees.
"I wish I knew where Mindy is." Desperate to do
something, she collected Vic's shoes, which were lying
in disarray beneath the dining table where he seemed
to have kicked them off, and placed them neatly by the
door to the kitchen, then picked up the tube of first-aid
ointment lying on the floor. When she was done, she
had to go back to thinking about Vic lying before her
and Mindy nowhere to be found.

The sound of the siren grew from a thin whine to an

ear-splitting wail as the ambulance pulled into the driveway. Becka propped open the front door, then stood aside as men and women in EMT uniforms hurried back and forth, calling out directions, listening to static on their receivers, trying different methods to rouse Vic Rabelard.

JOE SILVA STEPPED BACK from the ambulance as the technician adjusted the brace on the dolly and then climbed in. Joe had a glimpse of a black sock with a worn spot beneath the big toe before the door slammed and the ambulance sped down Basker Court and onto Trask Street, its siren blaring. The chief rearranged his hat on his head, relieving an insistent pressure aggravated by the heat.

"Is he going to be all right?" Becka asked, coming up behind him. Joe had sent the man home barely twelve hours earlier without spending any time thinking about Vic Rabelard's bizarre behavior—as well as Eliot Keogh's—beyond getting them parted and calmed down, and was just then wondering with mild regret if he had missed something significant last night, anything that might have indicated that Vic's health was precarious or endangered.

"They'll do everything they can," he said. Banal. And yet it was the truth. The EMT crew would do everything they could and then the doctors would carry on. But at no time would anyone want to step forward and say, We don't know what's happening. We don't know how things will be in even an hour from now. So instead we offer reassurances to ease you over the fear and unknown. Joe couldn't say any of this; he didn't have to either. The sparkle of hope dulled in Becka's eyes. "Did you find him?" he asked.

She nodded, staring at the now empty street. The neighbors who had clustered a few feet from the ambulance had drifted back to their homes. To every question about locating Mrs. Rabelard, each had shaken a frowning face, looked around, tried to think of some answer to help the chief, then given it up as wasted effort and returned to scanning the open door and windows of the house for signs of activity. Becka slipped her hands into her pockets.

"Maybe I'd better take a look inside," Joe said. "The EMT crew wasn't sure what happened to Mr. Rabelard." He started to move to the front door. The brick path had been meticulously weeded recently, along with the flower bed in the front of the house. The stucco finish was an off-white without a single feather line or stain. Everything contributed to a feeling of prosperity and agreeableness.

"Someone has to call the girls," Becka said half to herself. Joe waited for an explanation. "That's why I came over. They called me because no one picked them up at their friend's house and no one answered the phone here when they called." She looked through the open front door, exactly like her own. "Vicky, the older one, sounded impatient, like she knew her parents couldn't do anything right and here was more proof of it. She's at that age." She paused, thinking she should smile. "She obviously has no idea anything is wrong."

"Do you know where Mrs. Rabelard might be?" Joe asked as he followed her into the house.

"No," Becka said, stopping and turning to him. "She didn't show up last night at the reunion party. But it doesn't look like anything's wrong." She entered the dining room. The EMT crew had pushed aside chairs and the dining room table in order to move easily around Vic, and the room was still in disarray. Becka sat in a chair in one corner, resting her head against the wall behind her, her eyes closed.

"They said he was in a coma. A deep coma," Becka said, looking over to the spot where Vic had most recently lain. "She kept saying that—the woman. He was in a deep coma. She wanted to know if he was diabetic or took drugs or anything like that." A look of incredulity passed over her face. "Can you imagine? Vic taking drugs?"

"I didn't know Mr. Rabelard," Joe said as he looked over the room.

"He was a straight arrow. Well, he wasn't into drugs," Becka said. Joe glanced at her, struck by the tone of her voice.

"They'll need to talk to Mrs. Rabelard," Joe said. "Do you think you can find her?"

"I don't know. I can't think where she could be. We usually take a walk together Saturday mornings but I told her I couldn't this week because of the reunion." Becka pushed away the curly light brown hair that lay close to her face, sweat matting it flat to her forehead and temples. To Joe she seemed much hotter than the weather warranted, hot as it was.

"Did Mrs. Rabelard tell you what she was going to do instead?" Joe asked. Becka shook her head. She was wearing a cotton blouse and shorts that brushed the tops of her knees, more clothing than she'd worn in days. She wouldn't admit to herself that Vic's attack bothered her, but she was glad she had given in to a conservative reflex this morning. She felt shy in Chief Silva's presence.

"All she said was that it was just as well that I couldn't go this morning," Becka said. "So I assumed she had other plans, but I didn't ask her what they were. I should have, but I've gotten so used to her lack of interest in that kind of thing that I've gotten out of the habit with her.'' Becka's voice started to rise.

"How were things arranged when you found him?'' Joe asked, hoping to interrupt her headlong rush into confusion. "Where was Vic? Sitting at the dining table?''

"No,'' Becka replied, walking to the center of the room. "He was lying on the floor. Right there.'' She pointed to an area of the rug and waved her hand over a large corner of it.

"And the table and chairs?'' Joe asked.

"Where they always were,'' Becka replied. "You can see the dents in the rug.'' Joe followed the line of her pointing finger.

"And the shoes? They were there?'' he asked, indicating the brown loafers placed side by side near the door.

"I did that,'' Becka said, looking down at them. "I can't think why. It seemed the right thing to do. I was just waiting here. I had to do something.'' The feelings of an hour ago began to come back to her. "I don't know what to do. What should I tell the girls? They're waiting for me to call them back.''

"Perhaps Mrs. Rabelard is staying with friends,'' Joe suggested. "You must know who her other friends are. Someone may know where she is. If you start phoning now, I'll stop by before I leave.'' Becka let herself be ushered out the door.

Joe assured himself that she was not about to return to the Rabelard house before he gave all his attention to the dining room. He repositioned the table, replaced the chairs, and inspected the shoes. Then he knelt down to inspect the spot where Vic had fallen.

This wasn't, strictly speaking, a crime scene; there was, as far as he could tell, no crime, but the senior EMT had been uneasy, hedging every comment with qualifications about his limited experience, restricted training, and legal requirements. He was plainly nervous. Instead of making Joe less curious, the EMT made him more so. The complication of Mrs. Rabelard's apparent disappearance—though part of him insisted she would show up with a perfectly reasonable (or unreasonable) explanation—stimulated his concern, and he began to inspect the well-cared-for room with a professional eye.

The modern cherry table seated six; a matching sideboard was decorated with half a dozen plates with bright borders. The windows were draped with red silk swags, and the gray rug caught the gray stripes in the multicolored wallpaper. It was a comfortable room that spoke of boldness and confidence as well as warmth and family.

The EMT crew had been careful not to damage or disturb the items on the table, and they seemed to rest where Vic Rabelard had left them. A small plate held the stale bread crusts of a sandwich; a tall glass with a heavy bottom held a light brown liquid that looked like iced tea or a soft drink diluted by ice; a pair of men's eyeglasses sat nearby. A paper napkin lay crumpled on the floor. Joe picked it up and dropped it on the table. Following instinct more than physical signs, Joe bagged the remnants of food and drink for inspection by the lab, then moved on to the kitchen. He did the same there, inspecting and bagging food from the refrigerator, checking the gas stove, searching for some sign of what might have sent an apparently healthy man into a coma. After an hour he loaded a box of samples into his car and locked it.

Joe returned to the house and knelt down again near the table. He wanted to see Vic Rabelard's medical crisis as an accident in an otherwise ordinary life but his instincts told him that was wrong. Vic had lain on the floor in a coma for perhaps ten hours or more. He was wearing the same clothes as yesterday, the dining room lights were on during a bright, sunny morning, and food and drink had been sitting for hours on the table. The previous night he had been in a senseless fight in a bar, where he went in search of his wife, whom he did not want to declare missing but sought hopelessly on his own. There had been another fight not too many hours earlier, before the fight in the bar. Now his wife was missing and Vic was in a coma. At the very least Mrs. Rabelard had picked an inopportune time to spend the night elsewhere without telling anyone of her plans.

There was no sign of a struggle or a fight in the house, but Vic had lain alone for most of the night—alone and untended. It reminded Joe of the night he had found a man who appeared to be asleep behind a dumpster in Boston. He had lain down with a dirty coat over him, perhaps thinking he was going to sleep. Joe always wondered if the man knew that it was his last night, if he was troubled, as he settled onto a shifting stack of flattened cardboard boxes, that no relative, no friend knew where he was. Did he understand what was happening to him? Did he yearn to call out to a businessman passing by on the sidewalk to come to him, stay beside him for that one moment when God lets go our hand in order to embrace us with both arms?

Joe stood up, took one last look around, and shut off the lights that had been burning since last night. He picked up the eyeglasses, inspecting their lenses, for the nearsighted. Joe folded them up, bagged them, and added them to the box in the cruiser. Another five minutes or so looking around the downstairs convinced him he had seen everything he needed. A pair of keys hung on a peg in the kitchen; he locked the front door and went out the back, locking it behind him and taking the keys with him, then walked down the driveway to the garage. He knew Vic Rabelard's white pickup was still parked on Main Street, waiting to be claimed. There was no second car parked here. The garage was orderly, a few gardening tools hanging on the joists, two snow shovels leaning in a corner, a lawnmower parked against the far wall. Joe, not really expecting to find anything, so not disappointed, crossed to the Chase home, ringing the bell a few minutes after ten o'clock. Becka answered the door. She looked tired and drawn.

"No one's seen Mindy," she said without preamble. "I've talked to Mrs. Conway, and she's told the girls as little as she can and they're going to stay where they are for now. I've promised to go over, but they're real scared." Joe followed her into the kitchen; a sheet of paper with a list of names, most of them crossed off, sat beside a cordless phone on the table. "I can't understand where she could be. What's going to happen?"

"Well, first off," Joe said, trying to keep her calm, "I'm taking some things for testing." He too didn't like the idea that Mrs. Rabelard was nowhere to be found. "But as for Mr. Rabelard, I think we'll just have to wait for the doctors to tell us. It's too soon to start worrying one way or the other."

Becka nodded. "I told the girls I'd take them up to see their father as soon as the doctor said it was okay." She offered Joe coffee from a full pot, but he declined.

"If I'm going to be looking for Mrs. Rabelard," he said, "it might help if I knew what kind of car she drives."

"Mindy's car? It's a red Escort. She got it last year."

"Do you happen to know the license plate?" Joe asked. Becka shook her head and eased herself into a chair.

"You don't think she's had an accident, do you?"

"It's just a precaution. If the car isn't here, then most likely she's driving it. Anyway, it's a place to begin looking," Joe said. It was an ordinary step in any situation, but he was surprised by the woman's reaction. She turned pale.

JOE DREW UP AT the stop sign at the end of Trask Street, prepared to turn right; instead the patrol car sat. He wasn't sure but he thought he had recently seen a red Escort where he didn't expect to. Last night. The trouble with trying to extract one memory from last night was that he had spent most of it in the company of Gwen MacDuffy, who compelled him to focus all his attentions on one person—her. Therefore, he must have seen the car either before he picked her up or after he took her home.

A car honked behind him; he looked in the rearview mirror. An elderly woman was leaning forward, peering at the patrol car over the steering wheel in search of a reason for the delay. Joe returned to the problem of the red Escort and swung left.

He drove slowly through the town, past the shops

catering more to tourists than townspeople and the old drugstore and on past a gas station, the post office, more stores, and across the train tracks. To his left was the train station. He turned in and drove straight to the red Escort parked at the other end of the platform shelter. The car had caught his eye when he had driven Gwen MacDuffy home last night because the car sat alone in the station parking lot, like the last child waiting in front of a school for a wayward parent to collect her. He pulled up behind the car and climbed out.

The red car was locked. Inside it was clean; no school papers or empty soft drink cans; no abandoned bathing suits lay heaped on the floor front or back. The trunk was also locked. Joe took down the license plate number and headed for the police station, a little depressed because Vic Rabelard seemed to have been right after all.

Until that moment Joe had forgotten precisely what Vic had said to him in the Loblolly Bar. His wife was leaving him, for another man, he had said. But certainly he seemed to be right about the first part: she had left him the night before, driving to the train station and leaving her car while she either drove off with someone else or caught a train to Boston. It was a neat, prosaic scenario, and all conjecture. Anyone could have driven the red car to the train station; it didn't have to be Mindy Rabelard's, and Mindy could have gone anywhere or nowhere. She could be buried in the Rabelard cellar for all Joe knew. He pulled into his parking space behind the nineteenth-century police station that continued to serve the town of Mellingham despite narrow doorways, leaking windows, rolling and creaking floors as well as the obligatory cramped offices and unreliable plumbing. Either you grew fond of the building, like an exasperating cousin, or you went crazy.

"There's a box in the trunk, samples for testing," the chief said to Officer Maxwell, who descended from his perch behind the main desk to collect the goods. "Get someone to take it over to the lab."

"Yes sir." Tall and thin with coarse brown hair that seemed to grab his skull, Maxwell always looked like he was recalling an especially entertaining tale and was just about to reach the punch line. Consequently, he always had a smile lingering around the corners of his mouth. Irritation, even disappointment at a friend's grumpiness were expressions foreign to his nature. He was the only person on the force unaffected by the change that had come over Sergeant Dupoulis since Joe had had to order him to take off some weight or face undefined sanctions from the board of selectmen.

It was a problem that had lingered for months, with Ken growing quieter and quieter, grumpier and grumpier, as he became thinner and thinner. With each pound he seemed to be less present as well as less. He was disappearing in more ways than one, and Joe had put off talking to him about it for as long as he dared. Watching Maxwell go out to the cruiser suggested a solution. Joe promised himself he would act—finally—as he went on to his office.

In the next few minutes Joe confirmed that the car was indeed owned by and registered to Vic Rabelard, and received a general description of Mindy Rabelard taken from her driver's license record. He had failed to acquire a photograph of her from the house, however, and some idea of where she might have gone from friends or family. The obvious next step of questioning her daughters did not appeal to him at all, and he cast around in his mind for an alternative.

A summer Saturday in Mellingham, particularly if it was fine, belonged to the tourists; traffic crawled down Main Street and parents posed their children in front of the polished granite trough. He had once thought of them as innocents safely protected from the harsher reality of life, people whose innocence was his responsibility, but that, he knew, was a self-serving delusion. The father posing his daughter next to his son, gently encouraging her to move just one inch closer, could be holding in abeyance grief over the loss of a parent, rage at his wife, revenge against a business partner for a deal gone bad. Mindy Rabelard, ever beautiful with her serene smile, was turning out to be an expert at deception. But of what? And of whom?

BECKA CHASE HAD ALWAYS considered herself a strong woman. She had taken self-defense training, marched at midnight in candlelight vigils, volunteered at shelters; she had trained herself in fortitude and understanding. There was not much she had overlooked in the 1970s, her personal decade of growth, exploration, and chaos, though to be honest all this was registered as both entertainment and business at the time. She looked for the best of her learned qualities now as she tried to keep at bay the mounting tragedies of the Rabelards, which seemed to threaten to tumble down upon her. The convenient belief that a family tragedy ended at a neighbor's property line had turned out to be as insubstantial as an empty milk carton.

The traffic on Trask Street picked up around noon. Becka attended to every car driving toward or away from Mellingham. The screen door creaked and whispered as the house breathed; the furnace came on, burned contentedly for a few minutes, storing up hot water, then shut off with a sharp click. The mailman riffled through his blue canvas bag as he approached the front door, then ran up the steps and dropped the bundle into the black metal box. He did the same next door. Becka wondered if she should collect the Rabelards' mail, then decided no, that would be intrusive. She let the mail sit. Not until the mailman was back on Trask Street did Becka rise from the kitchen table.

Becka collected her own mail and arranged it in its usual pattern on the hall table: circulars in one pile, bills and letters in a second, and Tony's in a third. She tapped this last pile with her index finger, then with a huff of determination gathered up the letters and carried them upstairs. She knew her son was still in bed, since he had made no sound and left no dirty dishes in the sink. She meant to talk to him about that, reminding him that he was now at a point where he had to carry as much of the household responsibility as any other adult, but whenever she got this far in her private conversations she was stymied. Hugh did next to nothing around the house and Tony knew it. She would have to find another line to reel in her son's behavior.

Becka rapped lightly on Tony's bedroom door, listened for a response, then slowly opened it. The room had been Tony's from the day they moved in. He laid claim to it as though only this space could keep desperation at bay; it was the only time Becka had seen just how deeply the divorce had affected him. Over the years his room had undergone numerous transformations; posters had gone up, come down, ceiling and walls had been painted blue, then red, black and white (briefly), and finally off-white. Clothing had moved from drawers to floor to under-bed and finally to the closet and a bureau. Some of the toys and computer games still lurked in corners, but gradually her son's room was progressing from a youth's den to a young man's bedroom. Tony rolled over and stared at his mother with gimlet eyes, blinked and sat up. Becka handed him his mail and sat on the edge of the bed with one foot tucked beneath her.

Tony flipped through the envelopes, then looked up at his mother. "Was there something you wanted to know about?" he asked. Becka shook her head and looked out the window. From here she could look down inside the Rabelards' kitchen. It looked like part of a doll's house with its brightly colored tile counters and linoleum floor.

"Vic's in the hospital," Becka said, turning back to her son. His eyes flickered with shock.

"He's in the hospital?"

"You slept through an ambulance—coming and going."

"What happened?" Tony sat up straighter, positioning a pillow behind his back.

"They don't know. He's in a coma." The restraint and wishful optimism she had been clinging to fell away like the bright plumage of a dying bird. She felt weary and frightened. The words rushed out of her. "I found him. This morning. He was lying in the dining room. They have no idea what happened to him. He looked awful. I had no idea sickness was so ugly. I mean, it's not like an old person who breaks a hip or has a stroke. This was something else. He looked so different. I don't know how I even knew him."

"It's okay, Mom. Don't let it get to you."

"You didn't see him." She shook her head. "I

didn't realize until just now how much it upset me."
She took a deep breath.

"What did they say?" Tony asked.

"They don't know what happened to him. You
know those marks all over him?" Tony nodded. "He
was in a fight yesterday. With Eliot Keogh. You don't
know him. He was in my class. He came back for the
reunion."

"Is that what did it?"

Becka shrugged. "Who knows?" She stared down
at the folded spread at the end of the bed for a moment.
A consciousness-raising session long ago in 1976, a
year she and her friends had chosen for their own personal declaration of independence, had led to the conclusion that any anger directed at men was justified
simply because the world created by and for them acted
out violence against women every minute of every day.
Not until she saw Vic lying on the floor did Becka truly
believe men could be as vulnerable and as worthy of
compassion as women. Instead of feeling even a mild
revenge at Vic's collapse, as she was told she would
someday, the events of the weekend so far, beginning
with Vic's bizarre attack, had stretched her feelings so
thin that she was afraid she would feather and shred
into nothing.

"Mom, are you okay?"

"Mindy's gone. She didn't show up last night. Vic
came looking for her when she didn't come home after
taking the girls over to their friend's. No one seems to
know where she is." She paused, looked at him, her
eyes searching. Tony shook his head.

"I didn't see her. I went out around eight, down the
beach. She wasn't over there when I left, at least I

didn't see her car, and I didn't pass her anywhere when I was out."

Becka looked disappointed. "The girls are staying with their friends."

"You said that," Tony commented. "It'll work out, Mom." Becka warmed at the words. For a moment she could believe it.

"What does the letter from Maine say?" she asked, pulling herself back into the present. Tony tore open the envelope and pulled out a thick sheet of paper. He read the letter quickly.

"I'm up for the second round of interviews," he said, still reading. The glow of pleasant surprise moved over his face.

"Honey, that's wonderful." Becka squeezed his ankles through the sheet. "I knew you could do it." Tony nodded slowly, a tinge of bewilderment in his eyes as he reread the letter. "It just takes a little while."

"Yeah," Tony agreed, putting the letter away. Becka listened to the crinkle of good cotton rag slide into its envelope.

"I didn't get around to asking you last night. Didn't you get something yesterday?" she asked. "I sort of remember putting something out." Tony frowned, shook his head.

"Just the usual stuff. Junk. My phone bill," he said, nodding to the phone on the desk by his computer. Becka nodded, looked around the room, then back at the remaining letters and circulars sitting in Tony's lap. He gazed at her.

"Well, that's that," Becka said, suddenly at a loss for words.

A PLEASANT SATURDAY morning invariably draws a dozen or so people of various ages to the edge of the inner harbor, where they sit on the huge granite blocks of the sea wall and watch friends or family wrestle with a frayed painter holding an aging skiff to the dock, or where they sit on canvas chairs and speculate on why Charlie Foster hasn't taken his putt-putt out in three days or has taken it out an hour earlier this morning. It doesn't matter which. Charlie Foster is a colorful guy and he's fun to talk about.

Chief Silva could see them entertaining themselves from his office window, and whenever he came up against a problem that was new to him, he was tempted to leave his office and stroll the village green or the harbor's edge in search of an old-timer who could tell him what the department had done about this matter before 1985, or perhaps 1955 or even 1935. If he mentioned his own uncertainty, he usually got a quizzical expression of disbelief in reply. He chalked it up to his failure to grasp immediately what was as basic as the alphabet to a native.

At present he was trying to decide if he should grant a license for a fortune-teller to set up a stall during the Fourth of July weekend as part of the local carnival. The application was in order, the woman had no police record in this area that he could find, and she had been a professional fortune-teller for thirty-three years. That was what bothered him.

Joe liked to think he was a fair-minded man. He knew that some people had an uncanny ability to understand the lives of others, but he did not believe this was to be found in palms or tarot cards. He also knew that some people could open themselves up to a level of feeling and sensing that led to inexplicable discoveries. Still others could trigger a healing faith in a stranger. Nevertheless, he had the normal suspicion of those who tell fortunes for a living and their tendency to prey on credulous, needy people. The problem was, he had been approached by a town committee to license a variety of new activities this year in order to salvage a sagging weekend that had become a fundraiser for local groups. Joe wasn't the least unhappy that interest in the carnival was waning; policing it was a headache. He put the application for a license away and reached for the telephone.

The EMT who had transported Vic Rabelard earlier this morning had been unable to give him any guidance about following up, so Joe had waited what he considered a reasonable period of time and now was anxious to learn whatever he could. After being passed from receptionist to nurse to attendant to nurse, he finally got the doctor in charge. Joe turned over his hourglass, to measure how long it took before Dr. Wintress's reservations gave way to loquacity. Even a police chief has a right to amuse himself.

Time: three minutes. It must be the man's lunch hour, Joe concluded.

"I'm not sure I should be talking to you," the doctor said. Joe helped him over that hurdle. "I'll tell you, we tested him for everything," the doctor explained, sounding impatient as he recalled his first dilemma of the morning. "He's anemic but otherwise he seems to be in good health. No drugs in his system. But we're still testing."

"He'd been in a fight," Joe prompted.

"Yeah, right. All the lesions were clean. He kept them clean." The admiration in his voice was obvious.

"Could that have anything to do with it?"

"The fight? Possibly. A blow to the temple. We're

still testing. He hasn't come out of it.'' He spoke with low, clipped syllables, as though he were uncomfortable with the subject and wanted to get away. "You should get his wife in here," he suddenly said, as though it had just occurred to him. "We may need her signature."

"We're trying to locate her." Joe could hear shuffling on the other end of the line, as though Dr. Wintress had shifted the receiver in order to hear more clearly.

"She's missing? You mean she left without telling anyone when she'd be back or she packed up and left?"

Silva was intrigued by the alternatives the doctor offered, the swiftness with which he moved to the most melodramatic possibilities. "The first one. It doesn't look like she took anything, including her car."

"We may need someone to authorize a procedure," the doctor went on. "Any other relatives?"

"Two teenage girls."

Dr. Wintress groaned. "Not good."

"And a business partner."

"Better." The telephone receiver seemed to be in transit again. "We have his medical records here. No sign that he has any untreated condition that could lead to coma." Joe waited. So far he had almost nothing except a doctor who would be willing to talk if he had something to talk about. The irony did not escape Joe.

"He'd been eating and drinking before he collapsed," Joe said after waiting for the other man to continue. "I sent everything up to the police lab."

"Let me know." Joe extracted the same promise from him and thanked him.

The phone call left Joe no better off than he had

been before. Both he and Dr. Wintress were avoiding confronting the one clear possibility—the fight between Eliot Keogh and Vic Rabelard had injured Vic enough to lead to his collapse, and unless he recovered the police would only have Eliot Keogh's version of events. Joe decided to change his plans for the evening.

Joe had never attended a reunion of any sort, but he had observed plenty of them. Such an occasion seemed a reasonable pleasure for those who had developed an allegiance to a particular institution, but Joe never had. He had liked his old high school as much as seemed healthy for a young man who was determined to get away, and he honored his university for helping him get what he wanted, but he was not a man for nostalgia. His life was in the present and going back to see how others had fared smacked to him of one more opportunity to indulge in envy or braggadocio or some other emotion he'd rather not cultivate in himself. That was ungenerous, he knew, but it was a measure of how uneasy the prospect of a reunion made him that he was willing to rationalize it in this way. Every few years the invitations and announcements arrived and he threw them away, unopened. Watching the Mellingham High School class of 1969 last night at the Loblolly Bar convinced him he was right.

FEW PARTS OF THE Tveshter Paper Mill reminded Hugh Chase of the Herman Melville story these days. Only the dark stained wainscoting in the stairwells consistently brought to mind ''The Paradise of Bachelors and the Tartarus of Maids,'' and then only when he passed up and down the stairs slowly enough to let his mind turn to something other than his work. The mill seemed almost quiet here, the hum of the dryers, the churning of the beaters, contained beyond thick doors.

He had been on his way to inspect a new dandy roll, the twenty-foot long cylinder of stiff wire gauze that imprints the watermark, at the instigation of an employee who thought he noticed damage on one end, when the bells had first called him back to his office. He had expected a very different phone call, since it was Saturday morning—perhaps a customer in New York dissatisfied with the sizing on a recent shipment, the laboratory supply company that needed clarification on an order, the insurance inspector rescheduling his visit. The second time he was called back to the phone he had been on his way upstairs to inspect a storage room. This time it was his wife, Becka, relating in a manner both stunned and anxious that she had found Vic Rabelard unconscious on his dining room floor.

"I don't know what could have happened to him," Becka said. "And I can't find Mindy. No one knows where she is." He barely heard her, only fragments of words, disconnected sounds, reaching him. He grasped that Chief Silva was there, somewhere in the neighborhood; he couldn't be sure exactly where or why, and he couldn't focus on it. His mind was on a storage area one flight up; the dandy roll two flights below was forgotten. In the end he knew Becka had said goodbye when he heard the dial tone.

A red button blinked on the gray machine on his desk. Hugh punched it.

"Am I right?" Richard Ostell said as soon as Hugh answered. "Of course, I am."

"I don't know. I haven't been up there yet," Hugh said.

"Aw gee, Hugh. Did I interrupt your coffee break?"

"Becka just called. Vic's in the hospital."

The two men listened to the silence along the phone line. Outside his window Hugh could see the shallow river working its way over boulders and pebbles, its greater body of water diverted into the canal on the other side of the building. Years ago, he reminded himself every once in a while, the water here overflowed its banks, finding only scrub and trees when it did so. There was mud.

"What do you mean he's in the hospital?" Richard asked, his voice low and soft.

"Becka found him unconscious and called an ambulance. They don't know what's wrong with him."

"Oh, no," Richard exclaimed. The bells rang. Hugh started to count—one, two, three, but the bells seemed to go on and on and on, up to five, then seven, then twelve. Bells were echoing along the halls, buzzers were bleating through the rag room. The light on his telephone flickered; he reached out to cut off the other line, then stayed his hand.

"I have another call," Hugh said.

"Get up there and take a look. I have to know," Richard said, his voice even and tense. "Especially now." Hugh promised he would and rang off, then transferred the other call to another line without answering it. Before he could be waylaid again, he slipped down the hall, through the fire door, and up one flight to a low-ceilinged room empty of workers. The cutting machines lay idle, the conveyer belt carrying boxed stock to the second floor also idle, a row of vacuum-wrapped boxes of stationery poised at the mouth of a tunnel to the packing room below. He turned a corner and flicked on the light over a storage area. The tall, distant windows gave sufficient light, but touching the switch and standing in the glare substantiated what he saw before him—a bare wooden floor and three bare walls of dark wood. At the open end, near him, stood a stack of wooden pallets. Hugh smashed his fist into the doorjamb and swore.

From the far end of the cavernous room into which the space opened came footsteps. A woman came into view, spotted Hugh and stopped, then waved. He lifted his right hand.

"Splinter," he said, waving his hand. She offered first aid, which he declined, and returned to her station.

He supposed he couldn't blame her. For almost twenty years he had moved through the Tveshter Paper Mill doing every job that had to be done until he knew everything about the mill and its manufacturing, except perhaps who machined the wood paneling in the original building. It was what his father had wanted all along, had counted on, had believed would happen regardless of the changes in politics or the economy. Washington might have riots, the language of the country might change from English to Tagalog, volcanoes could erupt in Alabama, but the Tveshter Paper Mill would continue and the Chases with it.

Hugh turned back to the stairs. On Saturdays few employees came in to work in the offices; usually the highest-ranking employee was a supervisor on the floor or someone in the lab unwilling to give up on an experiment even for a weekend. Today was typical. To the sound of his own footsteps he turned into a small office, switched on the light, and sat down at the desk. He turned on the computer and called up the file for the Lawrence Superior Paper Company, scanning the orders, discounts given, dates of shipment. It was not a long record, and the computer file did not contain the details Hugh was looking for.

Behind him stood new metal filing cabinets. He pulled open the third drawer, pulled out the Laspac file but didn't find what he was looking for there. The bells sounded—four, one, three. He replaced the file and closed the drawer. Accounting was not a department he had spent much time in, learning the basic procedures and working with the previous accountant before moving into sales. When the new man had joined them years ago, Hugh greeted him but no more. Now he wished he had spent time learning his peculiarities: Did he like to file on Friday? Did he have an aversion to blue ink? Did he code his forms and read only the codes? At what point did they enter the permanent record? Where did he keep hard copies after a week? A month? A year?

Hugh moved through the boxes of unfiled records atop the file cabinet until he came to the last one. He carried this box to the desk and began to thumb through the contents. The sound of a fire door opening was followed by the tinny strains of music from an earphone hanging loose. The footsteps passed to a soda machine in the reception area; a can slid and clunked its way to the opening. The steps retreated to the fire door.

On the desk Hugh lay the most recent order from the Lawrence Superior Paper Company, each detail in the entry printed in the departmental secretary's neat, mature hand. The terms were standard—net less 2 percent if payment is made within twenty days. Otherwise, net in twenty-one days. Hugh went back to the box, searching for any more surprises—for himself or for Richard. He passed orders for two new customers: an order for fine rag paper for a printer in Michigan and an order for onionskin for a company in the Philippines; all the others were familiar to him from years of association. Every form was in order, correct, reputable, to be expected. Except one.

He shuffled the forms back into a neat pile, one after the other falling into place, each one just like its counterparts from years past. Except one.

Hugh leaned forward and drew out a pink sheet, laying it on top of the Laspac form. Each item was neatly typed, every box on the form filled in, the initials firmly written across the bottom. How had he missed this the first time?

FOUR

Saturday Afternoon

By SATURDAY AFTERNOON Eliot Keogh had forgotten about Vic Rabelard, putting him down as a wild man who just happened to need someone to pick on, and passed into general anger at a world that did not credit him with all that he was due. He had breakfast in the Agawam Inn, on the veranda, savoring the memory of the last time he had crossed the wide gray-painted boards—he had been soliciting support for the high school band—and wondering if he would get the chance to point that out to Mr. Campbell.

He held this sense of wonder throughout the morning while he walked to the beach, visited the library, made lists of names and addresses, walked the residential streets of Mellingham, and endured abrupt responses to what he regarded as entirely reasonable questions of homeowners. Late in the morning he dodged an ambulance on Trask Street, but otherwise encountered less excitement than a puppy in an office parking lot on a sunny Sunday afternoon. He nodded to the few people he passed and tried to figure out what was happening to him. A person who seemed to be him was running deep in a track he thought he had dug only in his imagination.

Some years back his wife had told him he was driven. She didn't mean it as a criticism, only as an observation, and he had agreed with her assessment. He was driven. He had a goal that meant more to him than any amount of money he might make, so he had come home to Mellingham to reach for it once more and show off his success. This was the usual fatuous fantasy of the middle-aged, he told himself. This trip was not, he insisted in the less generous corner of his heart, an opportunity for redemption for anyone. Nor was it a silent rebuke to those who had not stood by him years ago. It was a search for truth.

Only as he walked past Victorian homes, colonials, more recent Capes set back from the street by a tidy lawn, did other feelings pulse and beat against his chest for attention. These were less virtuous feelings, tied to confusion and shame over events of many years ago. A man answered the door to him with a curt no; Eliot backed away and crossed a name off his list. A little girl walking a dog jerked the animal's leash and drew away from him. He realized then he must be glaring at her, the sidewalk, the traffic. He turned again, walked past a greenhouse. The sign was different, signaling a new owner, perhaps. He felt oddly betrayed; the town had changed without his knowing.

By the time he got back to the Inn, with more than half the names on his list crossed out, he was tired and stiff from walking all morning, a form of exercise, along with every other kind, he had long ago given up. At this rate, he'd be too tired to enjoy the rest of the weekend. He strode to his car, unlocked it, and started searching through it, running his hand along the synthetic carpeting under the front seats, peering through the cracks between the metal base and the cushion, leaning over the gear shift to look on the floor in the back. He was leaning in the back door, searching along the back seat, when Chief Silva appeared in the window opposite him. Eliot bumped his shoulders extricating himself from the back seat and tried to forget his embarrassment of the night before. At least, he didn't know this policeman from his youth, which was a minor blessing. Eliot greeted Silva with the smile that had ensured success for him and his paper mill for the last twenty years.

"I was just thinking about going out for lunch," Eliot said. "Find out what's new around here after all these years. I bought a tour guide for the area, but I can't seem to find it." Chief Silva commiserated, and the two men repaired to the veranda; Joe sat down without comment while Eliot babbled on about how much the area had changed in the last twenty-five years. Joe listened. Eliot's confidence wavered like the needle on a barometer.

"That was quite a hubbub last night," Joe said. Eliot's smile disappeared. "Can you tell me again how it came about?"

Eliot tried to think quickly, to come up with something to bring an end to this problem dogging him.

Joe said, "He's in the hospital. In a coma." Eliot's entire body sagged. Coming back had been a mistake. Without even trying, Eliot had fallen from one disaster into another. Mellingham was still bad luck for the Keoghs.

"He attacked me," Eliot said. "I never saw him before in my life. Out of nowhere he attacked me."

"Can you think of any reason?" Joe asked.

"He didn't like my car," Eliot said seriously, "and he said he wasn't going to let me hurt Mindy." He rubbed the palms of his hands along his thighs. His light khaki slacks were losing their crease in the heat.

"And Mindy is?"

"I have no idea. I was just taking a nap."

"You lost me," Joe said. Eliot didn't hear him; a whistling in his head blocked out all other sound—the voices of girls walking by to the beach, gravel crunching under an arriving car, a horn tooting in the harbor for a launch to collect the sailors. Eliot leaned forward and spoke in a low, sharp voice.

"I was just sitting there at the Pickering Preserve. I must have fallen asleep. This guy—Vic Rabelard, you said his name was—he woke me up, said something about not bothering Mindy, and started hitting me. He's a crazy man. I got away as soon as I could. But he was all right when I left. Honest. I mean it."

"When was this fight?"

"Yesterday afternoon, right after I arrived. It wasn't even three o'clock. I thought I'd just stop off at the Preserve," Eliot said, remembering the single impulsive act of the last several years. "I had some happy times there, hunting, fishing."

"And last night?" he asked, with growing interest.

"Out of the blue. Just like I told you. He attacked me. He's obsessed with his wife. He's convinced everyone's out to steal her from him. He's a crazy man." Eliot's strength of will came back with a vengeance. He might be guilty of a lot of things, but he never was and never would be guilty of stealing another man's wife.

"You're both members of the same high school class, but you don't seem to remember each other," Joe said. Eliot shifted in the rattan chair.

"Actually, I left before my senior year. I was included in the reunion only because everyone remembers me. I had a lot of friends here.'' He clapped his hands onto the rattan arms. ''So, that's about it.''

''You kept up with your friends after you left,'' Joe said, knowing when he was on to something. Eliot held his gaze steady, then slowly shook his head.

''You know how things are,'' Eliot said, again starting to rise. ''Kids fall out of touch. A card now and then.''

''Why did you leave?'' Joe asked.

Eliot paused. ''My family moved.''

''Why then? Parents usually let children graduate from a school before they move,'' Joe said. ''Especially high school, especially back then.'' He didn't know if it was true, but it sounded good.

''I should never have come back,'' Eliot said as much to himself as to Silva. He gave the chief an appraising look as his body sagged back into his chair, filling the curves and bends of the rattan frame. Inside the Inn men and women were calling out to each other to move the table this way, arrange the books over there. Eliot had been listening to them off and on while Chief Silva questioned him, wishing he had had the forethought to donate something to the auction, a trifle perhaps to show what he had achieved, to erase the other impression still lingering, he was sure. Now he was glad he hadn't. His donation would probably become known as the jailbird's toy.

''Do you want to fill me in,'' Joe asked, ''or should I ask Polly Jarman?''

''Polly?'' Eliot laughed. ''Poor Polly. She'd be shocked at you for bringing up something so indelicate. Besides she's probably one of the few people who doesn't know more than the bare outline. Polly lives in her own separate world.''

"Then you'd better tell me.'' The two men were alone on the veranda, the sun was striking down on them, two seagulls delicately picked their way across the saltwater marsh.

"It doesn't have anything to do with this Rabelard guy.''

"This is background information I can get from you or from someone else.''

Eliot shrugged, sighed heavily. "All right. Just before my senior year my father got into trouble at work. He worked for a paper mill in New Hampshire. When the mill first started looking into things he moved us up there so he could be closer to what was going on. He thought it'd be easier to defend himself against the charges.''

"Was it?'' Joe asked.

Eliot shook his head. "He was convicted in the end.'' He paused, listening to the people laughing nearby. "From a big high to a big low.''

"And you think that it was common knowledge?''

"I'm sure it was,'' Eliot replied bitterly. "What does it matter, anyway? It killed my mother. She couldn't face my father going to prison.''

"I'm sorry.'' Joe waited for the other man to compose himself. "You haven't told me anything yet to explain how Mr. Rabelard fits in.''

"He doesn't.'' Eliot took a deep breath. "I never saw him before. I don't know who he is. He has nothing to do with me.'' Eliot waited for Joe to comment. "Look, I came back to show my old classmates that I'd made something out of my life.'' Eliot caught his breath, then hurried on. "Whatever happens to you when you're a teenager stays with you. So finally you do something about it or it eats you up. I came back to prove something to myself, that's all."

Joe was willing to accept this explanation for the moment, for certainly he had seen enough men like Eliot Keogh struggling to redeem themselves in the eyes of people whose opinions shouldn't matter to them at all. But one part of Joe kept wondering about the rest of the story.

"I suppose it sounds shallow to you," Eliot said. "Okay. I went to work for the same mill just to prove something, what I don't know." He wasn't smiling. His breath was coming in short gasps. "Maybe I wanted to redeem my father, show them they had to be wrong." He kept his eye on Joe and his breath grew ragged.

"That doesn't help me with my problem," Joe said. "I don't see how Vic Rabelard fits in."

"I don't know anything about him." Eliot leaned forward and threw out his hands. "I never saw him before in my life. He just attacked me out of the blue. I never hit him in the bar last night. He was all right when you broke it up." Joe nodded, recalling the end of the fight. The Syzyckys had deftly removed Vic from the bar and sent him home in a taxi. Apart from a momentary scare and disrupted conversations, the entire incident seemed harmless, yet it was the last time anyone had seen Vic Rabelard in a relatively normal state, able to walk and talk and answer questions.

"What did you do for the rest of the evening?" Joe asked, changing directions.

"I stayed at the Loblolly Bar with Richard Ostell and Hugh Chase." The happy grin Silva had glimpsed for a single moment the night before came back, uncontaminated by any other emotion. ''They haven't changed,'' Eliot said. ''They're just the same as they always were.''

''What time did you leave?''

''Midnight. A little before. Maybe ten of or around there.''

''And you drove straight back here.''

''No, I walked. Richard came part way with me. He parked down near the train station,'' Eliot said. ''I walked the rest of the way alone. Got back here a little after midnight. You can ask the man on the desk. He'll tell you.''

Yes, thought Silva, I can and I will.

At the end of their conversation, Eliot Keogh was relaxed, confident, a sense of purpose restored. The truth about his father was out in the open, and he didn't feel anywhere near as bad as he thought he would. It came to him only later that afternoon that he was not guilty of a crime; his father was. For that he would grieve. And when he put that aside, he would consider what the confusion of shame and guilt had done to his own life. He had followed a red line hand drawn on a map, followed it devotedly as though it were a true road testified to by surveyors and cartographers. Every day he went to work with a single goal; his wife told him he was obsessed with trying to prove that this Keogh was different—honest, reliable, aboveboard. He didn't argue with her about it. Sometimes he could even admit there was some truth to the charge. Some. He could see now it had been an unnecessary burden, this need to prove himself, using up time and energy wanted elsewhere. Free of that weight, he could focus his attentions on his deepest concerns.

Eliot set aside his list of names and addresses, and

borrowed a guidebook from the desk; he grew lighter and lighter as the afternoon progressed, and for the first time in his adult life he didn't automatically seek the goodwill of every stranger he met.

REGINALD CAMPBELL, owner of the Agawam Inn, had one distinctive feature: he had grown up in Mellingham and moved away as an adult. This was unheard of. He later redeemed himself by moving back. With a tidy inheritance, he purchased the Agawam Inn and settled into what he thought would be a quiet life of hostelry. In short, he was a man with problems, several of them.

First, Reginald Campbell spoke as both an old-timer and a newcomer. He was shocked when he awoke one morning to discover there was only one grocery store left in town instead of the four he had grown up with, and he saw no reason why anyone would oppose a new town hall. After all, the old one was a mess, to put it bluntly; it needed a coat of paint, access for the handicapped, floors that didn't roll like the gentle swells six days after a hurricane, and storage (not more or better, just any kind of storage). The battle that ensued mystified him, and he was personally disappointed when the new town hall went the way of all modernity in Mellingham.

Second, the novice hosteler considered the Agawam Inn his own property. This was a major mistake. Mr. Campbell's attempts to redecorate had brought howls of protest and a steady stream of visitors who insisted on spending morning or afternoon settled in his lobby and public rooms. The 1920s early art deco remained, to be cherished by all. Well, almost all.

Third, Reginald believed there was a magic formula to success, and whenever he thought he had found it, he pounced. He was decisive, unyielding when he was going after what he wanted, but when it failed, he shrugged his shoulders and turned his attention elsewhere. He had been doing this long enough for those who wanted to know how to get around him to learn how to do so. As a result, his inn was filled with a variety of services and offerings each of which had been at one time the answer to his prayers. He was at the moment without a magic formula to believe in, and so sat morosely on the veranda outside his office, staring at the view of the harbor beyond. The Agawam Inn might not have luxurious rooms, four-star cuisine (one, perhaps two stars), or extensive grounds. But it did have one of the most perfect vistas on any coast anywhere—a well-protected harbor laid out like a nest of three bowls, each larger than the other until the tiny vessel, tacking patiently or, more bravely, its sails close-hauled, set off into the open sea.

That was how Reginald had expected his life to proceed. He set off closehauled into the world, only to find that tacking was wiser, if less interesting. Rarely now did he wonder about the day when he would turn into a broad reach, the wind at his back and spinnaker filling out majestically, as he rode the rolling swells home. He wriggled his toes in his topsiders resting on the veranda railing, cutting off momentarily the tiny boat tacking past the Yacht Club in the distance while he waited for the next crisis in the class of 1969.

At the sound of a knock on his office door, Mr. Campbell rolled his head back against the chair and waited for the receptionist to usher in his next problem. "Chief Silva?" he echoed, jumping up from his chair. The receptionist closed the door.

"Daydreaming," Mr. Campbell said. "Don't get out

on the water as much as I'd like." Joe explained the purpose of his visit while his host showed him to a chair.

"Eliot Keogh?" Mr. Campbell whistled. "He's registered. Yes, he left his car here all evening. Got in around midnight, maybe a few minutes this side or that." Sitting on the desk late at night was not one of Mr. Campbell's favorite occupations. It reminded him just how different the reality of hostelry was from his dreams. "There isn't going to be any more trouble, is there?"

"I didn't know there'd been any," Joe said. Mr. Campbell rolled his eyes. "Maybe you'd better tell me what you're referring to."

"I didn't know it at the time, but that's the man Vic Rabelard was looking for."

"Vic Rabelard and Eliot Keogh know each other," Joe said. He did not at all like what he was hearing. Mr. Campbell nodded vigorously.

"He came in here yesterday afternoon about three-thirty looking for a Canadian." Mr. Campbell shook his head, then grew interested in recalling the details of the encounter.

"Who came in looking for a Canadian?" Joe asked.

"Mr. Rabelard, of course."

Joe held his tongue. The intelligence of the average citizen when called upon to relate events in a precise manner seemed to permute like chocolate under the sun.

"I had to persuade him that no one from Canada was registered. So he left."

"Vic Rabelard came here yesterday looking for a Canadian. Fine." Joe frowned. "What has this to do with Eliot Keogh?"

"Eliot Keogh registered about half an hour later. His car has a Quebec license plate but he said it was a rental. Said he couldn't get anything else even though the agency promised him a car. Guess it's a big weekend for lots of people." Reginald paused. "When he arrived, I just assumed he was the man Rabelard was looking for. Besides, he was a mess."

"Who?"

"Eliot Keogh. When he showed up here to register late yesterday afternoon, he looked like he'd been in a brawl. He tried to hide it but his clothes were filthy. His shirt was torn and he had cuts all over him."

"And you think Mr. Rabelard was responsible," Joe said, trying not to let the other man see that for once jumping to a conclusion had landed him right on the answer.

"Well, ah, sure." Mr. Campbell moved uneasily in his chair. "Of course, I have no direct evidence for this, which I suppose is the same as finding out that I'm wrong." He laughed. "Pretty sloppy thinking, from your perspective, I suppose. I've got this reunion on my mind. They've taken over the whole dining room and most of the other rooms. And they all keep asking me what happened to this place or that place. They've got better memories than the IRS." Mr. Campbell laughed again and hurried on. "Anyway, I came in here to escape. Just now, I mean."

"I'm sure it's very trying," Joe said. "Did Mr. Rabelard give you any idea of who he was looking for other than a Canadian? Mr. Rabelard is in the hospital right now and we're trying to figure out what might have happened. Did he mention where he was going, anyone else he wanted?"

Mr. Campbell shook his head; all this meant nothing

to him. His interest stopped at the end of the driveway, along with his information.

"We're also trying to locate Mrs. Rabelard. The hospital," Joe said, leaving the sentence unfinished and the other man to draw his own implications. Immediately, Reginald Campbell's patchy pink face lit up.

"Mindy? Great gal," he said.

"Then you know her?" Joe said.

"Oh sure. She was working here about the time I bought the place. Great gal. Probably met Vic here. Oh sure, I know Mindy."

"Maybe you can help then. Where would she have gone? To her parents? Other relatives?"

"Hmmm." Reginald twisted his face into intense thought. He had been away from Mellingham long enough to lose the barrier that many wealthy Mellites erected in the face of doubt, unpleasantness, disagreement. He lifted his thick red brows, then pulled them down close to the bridge of his nose. At least it gave Joe something to watch while he waited. "Now what you just said, that reminds me of something about Mindy." He went over to an old filing cabinet, pulling out the bottom drawer. "Most of my employees stay forever. Even after they get married." He spoke with a mixture of disbelief and despair as he opened a file and flipped through yellowing sheets of various sizes. "Have you ever tried to fire anyone in this town? No, of course, you haven't." The hosteler turned back to his files and continued to flip through them. "Ah, that's what it was."

"That's what what was?" Joe prompted.

"She wouldn't fill out the forms. She wouldn't give me a social security number or date of birth or place of birth. She wouldn't give me anything." He handed the old sheet of paper across to Joe. At the top was printed the name Mindy Stoler and a local address in a firm hand. The date was December 1974. "I told her I'd have to let her go if she didn't get a social security card."

"Did she get one?"

"Nope. She ignored me."

"So you fired her."

"Nope. She moved on, worked someplace else for a while, came back. Still wouldn't give me a number. Then she married Vic, so that settled it. At least for me." It seemed to have settled the matter for him a second time; he pushed the drawer back into the filing cabinet with his shoe and returned to his seat. "I was sorry to lose her. Good worker. A charmer. Customers all liked her. But she had a real blind spot about that social security card." He leaned back, reflecting on the first months of his return. " 'Course she was only one of the problems I had right after I took over. And not even the most important one. You should have seen the food bills."

"How long was she here, at the Inn?" Joe asked, ignoring Mr. Campbell's meanderings; he tried to re-call exactly when social security cards became a re-quirement for employment. He remembered plenty of summer jobs before he applied for one.

"Mindy? All together, both times? Maybe a year or two. Not much longer."

"Did she ever talk about her family or where she grew up?" Joe asked.

The other man shook his head, relieved to change the subject. "I wouldn't remember, but I doubt it. She talked about the town, asked a lot of questions. Most of them I couldn't answer. But she was a good worker.

I was sorry to lose her. Threw herself into her job. Hundred percent reliable. Except about that social security card business. You know, if she weren't so open a person I might have thought she was hiding something.''

JOE SILVA PULLED UP in front of the Rabelard home just as he finished his radio call to Sergeant Dupoulis. Next door Becka Chase was loading her car with boxes.

"The auction," she said by way of explanation to him as he approached. "Almost the last trip." Joe commiserated.

"Have you located Mrs. Rabelard yet?" Joe knew what her answer would be.

She shook her head, her cheerfulness a thin veneer ready to split. "I called everyone I could think of. The girls are being really good about it, but they can't be brave forever.''

"It might help if I knew where she might go. Her parents, perhaps. Siblings. Childhood friends," he said, watching Becka draw away from him. She was wearing the same blouse and shorts she'd had on earlier; she shoved her hands into her pockets.

"I don't know. I honestly don't. She never said where her parents lived or where she grew up." Becka gazed over at the open trunk of her car. "She never said much of anything about her early years." She turned to Joe. "I never even thought much about it— until yesterday.''

"What happened yesterday?" Joe asked. He hated it when a resident made a casual comment that left him feeling he had missed most of the serious business of the town; he had a mental picture of dozens of tiny events of momentous consequences popping off around Mellingham, all of them unknown to him until it was too late. "I need to know, Mrs. Chase."

"I didn't mean to make it sound so, so mysterious," she said. "Once in a while you have a disagreement with a friend and you find out you weren't really friends after all. It was all just on the surface. It wasn't anything important."

"Perhaps if you tell me," Joe said, keeping any hint of impatience out of his voice. "What did happen?"

"Nothing, really." She shrugged.

Joe wondered if there could ever be a more innocuous prelude to a critical event. "Then it won't matter if I know."

"I guess not," Becka said. She leaned against the car and crossed her long legs at the ankles. She had the beauty of a woman in her early forties, when the body knows that this is its last chance to reproduce. Like a tree that sends forth its most glorious bouquet just before it dies, perhaps to deny its impending decline, Becka was shining with the beauty only an older woman can show. She glanced away, then said, "He came on to me."

Joe waited.

"That isn't like Vic, at least not since he got married," she said, looking at Joe when she realized he wasn't shocked. "I asked Mindy later if something was bothering him and she said no. It dawned on me right then that I really don't know her at all. We've been close all these years—maybe a dozen years—and I really know nothing about her." She folded her arms loosely across her chest, deep into her own thoughts.

"She must have told you something about her family, where she went to school, that sort of thing." Joe was getting worried. A woman without a social security number or a past could prove very hard to trace. Becka shook her head.

"She's very generous with her time and attention. But she has never said a word about herself." She grew angry. "You know, I used to be hurt. I thought it was because she didn't trust me as a friend. Now I feel cheated. Used. It should have been reciprocal. Two ways, you know?"

Becka seemed to get angrier the more she thought about it. She repeated her complaints. She slammed the trunk and cursed as she climbed into the driver's seat, hunching over the steering wheel. At Joe's insistence she took a few deep breaths and calmed down. He had come in search of a photograph of Mindy Rabelard, which Becka swore she didn't have, using it as further evidence of the duplicity practiced by her neighbor. Without a halt of surprise or wonder, she rushed head-long into one more resentful condemnation of Mindy before driving away.

With the permission of the Rabelard attorney to enter the Rabelard home now on file at the police station, Joe let himself into the white-stucco house and set to work finding some aid for his search for the missing woman. The home was well furnished, without the clutter that seemed to multiply spontaneously in homes long occupied by the same family. He found photographs of the two girls at various ages engaged in diverse activities, with and without their father. In only one photograph did the girls appear with a woman who might have been identifiable as their stepmother, beneath the wide-brimmed hat, oversized sunglasses, and blowing hair. Joe turned to a small desk in the living room, searched through orderly stacks of old receipts, family papers, and personal letters. He moved to the upstairs bedrooms, continued his methodical search. Still, he found nothing.

Now he was worried.

BY THE MIDDLE OF Saturday afternoon Richard Ostell began to feel that life was again under control. An observer might point out that this was an optimistic attitude at best, but Richard was not one to settle for anything less. If he understood a situation, it was under his control. He couldn't imagine reacting in any other way. If you saw the target, it was yours and you went for it.

Richard had gone through life with this philosophy, never stopping to wonder if the target was what he wanted or regretting time spent chasing the wrong goal. He married Becka right out of high school for a lot of reasons, and when she told him she'd had enough, he buried his grief and set his sights on the divorce she hung before his eyes—another target hit with startling accuracy and speed. And after the divorce Becka did none of the things he expected of her—no new boyfriend, no sudden trips away. His gentlemanly assumption that she was in love with someone else came to nothing; it was the one error of thinking that gnawed at him, no, worse, cut out his heart. He let her go thinking she loved someone else more, and then found she loved no one else; she just didn't want to be married to him.

He set aside the pain of his loss, and tried to be a good father to Tony. Richard felt entirely differently about his son from how he felt about everything else in his life—his family, friends, work, everything. He might josh Becka until she lost her temper, push Hugh an inch beyond safety, scare Vic into checking his insurance policies, but Tony was a different matter.

Richard swung his feet off the desk and loped over to the filing cabinet in the corner. He plucked one of the large reference books from the top and started paging through it. The building was empty except for him, and the phone had finally stopped ringing. He rarely did any business on Saturday mornings, but he would have to be on that phone early on Monday if he was going to move the last load to arrive yesterday afternoon. Outside the window the heat sat heavily on tree branches; the birds were quiet. Some years ago when he was afraid he was losing one of his larger mills, he had looked out on the woods and seen pulp—not trees, but supplies. Only then did he realize how edgy he'd become.

Richard turned to the listings he wanted and ran his finger down the SEC codes, noting the most likely prospects for yesterday's delivery. The list was long and the possibilities seemed endless but he knew it wasn't so. In each year of his life he felt more and more squeezed. What had been possible once, even probable, for anyone was now barely a glimmer of an idea for a rare few. Opportunities were shrinking even as people were becoming more knowledgeable, more competent, more willing. He still thought in terms of the world as it had seemed to him in the early 1970s, when a man could drop out for a year and then come back to a good job of his choice. That time was gone but the memory was permanent. He turned the page. A car drove into the dirt parking lot. A door slammed. Tony, Richard guessed, and went to unlock the main door.

"Wandering around looking for trouble, eh?"

Richard said to his son as he held the door open for him. He wondered if he'd ever be able to tell him how much he loved him. It gnawed at him that his son might go through life not knowing how important he was to him. Richard lost his own parents early and knew what it meant to wonder about them and what they thought of their only son.

"I heard about Vic this morning," Tony said, entering the office. "Mom told me. She found him, you know." Richard nodded. It had been one of the few solemn conversations he'd ever had with Becka; he wondered if she'd noticed. It gave him time to think about her, so he thought she sounded upset and perplexed and cranky, pretty much the way she always sounded near the end of their marriage.

"I called the hospital," Richard volunteered. It had been one of the most unpleasant moments of his life. It reminded him of the day his father died, when the nurses were trying to be solemn and discreet, but were really frustrated and busy, and he had to force his way past them to see his father before they moved him out of his room. "They're going to make me sign for him. Put me in hock for the rest of my life and Vic'll be off scot-free, living it up in the Caribbean after he recovers." Richard shook his head and grimaced. Tony laughed. It was what he had come for.

"Can I help? I thought maybe you could use some help now with Vic out of commission." He rested his hands in his jeans' pockets and looked around the office for some task to latch on to. His shoulders tilted in eagerness. "Any calls I can make?" Richard was visibly moved.

"Think I can't cope, eh?" Richard chuckled. "Trying to make me look old, huh?" Tony grinned.

The fact was Tony did make him feel old. Though just forty-two, Richard looked upon his nearly grown son the way an old man looks at a teenager. The young one is a stark announcement that no one's time lasts forever. If it hadn't been for Tony, Richard might not have noticed at all. He and Hugh and Eliot Keogh had been like brothers through school; then he and Vic and Hugh had remained friends for so long into adulthood that it seemed they had pulled out a special thread from the weave of life that would remain unfaded, unfrayed, unbroken, marking the story of their lives apart from others less fortunate.

"Mom's trying to get ready for the auction tonight, so I thought I'd stay out of her way," Tony said. "I'm moving some of my weights out of the basement into the garage now. At least for the summer."

"Hugh will like that," Richard said, grinning. "Did she find Mindy yet?"

Tony shook his head.

"She probably took the girls somewhere," Richard replied absently, absorbed in his growing list of names.

"No, she didn't," Tony broke in. "Mindy didn't show up this morning to pick the girls up after their sleepover and she hasn't called them either. She hasn't called anyone." Richard finished one page and moved his index finger to the next column. "Kinda creepy coincidence, don't you think?"

"What is?"

"Her disappearing just when Vic gets sick."

"I doubt there's anything to it," Richard replied, returning to his list. Where Mindy was concerned, he never expected much. She was a beautiful woman always perfectly composed who was the absolute center of Vic Rabelard's life, one who filled all the personal space around her husband without appearing in the least possessive. But she was. She hoarded every fiber of her being, deflected every approach like a white robe on a sunny day. She made Richard uneasy and he disliked her for it.

He disliked her for another reason, a more fundamental one. She made Vic happy, happier than Richard had ever been in his marriage or seen anyone else in any other marriage, and she made Becka happy, happier than Richard had ever made her, even during their first year. He barely knew what to do with the feelings Mindy aroused in him.

As THE REUNION WEEKEND progressed, Joe Silva found the high school reunion in Mellingham was having the same effect on him as it seemed to be having on the alumnae. And he understood why, or so he told himself. He had always avoided going back for a reunion because it meant going back to a person he did not know, had never known, and could not know. When he entered high school, he became a stranger among strangers. The entire experience might not have bothered him so much except that he knew the policy he encountered was not universal. Distant cousins in other parts of New England could not comprehend what he told them.

It was something everyone took for granted, grumbled about for a few days, and then tolerated to various degrees. But he reclaimed his identity as soon as he left high school and vowed not to let it happen again. Others didn't feel the same way. Joe Perry, originally, Perreira, shrugged once, then took his seat in front of Joe; behind him Cesar Rodriguez gave way to Charles Rogers, and Joe Silva became Joseph Wood, since there was already one Silva in the class, a girl whose Christian name was changed from Zaira to Sarah. No amount of protest made any difference. His younger brothers and sisters told him things changed a few years later—the 1960s had some lasting benefits—but still it rankled.

Joe turned his mind to more immediate problems. Eliot Keogh had seemed forthright, under some pressure, about his motives for coming back, and Joe was inclined to believe him when he insisted he didn't know Vic Rabelard. Becka Chase was perfectly open about Vic's behavior and how much it had upset her; she was equally open about Mindy Rabelard's friendship and secretiveness, and now her own anger and disillusionment. And yet Joe felt increasingly uneasy, whichever way he turned. That was what decided him.

He called in Sergeant Dupoulis, and braced himself.

In the last few months Ken Dupoulis had managed to take Chief Silva's advice about excessive weight gain to heart and had lost several pounds. In the process he had apparently lost his sense of humor. The quiet, serious young man, who was a store of miscellaneous facts, often bizarre, and local lore, now answered genial inquiries with ''Why do you want to know?'' His beloved Day-Glo sweatshirts bagged and sagged; one had actually been replaced with a plain navy sweatshirt, pathetically naked of any sayings clever or otherwise. Sergeant Dupoulis was turning into another person.

''We need to find Mindy Rabelard. Vic Rabelard is not improving,'' Joe said to the sergeant as he eased himself into a chair. Ken nodded. ''I couldn't find a picture of her in the house. Talk to the daughters; see if they have something.''

Ken dutifully flipped open his notebook and made a

few notes; he sat erect, his torso almost taut and straight. He looked exceedingly uncomfortable. Even worse, not one question passed his lips. It seemed to be one more mannerism that had replaced his earlier habits of dusting crumbs from his shirtfront or pulling at his waistband. Joe wondered how much of it was irritation wrought by hunger, sulkiness at having to give up one of his main pleasures, and an unsubtle attempt to punish his superior. A lot of things changed when a man lost weight.

"Have we ever taken a call about them? The name doesn't mean much to me officially."

"I think they keep pretty much to themselves," Dupoulis said. "No problems and no local involvement." Joe glanced at his sergeant, who had just spoken more words on the Rabelards than Joe had heard in the last week.

"Well, check back just to be sure. And then see what you can find out about Mrs. Rabelard's background, before she came to Mellingham. Mr. Campbell, at the Agawam, said she was working there when he bought the place about twenty years ago but she balked at giving him a social security number or anything else personal." Joe waited. Ken wrote.

"And rate Gordon's jokes mediocre, bad, or terrible."

"Sir?" Ken looked up, his face a study of innocent misapprehension.

"At the town hall. He's probably over there, in the basement, on one of his research kicks," Joe said. Gordon Davis, beloved but eccentric town clerk, told the worst jokes in town. People measured their intimacy with him by how they responded to them. Strangers laughed politely; his wife was brutally candid. The rest of the town fell somewhere between the two. "Just so I'll know you had his full attention."

"Of course, sir." Ken's face was stony but correctly polite.

"I don't know how much longer we can put up with you." Joe smiled. Ken didn't.

"I'll get on this right away, sir."

"You sound like a television program." Joe turned back to his desk. "And to think it's all my fault."

"Yes sir," Ken snapped out smartly.

FIVE

Saturday Evening

MOST OF US THINK we move anonymously through life, that if we are known it is a matter of choice. We assume we can purchase a few groceries, buy a map, and go about our business without causing a ripple in other people's lives. Anonymity cloaks us unless we unveil ourselves by writing a check or posing an inquiry that leads to conversation. If we remain within ourselves, we think we remain unknown. This is untrue. The stranger or casual acquaintance is sometimes better known, his or her actions more closely followed, than those of a friend.

Chief Silva was counting on this when he returned to the Loblolly Bar early Saturday evening after spotting Patricia Syzycky's car disappearing down the narrow service road running behind the building. She came at once to his knock at the front door and ushered him into the main bar. She was wearing a white blouse and tight black jeans.

"We're not open yet," Patricia said as she walked to the bar. The door to the kitchen swung open and Theodore Syzycky came prancing out, singing happily to himself as he danced his way toward the bar with a case of beer.

"I wanted to talk to you about last night," Joe said. Patricia stacked a tray of glasses behind the bar and turned to the chief.

"Those guys get in more trouble?" she asked.

"Vic Rabelard's in the hospital," Joe said. "In a coma."

"He was fine when he left here," Theodore said, resting his case of beer on a stool. He looked back and forth between the two with short, jerky motions. "Wasn't he, honey?" His eyebrows went up in a plea for agreement. Patricia nodded, not in the least perturbed by the chief's news.

"We settled him in the back of the taxi and sent him home," she said, looking for a cloth with which to clean the bar. "He was just fine. You saw him."

"That was about eight o'clock, wasn't it?" Joe asked.

"Just about," she agreed, still not interested.

"We're also having trouble locating his wife," Joe said. "She never showed up last night, I guess."

"She had other plans," Patricia said as her husband disappeared back into the kitchen.

"Is that a guess or do you know something?" Joe couldn't fathom the short and wiry Theodore Syzycky; the man seemed to be perpetually locked in a parallel world that featured most prominently an altered form of time, one that sped up and slowed down arbitrarily. Patricia Syzycky, on the other hand, was a sharp, practical woman who surveyed the passing scenes of life with bemused detachment; as a result, she could always be relied on for a straight answer. "I saw her down at the train station," Patricia said. "Maybe about this time yesterday." Joe looked at the clock over the bar. It was 5:38.

"What was she doing?"

"Nothing. Just sitting in her car." Patricia finished rubbing down one end of the bar and started to work her way back toward Joe. "I stopped to buy a paper."

"Did she see you?"

Patricia halted in her polishing and studied him. "Probably. I drove in and parked, so she would easily have seen me there by the paper dispensers. She knows me. I'm sure she knew it was me getting the paper."

"You waved to her," Joe said.

"We know each other. We're not friends." She didn't seem to care how her words sounded, but it was hardly possible to ignore. Joe wondered if Patricia, with her years of observing Mellites from behind the Loblolly Bar, had reached the same conclusion as Becka Chase but without the personal involvement, painful or otherwise.

"There's a 5:50," Joe said, half to himself, filing away Patricia's comment.

"5:54."

Joe acknowledged the correction. It was perfectly plausible that Mindy Rabelard got on the train to Boston for a weekend, but was it plausible that Vic didn't know or remember that that was where she was going? Was it plausible that her daughters didn't know?

"She had a bag in the car. On the front seat," Patricia said after watching Joe for a moment. "I could see it through the window, sitting up on the seat."

"You're sure?"

"It wasn't a purse." She exhibited no doubt whatsoever, and even less concern.

A suitcase changed everything. If Patricia's observational skills could be relied upon, then there was less likelihood of an accident and a greater chance of marital trouble. At least parts of Eliot Keogh's story now made sense. There was some problem between Mindy and Vic Rabelard, and he did seem to have grounds for worrying that his wife was leaving him. That might explain his unpredictable behavior Friday, but not his current state or Mindy's whereabouts. And it didn't explain her leaving behind, without any word, two teenage girls, even if they were stepchildren.

"You don't like her very much, do you?" he suddenly asked Patricia. Theodore had returned with another case of beer; he stopped when he heard Joe's question. Patricia continued to wipe the bar, stalling. Her husband deftly deposited his burden and skittered out of the bar. It was not lost upon Joe. Patricia laughed, murmured, shook her head.

"Theodore doesn't like seductive women. They make him nervous. He doesn't have any rules for how to treat them." She gave Joe the first shy smile he'd ever seen on her face. "He's very old-fashioned."

"Is that what she tried to do? Seduce your husband?"

Patricia shook her head and grinned. "No, nothing like that." She looked around the empty bar, then rested her eyes on Joe. "Let's say I have a low opinion of women who smile sweetly and wait for you to fall into their lap." Patricia crossed her arms over her chest, letting the dust rag dangle from her fingers.

"I've never heard that before, at least not about Mrs. Rabelard."

"You think I'm being catty," she said without any trace of embarrassment. "Too bad. Vic was besotted with her, and she was cool about it, like it was her due." She made a face. "It was disgusting." She moved away from the counter to answer the telephone, gave the hours of the bar, and returned to Joe. "She's a good mother. I give her that. Her girls are nice, well-behaved. But I don't like her much. And if she has run off without taking her girls, then maybe I'll have to revise my opinion of her maternal virtues."

"Her leaving the girls behind really has me worried. It could mean that she's in trouble, injured, or worse. I find it hard to believe she suddenly up and walked out on two children. We need to find her, and it's not going to be easy. The only thing I have is a physical description and your information about the train. I can't even get a photograph of her." He was less sanguine about his task than he had been an hour ago. "At least not one in which you can see what she looks like," he added, thinking about the photograph of Mindy and her two daughters in his pocket.

"She didn't like having her picture taken," Patricia said, coming out from behind the bar. "Which is probably why I kept at it until I got one." Joe had raised his hat to the middle of his chest, and there it rested while he absorbed Patricia's words. She watched him with a cocky smile and arms akimbo. "I can be very perverse when the spirit is upon me."

"You have a photograph?"

"Yessir. And good citizen that I am, I'm going to let you have it." She strode into the next room, her arms swinging at her sides, and over to the opposite wall, where a series of bulletin boards were decorated with snapshots of customers enjoying themselves. Pictures of fiftieth birthday parties were scattered among photos of small wedding groups, retirement celebrations, pals getting together, and one or the other Syzycky presiding over the bar. Patricia removed a tack and extracted one picture from a cluster, then replaced the tack. "That's her." She handed the photo to Joe.

Four people were seated at a table. The woman in the center was turned slightly to her right, with her eye speculatively fixed on a person outside the frame of the picture. Her black hair was tucked behind her ear and her porcelain white skin made everything else around her seem dark. To her left was Vic Rabelard, his face and body in shadows but his eyes fixed adoringly on his wife.

POLLY JARMAN scheduled cocktails at 6:00 at the Agawam Inn after a relatively free afternoon because, she was told, if the alumnae were worn out in the afternoon they wouldn't show up at all for the evening's festivities. With great effort, Polly reined in her managing mania and left her former classmates alone and to their own devices for the better part of the day. When the bar was nicely packed with guests, including her prize catch for the evening, Chief Joe Silva, Polly was in her element and entirely forgot the emptiness of the earlier part of the day. By 6:30 she was fairly floating from group to group. When she spied the young bartender looking a tad frazzled, she sped—to the extent that any physical body could speed its way through the crowd— over to be of assistance in her own way.

"You have enough glasses?" Polly inquired of the harried young man garbed in the obligatory black pants, white shirt, and black bow tie. He was serving a line of women as fast as he could, reaching for the bottle of white wine before the order passed from their lips. The women didn't notice their wants had been anticipated, so they uniformly recited their orders while continuing their conversations. When Gwen MacDuffy inquired about the possibility of getting a Castle Dip Cocktail, the young man gazed in affectionate wonder at her. Finally, a bit of variety.

"Oh, dear. I don't think we have that," Polly said. The thought of a breakdown in the first event of the evening drained the color from her cheeks; fortunately she was wearing makeup so it didn't show.

"She's been reading a lot of very bad 1920s detective fiction," Joe said coming up behind Gwen.

"There is no such thing as a bad detective story from the 1920s," Gwen said.

"And I thought you were a woman of discrimination," Joe said.

"How about a nice glass of wine," Polly said, nudging the bartender.

"Not at all," the young man said, eager to make use of the esoteric knowledge gained over six weeks, one night a week for three hours, in the bartending course at the local community college. While those in line behind her began to grumble and gripe, the bartender reaped the dividends of his educational investment, measuring into a shaker apple brandy (one-half glass), white creme de menthe (one-third glass), and pernod (three dashes), which he then poured, well shaken, into a cocktail glass. He handed Gwen her drink with a slight bow. Gwen nodded smugly to Joe and walked into the crowd while he collected his drink and paid.

"So how is it?" he inquired.

"Revolting."

"Good, it won't distract you," Joe said as he steered her through the cluster of alumnae to a group of chairs set along one wall. Of the four, two were occupied by Richard Ostell and Hugh Chase. The men glanced up and nodded to the newcomers.

"Let me try that," Joe said, taking Gwen's drink after they sat down.

"All morning?" Hugh said.

"All morning," Richard repeated. "I found the forms and his notes but I can barely read them." He stared at the border of the carpet stretched and frayed after years of use.

"You're sure that's what it is?" Hugh asked.

"Hugh, come on. It's me." Richard leaned back in his chair. He picked up his glass, saw that it was empty, and put it down on the small table beside him; he sank deeper into the soft chair.

Hugh pressed the thumb and forefinger of his left hand against his temples. "I looked through the files at Tveshter this morning." He seemed to notice Joe's black dress shoes then, but when he looked up, Joe was absorbed in conversation with Gwen.

"And?" Richard asked.

"And the whole order is there in triplicate in the accounting office."

Richard closed his eyes as he spoke, his face tilted up to the ceiling. "Tony came over this afternoon. He wanted to help out."

"He's a good kid."

"He wanted to give me a hand while Vic is out." Richard talked to the ceiling. He rolled his head to the side and looked at his friend. "The only thing he wants is to follow his old man into the business, and it's the one thing I can't give him."

"Well, if we don't get this straightened out, maybe we'll all get the chance to do something together," Hugh said, leaning forward and resting his forearms on his thighs. "Making shovels so we can dig ourselves out of this shit."

Richard reached out to grip his friend's arm. "Hey, man, it's only money."

BY EIGHT O'CLOCK the alumnae and their guests had settled into the Agawam Inn dining room, as much as they were able to settle to anything. Many had managed to recapture their youth, and were thus wandering from table to table, chatting with old friends and re-experiencing a long-forgotten sense of boundlessness. Polly Jarman probably gave everyone the idea, so restless was she during the first part of the evening. Joe was actually unhappy when she settled down to her dinner, since she settled herself on the empty chair between him and Eliot Keogh, leaving Joe to join the more general conversation Gwen had initiated with Becka and Hugh Chase.

Across from him Becka and Hugh Chase were evidence that the rule on the separation of married couples at a dinner party was well founded. Becka punctuated Hugh's comments with additions and corrections, and Hugh grew impatient when Becka's contribution grew into a narrative, sprawling into four sentences at least. Through it all Polly laughed her musical delight and Eliot studied the space between Hugh and Gwen.

"Actually, we should ask Eliot that," Polly said in response to Becka's assertion that sidewalks irrevocably changed a neighborhood. They were literally the fatal step toward urbanization. Hugh's face relaxed into a grin.

"Eliot?" Hugh looked at his morose friend. "You are the least observant person I have ever known, unless you've been holding out on us." Eliot shifted his gaze to his friend. "I suppose you could've changed a lot."

"Me? Change?" Eliot said, joining in the banter and throwing up his hands. He patted his hair, perhaps unconsciously checking to make sure that it was still combed neatly over his expanding bald spot.

"I'm sure Chief Silva would like to know," Polly continued. "He's only been here ten years."

"And he doesn't believe me when I tell him Mellingham is caught in a time warp," Gwen said. Her chestnut brown hair curled across her bare neck, glinting like the wineglass in front of her. Since first getting to know her almost a year ago, Joe had never thought to ask her how she felt when someone she knew came under suspicion for a crime. Whatever she might think, she was more than willing to play her part, and Joe gave himself up to the pleasure of enjoying her company while the others did his work for him.

"Is it?" Polly asked. "Is Mellingham completely unchanged, I mean?"

"It's one or the other," Becka said. "Either you've changed or the town's changed." The two choices struck her as the end of a great logical effort; she was delighted with the symmetry and tightness of the pairing, and with her own role in producing this intellectual bauble. The idea of pressing Eliot to choose seemed even more exciting, catching her imagination; she egged him on.

"I don't know why you think my opinion would be any better than anyone else's," Eliot said, wondering how he had gotten into this. Joe had been mildly curious about Eliot's views, but he was now more interested in Becka's rising but restrained intensity and Hugh's visible coolness.

"She does have a point, Eliot," Polly said in a voice wavering between maternal encouragement and mild reproof. "Today, almost everyone went to the mall, as though they couldn't go one weekend without shopping." Polly managed to get most of her shopping done weekday afternoons. "You walked all around town. I saw you." She smiled sweetly at him, pleased not only with his interest in his hometown but in her now having firsthand evidence of it.

Joe thought he saw alarm in Eliot's eyes.

"Where did you go?" Gwen asked.

"No place, really," Eliot replied. "I noticed the library—"

"You're too modest," Polly said, interrupting him. "I saw you all the way out by the Stewart Greenhouse and then out at the far end of Trask Street, and that was just this morning." Polly directed the last to the others at the table. "Doesn't that seem far?" she asked Becka.

"You have to answer us now," Becka said. Hugh drew back, studied his old friend.

"You never liked walking," Hugh said, mustering a smile. "I guess you have changed."

"I don't think he was strolling," Polly said in complete seriousness. "Weren't you doing some sort of research? Didn't you have some sort of list?" She saw nothing unusual in her question, but most of the others at the table were immediately uncomfortable, as though a wife had let slip an intimate and embarrassing detail about her husband's lovemaking. Becka started to talk, Gwen took up her water glass, Hugh reached across the table to arrange the salt and pepper shakers. The moment passed, but not before Eliot trembled with anger and Polly said, "Oh dear, I let out a secret, didn't I?"

"What were you looking for out on Trask?" Hugh asked.

"Nothing." Eliot tried to laugh. "I just thought I'd look up some old friends. You know, see if they're still around." Hugh considered the reply.

"Well, have new sidewalks changed the town or not?" Polly said.

"The Barrows used to live out there," Hugh said, ignoring Polly. "Is that who you were looking for?"

"They were friends of my parents," Eliot said. "Just thought I'd say hello."

"They moved away some time ago," Becka explained. "North Carolina, I think." It had finally occurred to her that the drift of the conversation had shifted, and they were pressing into territory that might not be hospitable. "Do you think we could get more coffee?" she asked Polly.

"Oh dear," Polly gasped, every instinct in the hostess alerted. "Haven't they come around a second time yet?" She craned her neck as she looked around the dining room. "You don't think they're slacking off?" She stood up. "I'd better check on a few things," she said. Gwen tapped Joe's ankle under the table with her shoe, but it was unnecessary. Becka poured more cream into her half-filled cup, making a mixture so light as to be offensive to most coffee drinkers.

"So, are you staying through Sunday?" Becka asked Eliot.

"I think so," Eliot replied. "Haven't had much of a chance to talk to you guys yet."

"Yeah, we need to sit down and talk," Becka said. "Let's do that." Both men mumbled agreement as she excused herself from the table. Hugh tapped a teaspoon on the tablecloth, then he too excused himself, to get another drink before the auction started.

"You must have covered a lot of territory today," Joe said. Before Eliot could also get away, Joe pulled an envelope from his jacket pocket and let Patricia Syzycky's picture of Mindy and Vic Rabelard slip onto the thick white cloth. Eliot picked it up. He looked hard at it, then lay it on the table.

"That's the man," Eliot said. "The one who attacked me yesterday, both times."

"You're certain," Joe said.

"Positive. I'll never forget him." He sounded sad rather than angry, regretful rather than vengeful. It was a memory he would like to see fade and somehow he knew it wouldn't.

"How about the woman?" Joe asked. "Do you recognize her?"

Eliot studied the picture again. He shook his head. "She's beautiful. Who is she?"

"His wife, Mindy Rabelard," Joe said.

Eliot whistled, his eyes widened, and he looked again at the porcelain face. "No wonder he thinks everyone's trying to run off with her." He shook his head again, this time sorrowfully, compassionately. "I couldn't stand it," he said. "If I thought every man was after my wife, it would kill me." He handed the picture back to Joe.

"So you've never seen her before," Joe said. Again, the answer he expected didn't come; the picture rested in his palm as he reached for the envelope.

"There is something familiar about her," Eliot said, scowling at his inability to remember.

"Then you have seen her," Joe said. Gwen leaned forward. Eliot sat. Around them alumnae were moving about, looking over the items in the auction soon to start in the next room, getting another drink from the bar, as waiters cleared the tables.

"She was in the truck," Eliot said, looking at Joe. "The white truck."

"When was this?" Joe asked.

"Friday, yesterday, when I got to Pickering Preserve." He paused to savor the recognition. "I remember thinking that it was just the same. The trees, the road, all of it except the sign. And then this white pickup came by and she was in it. She was looking straight at me. I remember she looked surprised."

"And?"

"There was a white pickup in the parking lot when I—" He paused. "When I got away. I didn't even think about it. I just got out of there as fast as I could. The same one? But why? I don't know either one of them."

IT IS A CLICHÉ of amateur psychology that teachers, actors, and lawyers share the same profession, the art of performing before strangers and persuading them to accept a particularly artful illusion. But what of the society matron, an equally old and honorable profession whose place in contemporary society is still assured though the title might evoke protests?

This was the career Polly Jarman adopted twenty-five years ago, and not once has she regretted her decision. Others have, but not Polly, and those others are simply dropped from her list of prospective guests whenever they become known to her. Tonight she was coming home, figuratively speaking, to her first audience, to classmates who knew her when she was still aspiring, refining her social energies on her friends' graduation parties, neighbors' backyard barbecues, her relatives' Friday night buffets. Occasionally, a recipient of her generous attentions might idly wonder if he or she would survive and think enviously of Polly's husband, who had long ago persuaded Polly to look upon her activities as a career and then pointed out dexterously that a professional never let work overflow into home life. Polly's husband thus rarely appeared at a social function, remaining at home in dark green overalls among his beloved miniature soldiers, arranging and rearranging them in various configurations according to the military strategy he was currently studying. Sometimes the only difference between Polly and her husband was where they applied their skills.

Polly had planned the auction to be the high point of the evening (and thus of the weekend), leading to a tapering off during the dance and a general winding down on Sunday. So far things were progressing reasonably well, and she even had one special coup. She imagined the round of applause she would receive later in the evening even as she herded the alumnae and guests into the bar, leaving the waiters to remove the tables for the dance and the alumnae and guests to grow feverish with excitement, she hoped, as the auction progressed. She was not, it must be admitted, an imaginative woman.

"Right over there," Polly said, pointing to a bare spot on the floor. A waiter set up the easel where she had indicated. Polly stepped onto a low platform that made her almost the tallest person in the room. She beamed in anticipation.

"So, Polly, are you the first trinket?" someone called out.

"Fifty bucks for a night with Polly," another yelled.

Polly turned a scornful face upon them, though it was hard to tell the object of her disdain—the low amount offered or the purpose for which it was tendered.

"You see before you," Polly began, "the contents of some of the finest homes in Mellingham and elsewhere." Polly ignored the groans and laughter. "All presented in aid of our scholarship fund, which, I might point out, was instituted by the Senior Class Committee, chaired by yours truly." Someone threw a pillow in her direction. "However, you do not see before you everything our generous supporters have to offer you this evening, including things you have wanted for decades, if I may say so."

"You have, so what is it?" a man called out. Polly ignored him.

"Give her a break," a woman said. "You wouldn't treat a man that way."

"Is this going to be another sexist attack?" the man replied. The woman turned to answer. Polly grabbed a classroom pointer and smacked the large pad of white newsprint sitting on the easel. The crack ricocheted around the room.

"That's it, you guys," she announced in stentorian tones. The room fell silent.

"Gee, Polly," a man in the front row said, "we thought maybe you'd changed after all these years." The room erupted in laughter and cheers.

"The only rule," Polly said, pushing onward, "is that you can't buy your own donations."

"Why not?" came the inevitable challenge.

"Because it's not fair. If you're bidding for your own property, it puts a damper on the evening," she said with an exasperated smile. "It's standard practice. Now, let us begin."

"Is there an award for the one who spends the most?"

The question was so reasonable, to Polly's way of thinking, that she was just about to reply when others urged her to get started. "All right, all right," she said, "but that is a good idea." Giving in to the chorus of groans, she reached for an antique leather traveling case.

Polly set about extracting money from her friends. It was actually quite easy; she'd had a lot of practice, and her old friends still liked her well enough to let her take advantage of them. Fully cognizant of this, Polly moved with celerity through the sale of a blue-and-white teapot, a set of wrenches, a first edition of *Pigeon Feathers* by John Updike, and a silver gadget whose purpose was a mystery, which allowed her to ask twice what it was worth.

"Now this," Polly said, holding up a large manila envelope, "is a very special object."

"Didn't she just say that?" someone called out from the back.

"It contains," Polly continued inexorably, "the only passing grade Richard Ostell ever received in English 302, Creative Writing." She waved the envelope to applause and pulled out a ten-page manuscript typed on thick, erasable bond paper. On the front, across the title and author, was scrawled in red ink a large D+ and the words "some improvement here, even though it is a genre story."

"One dollar," came the bid.

"Just a minute; I'm not through," Polly said, raising her hand. "The title is 'Nip Point Murder' and it's about a man who gets killed working in a paper mill. Now you can bid."

"Wait a minute," Richard Ostell said, pushing aside two classmates to get to the front. "Where'd you get that?" He seemed more bemused than angry, but definitely surprised.

"The school sent it to me," Polly said. "I asked for any old records of our class and this is part of what they sent. I also have some old school literary magazines from our years, which you can all bid on a little later."

"One dollar and ten cents," someone called out. Polly clucked in disapproval.

"Wait a minute—" Richard said.

"Too late," another said.

"Now if the members of the class of 1969 don't appreciate an undiscovered literary gem, perhaps some of our guests might?" Polly queried. Joe nudged Gwen, who looked quizzically at him, then called out a bid.

"Twenty dollars."

"Now that's better," Polly said. No one wanted to deprive Gwen of her treasure, so Richard's only literary success passed into Gwen MacDuffy's hands for the princely sum of twenty dollars. Polly then sold tickets for the ballet for half-price and a disapproving look. It was definitely not an artsy crowd.

"Now this is an interesting item," Polly said, holding up a small white envelope. She paused, smiling at her audience. "This is a secret." A man coughed, the laughter died, rose again, grew uneasy.

"We're waiting," a voice said in the back. Polly beamed; she finally had their full attention.

"During senior week, if you will recall, our beloved Mrs. Claflin was ready to give a special commendation for citizenship. But something happened." Polly paused. Joe wondered where she had learned her technique. "I wrote to her in Alabama, where she has retired to live with her daughter. She sent me the name, with the wish that we might finally make the award."

"One hundred dollars," Richard called out. The audience was impressed. So was Polly. For once she was almost at a loss for words.

"A what, a hundred? Did I hear you say one hundred, Richard?"

Richard nodded. "I'm going to trade it for my story." The audience cheered, and after a few more catcalls, the envelope was his.

"Open it," someone called.

"Not me," Richard replied. He made his way to the bar with the envelope clutched in his hand. Polly turned to a free resume writing service, inspired to force the bids higher.

"Bid on that," Hugh told Becka. "We'll give it to Tony." He left her and followed Richard to the bar; Becka did as she was told and was soon thirty-seven dollars poorer. She might have won her objective for less if she'd paid more attention to Polly and less to Hugh. Even Joe had lost interest in the bidding and maneuvered Gwen closer to the bar. Not until he felt a hand on his shoulder did he realize he had missed hearing his name called. He and Gwen turned toward the other end of the room, where Polly was bouncing on her toes with excitement.

"This is our final offering for the evening," Polly said. "The dance floor is ready but I've saved the best for last." She positively levitated with glee.

"She means you," her assistant said to Joe, before scurrying back to Polly's side.

"You?" Gwen repeated in dismay.

"How do you think I got us invited tonight?" Joe said, avoiding her eye.

"How did you get us invited exactly?" Gwen whispered to Joe as he started to move away.

"Chief of Police Joe Silva," Polly said to a thoroughly confused audience, "has volunteered two hours of his time to the highest bidder." Polly threw open her arms in joy; all eyes moved to Joe and Gwen, standing on the edge of the crowd. One woman tipped her head and gazed speculatively at him, another blinked and blinked and blinked. Everyone was nonplussed. All were delighted. The possibilities fairly overwhelmed the less honest members of the class of 1969.

A MERE TEN MINUTES after the last item had been handed over to its enthusiastic purchaser and payment tendered, most of the members of the class of 1969 were proving they still had the stamina of their younger selves on the dance floor. The disc jockey hired for the evening began with "Good Morning Starshine" and just followed the whoops and hollers thereafter. When Gwen was invited onto the floor, Joe took the opportunity to wander the perimeter of the room. He was back at their table when the dance ended.

"Come on, Joe, that was fun," Gwen said. "You look like you disapprove of dancing."

"I look that bad, huh?" Joe said. Gwen nodded. "Unintended." In truth he liked dancing, the old-fashioned sort and folk dancing especially. Rock didn't appeal to him. But that wasn't why he was scowling, as Gwen seemed to imply. Partly he was feeling guilty for having dragged her into this when they had planned a very different evening together, and partly, the heavier part, he had to admit, he was disappointed that the minutes immediately after the auction had not produced what he had hoped for.

"Have I missed something?" Gwen asked.

"No, that's the problem," Joe replied.

"Well, if you're going to be cryptic, you're going to pay for it," Gwen said. "And enough of looking so grim, Joe." She pulled him onto the dance floor. This was probably a better idea, he conceded, and certainly more fun, so he let himself be led through "Only the Strong Survive" and "Midnight Cowboy." When they returned to their table, Becka Chase stopped to talk to them, her earlier discomfort of the evening long gone.

"You realize," Becka said to Gwen, "that you paid more for that story than even the owner would have paid." She was aglow with pleasure, and Joe could see the popular teenage girl she must have been. It made him wonder why such girls and later women never seemed to have any confidence in life. The popular, attractive girls seemed to marry young, right after high school, perhaps as a leap of hope to preserve their adolescent world. It rarely worked out, yet no one passed that wisdom on to the next generation. Now Becka was coming to that age when she would have to find something more inside herself or chase vainly and fruitlessly after a past slipping away.

"It sounds like he wasn't very good," Gwen said.

"He was horrible, but he had such hopes," Becka said.

"Have you read it?" Joe asked.

"Probably, years ago," Becka said. She drew it toward her, read the title, then pushed it back. "That's a paper-making term. Nip point."

"It goes back that far, does it?" Gwen asked. "Their interest in the paper industry, I mean."

"Oh that. Yes, for sure." She nodded. "They all worked at Tveshter one summer—Richard, Hugh, and Eliot Keogh. The three musketeers at the Mill. Mr. Chase, Hugh's father, got them jobs." She had cooled down from her dancing; her face was no longer bright pink, her temples were drying, and her body was still.

"When was it, exactly?" Joe asked.

Becka rolled her eyes skyward, tapped an index finger against her pursed lips. "I think it must have been the summer before their senior year." She considered her answer. "Yup, that was it. And they've been insufferable ever since," she said with a light laugh. The music changed again, and Becka rose, off to find another partner.

Gwen fingered the short story sitting in the center of the table. "What has the paper industry to do with all this?" she asked.

"I'm not sure," Joe said, as indeed he was not. He bumped into it everywhere, and his instincts told him it mattered, but he couldn't figure out how.

"Is that why you wanted the short story?" Gwen asked.

"That was a hunch." Joe leaned back in his chair. "One that isn't panning out."

Gwen reached for the story, opened it to the first page and read a few lines. "It's not very good. No wonder no one else wanted it. It's not even funny bad." She pushed the story under the edge of her purse.

"I didn't think anyone would want it for its literary value," Joe said. "But the way Richard said he was going to try to buy it back, I was sure we'd have a few takers. Especially after I read it."

"You read it? When?"

"In Mr. Campbell's office while you were in the Ladies' Room."

"So you think it's worth stealing? Isn't that a little risky?"

"I also made a copy."

"Of course, I should have known," Gwen said. "And it's all been for nothing."

"Seems so." Ever since he had read the story, Joe was sure he had figured out at least part of what had happened, and who had to be involved. As soon as the music started, he had kept his eye on the manuscript and on the bar some distance beyond, where Hugh and Richard had settled themselves before the end of the auction. But the two men seemed content to stay there, engrossed in their own conversation, sipping beers, gazing around the room, then falling toward each other for two or three minutes of intense discussion. They never once looked toward Gwen and Joe. Joe was beginning to think he had it all wrong.

JOE COULDN'T REMEMBER the last time he slept on a boat. For years he couldn't stop thinking about it, waiting for the lift that pushed his insides up against the envelope of his body, feeling the pull on his head, like the yolk of an egg rocking against the shell, as the swell moved on, letting the boat fall into a trough. It was so much a part of his early life that he stopped noticing until the night he lay awake in his dorm room planning to take the civil service exam and realized he would never sleep on the sea again. It came to him as an absolute, a clear-cut, hard-edged fact tumbling down on him from the future. It seemed perfect and true and life altering.

He kept thinking about the earth beneath him, about whether it was there or not, after he drove Gwen home and headed home himself. The black-shingled colonial was dark except for a single light left burning at the back. Joe locked the front and back doors, and moved around the first-floor condo, enjoying the smells of the harbor and the sounds of the birds. When he finally settled in bed to make notes by a small lamp, the night had entered one of those periods that every culture knows but few name, that transitional time between more important phases of the day. It was *madrugada* to Joe, the time between one and four or five in the morning, when no respectable person should be doing anything but sleeping.

The notebook page was still blank after ten minutes, reminding him of how little he really knew. Vic Rabelard twice provoked a fight with Eliot Keogh, who insisted he did not know the other man. Rabelard returned to his home in a taxi around eight o'clock, sat down in the dining room with a sandwich and a glass of iced tea, and later collapsed. Becka Chase, a neighbor, found him in the morning, in a coma. The house was locked. Richard Ostell, Vic's partner, and Hugh Chase, his neighbor, had business worries. All of that seemed indisputable to Joe, and all of that told him next to nothing.

Furthermore, he was no closer to locating Mindy Rabelard, and no closer to finding out why she left in the first place. Certainly, if Vic were a jealous man, given to fits of possessiveness and bullying, Mindy may have simply grown tired of it and decided enough was enough. Now was the time to break away.

This idea at first seemed plausible and attractive, but the more Joe thought about it, the more he felt the viability of the idea reflected his own desperation. The department had never received any calls about the Rabelards—no domestics, no disturbance from a loud party, no boundary disputes with neighbors, and Joe was of the opinion that try as people might, distress chose its own path into public view and would not be thwarted. Whatever problems they might have had showed in ways that didn't require the police. Whatever forces had driven Vic to accost a stranger and Mindy to abandon husband, daughters, and a life had to be discernible in what was already known. And that meant Joe had to stop listening to the official version of the Rabelards' life, and start peeling through the illusions.

In the distance Joe could hear a line of freight cars moving down the tracks, traveling at a sluggish speed, a line once busy all through the day with local shipping. Even this little bit would end soon, and the commuter rail that was *de rigueur* for certain subcultures in Mellingham and critical transportation for underpaid office workers between small cities north of Boston would be in even greater jeopardy. And it may have carried off Mindy Rabelard without anyone even noticing.

The more Joe thought about the Rabelards, the more two things stood out. First, Mindy and Vic were very much a pair. Unlike other married couples of long standing, neither one had moved on to become an independent player in the life of the town. Both held back. Becka had confirmed this unintentionally Saturday morning in her deepening realization that her friend of many years had in fact held back her true self, pretending deeper friendship than was in fact there. Second, there were no photographs of Mindy in the house in which she was actually identifiable. Either she did not want to be known or— Or what? The result was the same whatever the motive: she was not known.

Joe turned out the light and the moonlight tiptoed into the room. Darkness took many forms—the midnight blackness in a city alley, the patchy grays in a suburban backyard beyond the reach of street lamps, the dull white splashes of moonlight across the marsh leading down to the harbor, where scraps of starlight glittered and faded through the night. It was a soft darkness, the last one, the kind that helped Joe think clearly. The lack of photographs prevented anyone from knowing who Mindy Rabelard really is, but tomorrow he would take the first step in identifying her and, with luck, that would tell him where she had gone. He had a few ideas. It was all beginning to make sense in a fantastic sort of way.

SIX

Sunday Morning

THE MESSAGE WAS on Joe's answering machine when he looked in the morning, though the call had been made early the night before. The Rabelard girls wanted to get some of their things. It was just the excuse Joe needed to explore the house again without drawing attention to what he was doing. The festivities of the night before had widened the scope of Joe's investigation rather than narrowing it; instead of coming away from the Agawam Inn with a more restricted list of questions and people to pose them to, he had found the range of his concerns spreading from Vic and the disappearance of his wife, to the man's business, history, and friends. Joe began to feel he had been wasting his time trying to figure out Vic and Mindy's relationship and should look at Vic's relations with others. The first step in his new direction was to re-examine old ground.

He had agreed to meet the girls at the house at ten o'clock, so he arrived at 8:30, after leaving orders for Sergeant Dupoulis to meet him at 9:30, and began his second search. He had come with the additional purpose of finding something that would give him proof of exactly who Mindy Rabelard was; it would be easier to do it this way than call in a team to dust the house, but if it came to that, he would do that too. The parents' bedroom seemed most promising, and Joe took a hairbrush, picture frame, tin box of sewing notions, and hand mirror, among other items.

In the cellar Joe hunted for records or other materials that might give him a clue to Vic Rabelard's business problems. All he found were four old yearbooks covered with mold and cobwebs, a box containing an old watch and its broken crystal, a compass, three pens with broken and dry tips, a high school ring with the date and initials sanded off, and a Civil War currency note in a wooden cigar box wrapped in an old newspaper from New Hampshire dated Friday, November 8, 1974. The paper began to crumble in Joe's fingers and he gently returned the package to the carton. By 9:30 a collection of items, gathered from upstairs and downstairs, was waiting in a box on the kitchen table when Sergeant Dupoulis pulled into the driveway.

Ken marched stiffly down the walk and up to the front door. The wiry waves of thick sandy hair that had once seemed to sit atop his pudgy body in order to assert the self-discipline invisible within now seemed lank compared to his rigid posture and well-pressed shirt. Joe missed the old Ken with all his extra pounds, the one with the stale doughnut in his desk drawer, or extra packets of sugar underneath the front seat of the cruiser, the mental list of the best restaurants within ten miles of any given town center north of Boston. But especially he missed the one with the good humor and enthusiasm.

"Sir?" Dupoulis said to the chief's greeting.

"I have to give you credit, Ken," Joe said with a smile. "You're starting to get to me."

"Sir?" Dupoulis replied. Joe led the way to the kitchen.

"That's for the lab," Joe said, indicating the collection of objects sitting in a box on the table. "We need to verify Mindy Rabelard's identity, if at all possible, see if her fingerprints are on file anywhere."

Dupoulis nodded and whipped out his notebook, flipping open the cover with a twist of his wrist. He dutifully made a note, then turned to an earlier page. The thick eyebrows that once moved, sometimes imperceptibly, with the wave of inner emotion and thought, had become haystacks, each straw cut from its invigorating root.

"The taxi driver confirms that he delivered Vic Rabelard to his back door at approximately 8:05, helped him partly up the backstairs, and watched him go inside. He believes he heard the victim lock the back door before he himself departed for another call." Ken gazed at Joe for a response.

"Just out of curiosity, Ken, how long can you keep this up?" Joe asked.

"I'm a trained officer, Sir." And with that, Ken hoisted the box of objects and headed for the front door, managing to conceal any hint of humor. At the screen door, he turned. "I do whatever it takes to keep my job, Sir." He disappeared down the steps, leaving Joe to ponder his Dupoulis dilemma while he listened to the sergeant drive away and waited for another car to arrive. When he heard car doors slam out front, he went to the door. A middle-aged woman was nudging two teenage girls toward the house, a hand on each girl's back and a reassuring smile on her face. This was Mrs. Conway, whose family had kept the girls and broken the news to them.

Vicky Rabelard and her younger sister, Dana, had the usual mix of insouciance and uncertainty of adolescence. They looked like their stepmother, with her black hair worn longer and looser, but in the way they moved, with a heavier, earthier step, they acknowledged their father. For the last twenty-four hours, their best friend's mother had served as a buffer between them and the truth of what was happening, to the extent that she or anyone else understood the complexity of the situation. The girls didn't question what they were told, or seem unduly worried, but Joe attributed that in part to the tact and care exercised by Mrs. Conway. They stood now on the sidewalk, their backpacks hanging from their hands clasped in front of them, looking like schoolgirls in any country of the world. Joe tried to explain to them what his interests were without alarming them.

Vicky and Dana listened attentively, asking only when they could visit their dad, after swallowing a question about their stepmother when the older one nudged the younger in the side. They hid behind the exaggerated politeness of the child, accepting everything Joe said. He finally gave up, not wanting to pierce the armor they were probably going to need as the week advanced. As soon as he ushered them inside, they ran up to their rooms, and then into one, and Joe knew they had asked to come back for more than clothes; they had really come for a single moment in which they could believe they were normal, that everything was going to be all right in a matter of days. They came for a safe place to speak of all the worries that passed between them as glances, lowered eyes, nervous pats of their hair curls. Joe felt like an eavesdropper on a privacy already tattered unfairly by life.

He pushed open the back door and walked across the lawn to get away.

The warmth and beauty of the day made it hard to imagine just how much misery was—had been—building in the white stucco house. The two girls, hanging onto normality by a thread, its strength no more than a smothered laugh, and no less, were about to face the loss of their entire family. In a matter of days, unless Vic recovered instantly and miraculously, the juggernaut of government interest would be set in motion: Vicky and Dana would be made wards of the state, sent to a foster home, their parent's assets liquidated to pay for their care, and the remainder held in trust. And no one, as far as Joe knew, was ready to even broach this truth to either one of them.

The grass was still green, not yet burned brown on top by the summer sun as it would be in another month; the lawn was clearly someone's pride. Joe felt the cushiony earth give beneath his soles as he crossed to the old stone barbecue, its grill clean of burnt food despite the pile of ashes below. The barbecue was made of cobblestones rather than bricks, and suggested a beehive oven in its shape. The design seemed unique to Joe, and he stepped back to get a better look. Shade from a tree on the Chase property stretched toward the barbecue but didn't quite reach, though the ground sparkled temptingly. Or did it? Joe reached down and picked up a straight pin.

"We're ready, Chief Silva." Vicky Rabelard stood on the edge of the lawn in a change of clothes, her hands in the pockets of her short denim skirt, her sandaled feet decorously aligned. "We're taking suitcases this time." Joe nodded, said okay, and a few other things that were expected of him, before silence fell.

Vicky darted back into the house and out the front door with her sister. In a moment the two were gone.

THE PREMONITION THAT had nagged at Becka Chase earlier in the week had proven twice, not once, to be accurate. The weekend was well on its way to turning into a disaster. Every time she thought things were going to work out, something tripped her up. Dinner had been awkward, particularly with Joe Silva and Gwen MacDuffy there, but the auction had turned into fun, a reprieve almost, until Richard spoiled it. Typical of him, she thought, as she moved to the window of her living room to see who was outside. Well, the dance had been fun. It almost made up for all the trouble that was brewing. At least it was Sunday, thought Becka, and the weekend was almost over.

She pulled aside a lacy curtain and watched the Rabelard girls file into their own home. They were taking it well, she knew, but probably because they didn't yet understand how serious things were. They would feel normal for an hour or so, chatting while sitting cross-legged on their own beds again, and Becka would make a point of seeing them later in the day, of reassuring them that everything would be fine when she believed now that nothing would ever be the same again. She went back to the kitchen and made herself another cup of coffee. Then she settled into a chair, propped her feet up on another one, and drew the light cotton blue robe around her, though it was nearing eighty already. Hugh was still asleep upstairs.

The evening at the Agawam Inn had ended on a far brighter note than she had expected. She forgot about Hugh and Richard's removal to the bar. Another time she might have been angry, but last night she let herself go to have fun. And she did—until Eliot Keogh came along, the new one. For all the years she had been telling herself that past is past, forget it and move on, Eliot made her into a liar. And he did it with a genuine smile of friendship.

Eliot Keogh invited her to her first school dance. At least that was how it was recorded in her memory. More accurately, the school was having a dance for junior high students, to which everyone was expected to go, and Eliot had asked to escort her, in her father's words. It was the culmination to her hopes, for she'd had a crush on Eliot since she'd first realized he lived closer to the train tracks than anyone else she knew. In the winter he could even see them from the kitchen window. Once she learned this, she persuaded him to invite her over to his house, in exchange for a peek at the burn scars on the backs of her thighs from falling against a radiator. She and Eliot sat in the rumpus room waiting for the train to come along and listening to Eliot's older brother complain about getting thrown off campus for smoking a weed. Becka thought he was weird, her father said it was the experimental college he attended, and Eliot just shrugged. It was another year before she figured out what the weed had been.

Her crush on Eliot lasted for several months, until she forgot about it, but he always remained in her heart the conventional, predictable, and inoffensive classmate who had blushed seconds before trying to give her her first kiss. She kept trying to imagine this version of Eliot Keogh while they danced at the Agawam Inn. Instead, the new Eliot kept intruding, trampling her sweet memories and tearing apart her fantasies. It wasn't that he was rude or overbearing or gauche. He was none of these; in fact, he treated her with the same shy deference he had exhibited as a twelve-year-old, and clearly thought of her in the same way. They were still the friends they had always been in school, at least in his mind.

Becka might have felt the same way except for the questions he asked—about Hugh, about Richard, about retired people Becka barely knew and hadn't thought about in years. She didn't want to think it but Eliot seemed jealous of his old friends. This had to be the only interpretation, and it depressed her so much that Hugh had to yell downstairs for her to answer the telephone that must have rung at least three times before she was roused. It was a rule that Hugh was not available on Sunday morning to the outside world, not even if the mill was burning down. Becka excavated the cordless phone from the pile of newspapers, baseball caps, and bottles of suntan lotion littering the kitchen table.

"Hello?" she said, still drugged by her memories.

"Hello. I'm calling about the Rabelard girls." The voice was distant, hidden partly beneath a blanket of static. Becka dropped her feet to the floor and sat upright in the chair.

"Vicky and Dana?" She scrambled around in her head for a plan. Should she ask the caller to wait while she rushed over to the Rabelards, or just offer to take a message?

"I want to know how they are." The voice was that of a woman, firm and precise.

Becka sat motionless, listening hard. "What do you want to know? I can give you their phone number. They're right next door." Becka rose, ready to bolt across the yard if asked.

"How are they?" the woman asked.

"They're fine. They're over there right now. I can get them for you." The tone in her voice begged the other woman to let her do this.

"No, that's not necessary," the woman said. "I just wanted to know if they're all right."

"They're fine," Becka said. "They think—"

Becka never had a chance to tell her what the two girls thought. The connection was severed. She stood by the kitchen table listening to the dial tone.

"Who was it?" Hugh called out from upstairs.

"It was Mindy," Becka said too softly for anyone else to hear. "Mindy Rabelard." She pushed the disconnect button and ran into the living room. In the corner was a small antique desk. Her fingers fumbled through the row of pigeonholes until she encountered the most recent telephone bill. She pulled it out and skimmed through the flyer advertising new services, praying no one she knew was thinking of calling her. When she found what she was looking for, she dropped the bill and punched star 57 on the telephone.

"What's going on down here?" Hugh said from the living room doorway. He was wearing a pair of cotton shorts, which he obviously had put on just to be able to go downstairs. His hair was tousled and his eyes were still swollen with sleep.

Becka ignored him as she listened for confirmation that the information about the call had been recorded. At the end of the recording, she called the Annoyance Call Bureau and left the details of the call—time, date, and receiver.

"What's going on, Becka?" Hugh said again. "First you let the phone ring, and now you're not answering the door."

"What?" He was a stranger standing there, a normal

husband wanting a normal response from a normal wife; she stared at him across the chasm of unshared experience.

"The back door. Someone's knocking at the back door," Hugh said.

"Okay," Becka said, still holding the phone. "I'd better go. At least I've brushed my teeth." She passed out of the room; Hugh went back upstairs. Through the open back door Becka saw Chief Silva before he saw her. She drew the bathrobe tighter across her chest as she invited him in.

"We like to sleep late on Sundays." She suddenly felt immoral for not being dressed or on her way to church.

"The Rabelard girls have just left," Joe said.

"I meant to come over and see them," Becka said, "but I had a phone call." His eyes registered nothing but courteous listening. "You don't understand. It was Mindy. I'm sure of it." She gripped the cordless phone with both hands.

"Slow down a minute," Joe cautioned her. "How do you know it was Mrs. Rabelard?"

"I recognized her voice. Not at first. There was a lot of static and she sounded so far away, but it was her. I'm sure of it."

"What did she say?" Joe asked, taking out his notebook.

"She wanted to know how Vicky and Dana were. That's all she wanted. I said they were next door and I had the phone number. That's when I realized who it was. She didn't want the phone number. She just wanted to know if the girls were all right."

"Did she ask about her husband?"

Becka shook her head. "Not a word. Only about the

girls.'' What she couldn't say, because she could barely believe it herself, was that Mindy was all right, that she had left the night before apparently of her own free will, and without telling anyone. Without a word to her daughters or her husband, she had just walked out of their lives, and the only twinge she felt she satisfied with a single telephone call a few hours later. Becka could not imagine being able to do this. ''She mustn't know about Vic.''

''That's entirely possible,'' Joe said. He knew what she was thinking, the shock she must be feeling at what another mother could do; he had felt it too, the first time he had traced down a woman who had abandoned her family.

''I traced it,'' Becka continued, taking a step closer to the chief. ''We just got one of those flyers from the phone company about their new services—punch this for repeat dialing, punch that for returning a call. One of them was for Call Trace. I'm sure I got it right.'' She looked down at the phone in her hand, now moist with the sweat from her feverish grip. ''I hope I did. I hope I did.''

CHIEF SILVA MADE a single phone call on a regular telephone in the front hall of the Chase home, declining the use of Becka's cordless phone even after she sponged it off and wiped it dry. He wanted to speak to her again, he said, but first he would follow up on the phone call. He was gone by eleven o'clock, just as Tony was starting to perceive the activity in the house was out of the ordinary for Sunday morning.

''Did something happen?'' Tony asked his mother as he wandered into the kitchen just after Chief Silva had left.

"Chief Silva was here," Hugh said, coming in behind him. He had given up trying to get any more sleep after the last interruption. Unlike many who claimed to sleep late, Hugh really did. He did not derive pleasure from lingering on the edges of wakefulness while activity surged around him and savoring his freedom not to be drawn into it. Once he was aware of anyone doing anything, he felt compelled to rise and act, thereby making his own modest contribution to the challenge against the planet's slide into entropy. He thus had only two mental states of any duration, sleep and wakefulness, and was chronically irritated by having to wait for both Tony and his mother to cross that long expanse of semi-consciousness over which they stumbled every morning.

"What did he want?" Tony asked. He poured himself a glass of grapefruit juice and drank it at the sink, facing the window overlooking the backyard.

"Chief Silva?" Becka asked. She was tired now, the excitement of having once again, however briefly, touched Mindy had given way to a mild shock; her best friend never asked to speak to her own children, never inquired about her husband, never acknowledged who she was. "It was about Mindy and Vic." She spoke without inflection; she thought she'd never get over this single, unassimilable view into Mindy's character. "I'd better get dressed." She rose and caught Hugh's eye as she passed from the room; he nodded, listening to her sweating bare feet pull against the heat-sticky linoleum floor.

"Have a good time last night?" Hugh asked his stepson.

"Yup." Tony deposited his glass in the sink and ran water in it. "How was the reunion?" He moved to the refrigerator and chose a bagel from a plastic bag sitting on an upper shelf.

"Fun. Your mother had a great time. You know how she loves to dance," Hugh said. Tony grinned. He liked that side of his mother; it made her human.

"Was Dad there?"

"Oh, yeah," Hugh replied. "He wouldn't miss it." He poured himself a cup of coffee and pushed the package of cream cheese across the table to his stepson. Tony went about fixing the rest of his breakfast, late as it was, happily absorbed in his own thoughts. It was a quality Hugh recognized in the boy at once; as long as the surrounding world did not seem to threaten his immediate well-being, Tony tuned it out. He had done this since he was a small boy, with obvious benefits for his mother and the various men she had dated after her divorce. In simple terms, Tony did not recognize or feel the need to acknowledge undercurrents unless they gave signs of washing right over him. He left his mother in her world and kept himself in his. Only this morning did Hugh wish his stepson were more attuned to the atmosphere around him. Tony took a bite of his bagel.

"Your father said you were over at Laspac yesterday," Hugh continued. Tony bobbed in reply, swallowed.

"He's gonna take me on," Tony replied with a cheerful grin.

"That's what he said you wanted," Hugh said. Tony took another bite, his cheery mood unperturbed by Hugh's somber look. Hugh had never been one to pontificate on how others should raise their children, being all too aware that he had taken on a child already well on his way to personhood rather than having and raising one of his own with Becka. But now he thought he knew just how difficult it must be. He knew what he had to say but he kept bumping up against a barrier that made it impossible to speak. Words were dust in the air; the simple, obvious admonishment was an assault upon a person. Hugh was silent, inept in speech and act, terrified that this companionable boy would suddenly turn on him, transmogrify into an angry, threatening stranger.

"Yeah," Tony grinned. "Great, huh?"

"Of course, it may take your father a while to come up with a starting date." Hugh felt his stomach turn over at his prevarication, but in his mind he reassured himself that he had spoken with courage. It was a relief to get it out, sort of.

"Starting date?"

Hugh took a deep breath. "Right. A date when you can actually start working at Laspac," he said, trying to dig himself out of his own lie. "That could be quite a while into the future."

"Oh, no. I mean to start right away."

Tony wasn't going to help him, it seemed. Hugh tried again. "That's not going to be possible, not just yet." Tony blanched; Hugh could feel the conversation slipping away from him. Tony wasn't an employee who had to keep his temper, had to put a good face on everything; he was a stepson confronting a painful disappointment in his own home.

"Yes, it is," Tony said. He stared hard at Hugh. "He needs me. My father needs me."

"Well, yes. He needs all of us to give him a lot of moral support." Hugh wondered if every parent turned into a moral coward at some point. Perhaps the test came to everyone, and everyone failed, but the issue was the degree of failure and when it occurred. Was it worse to fail Tony now or earlier in his life? Had Hugh in fact already failed him in such a way that the discovery at this moment was inevitable?

"I don't mean that, that moral support stuff," Tony insisted. "I mean he needs me now in the business. Vic is sick. Dad needs my help."

In his plea, Tony finally broke through Hugh's self-consciousness. The older man ached for his wife's child.

"He wants to hire you, Tony, but he can't. The business is in a bad way, and your Dad is fighting for every penny, for every sale. He can't take any risks now, not with Vic in the hospital. If the mills found out he was bringing in someone right now, the whole thing could collapse. Everything right out the window."

"No." Tony's eyes watered; his mouth worked in protest. "No. He can't do that. He's my father. He can't keep me out. Not now."

"He has to, Tony. He has no choice."

IF IT HAD BEEN at all possible, Chief Silva would have sped back to the station, but it was just a few minutes before eleven o'clock and worshippers were still vying for parking spaces and rushing into the Baptist and Congregational churches while the stragglers from the last mass at the Catholic Church were enjoying the Sunday sunshine. Next month the chaos would worsen when the Protestant churches adopted their summer hours. Joe waited for an eddy of children and parents to move across the street before he turned into the police station.

Becka's chance recognition of Mindy Rabelard's voice propelled Joe into the office; he hoped this call might give him just the information he needed in locating her, if he could get the phone company to agree. The cheerful voice on the line boosted his optimism. Seconds later, when the operator balked, then went silent, Joe knew he had expected too much. Call Trace was a great service but it was understandably hedged in by restrictions and qualifications.

"I couldn't answer your question anyway," the operator finally said; he sounded like a young man in his twenties.

"You need two calls in thirty days," Joe said, anticipating the other man.

"Yes sir, but in this case two calls wouldn't help," the operator said. "The call was out of state."

"You can't trace out-of-state calls?" Joe asked.

"Not yet, sir."

Well, at least it was something, Joe concluded as he hung up the receiver. It wasn't much, but it was something. If Becka Chase was right, and Joe had no reason to doubt her, Mindy Rabelard had called to check up on her children; she had traveled out of state in the last forty hours and didn't know about Vic. Unless she knew enough and didn't have to ask.

Joe went to the outer office and poured himself a cup of coffee. The small table that was home to the various brews of coffee Officer Daley experimented with stood well behind the main desk, hidden from view of the complaining, fretting, or bleeding residents seeking solace. Joe pondered the empty space usually filled with Sergeant Dupoulis's Sunday morning contribution. His diet was hard on everyone. Joe added milk to his mug and returned to his office.

The telephone call to Becka was disturbing, for it gave the illusion of an answer without being any answer at all. Becka hadn't recognized the other woman's voice at once, which left open the possibility that it hadn't really been Mindy but someone trying to sound like her. Joe knew it was a leap but it was possible that Vic was responsible for Mindy's disappearance and the phone call was a ruse to cover it up. It wasn't all that remote a possibility. The only problem with this was that Patricia Syzycky had seen Mindy alone at the train station and Vic had been unconscious since a few hours after his wife's departure. Joe had no trouble imagining a jealous husband murdering his wife in a rage, then hiding her body and faking a call (he only had to drive to New Hampshire to thwart the phone company), but Vic was in the hospital Saturday morning, and if he had an accomplice, she was operating on her own now. The scenario answered all the questions, but it was too far-fetched for Joe.

If Mindy was not the victim, then she might well be the perpetrator. Until he got some response from the lab later in the day, he could only speculate on Mindy's role in her husband's condition. If she prepared a tainted meal for him before she left, that would explain why she didn't ask about him at all, only her step-daughters. She could have prepared the food and drink before she drove her daughters to their friend's house and went on to the train. Once her husband ate the food that evening, it would no longer be a danger to anyone else. Mindy would be taking a risk, but a limited one, with the girls out of the house. She would be out of the state by the time the damage was done, and a single call could tell her if her plan had worked. She would assume that if her daughters were all right, then Vic wasn't. Hence the nature of her question to Becka. Mindy didn't have to ask about Vic. She could deduce it from the answer to a different question. Or so she might think. Joe sipped his coffee and mulled over Occam's razor.

It was also possible, he supposed, that Mindy had simply decided to leave her husband this weekend, and Vic's condition was coincidental. He had suffered some medical problem that was too obscure to be immediately noticed, but would eventually come to light. The police were chasing butterflies, Joe decided. He let this thought play around in his mind for a while, but it found no place to settle. In the end, he didn't believe it. Coincidences made him uneasy. There was always something more to them, and that meant he had to go back to thinking about all those who'd had contact with Vic in the hours or days prior to his collapse.

Sergeant Dupoulis arrived in response to Joe's call and seated himself with such a rigid posture that Joe was inclined to believe he'd been injured. Before he could inquire, however, Ken shot Joe a look of long suffering and resentment that reassured the chief that all was well, in a manner of speaking. It was only the sergeant's diet.

"How much more do you have to go?" Joe asked, trying to be sympathetic.

"I've arrived," Dupoulis said solemnly. "I'm now on maintenance." He pulled at his collar. "It takes a while for it to show," he added as Joe's eyes swept over him.

"Well, don't think we don't all feel for you," Joe said, thinking about the pastries that weren't there anymore. "We're with you every inch of the way."

"Thank you, sir," Ken said in his least friendly voice. "I appreciate that. About Eliot Keogh. He's been asking about people who used to live here about the time his parents moved away. Going door to door in some areas.''

"That seems a bit extreme, but it's not illegal.'' Joe paused. "There doesn't seem to be any real harm in it.'' Joe idly wondered if Ken's attitude was affecting his work; the sergeant was usually intense in his reports by now.

"It's what he's asking that's interesting,'' Ken said.

"What's that?''

"He's asking if any of them came into a lot of money,'' Ken said. "If they moved away because they inherited a lot of money or won the Irish sweepstakes or won the jackpot in Las Vegas. There wasn't a lottery back then.''

"So none of this is random, just an old friend looking up other old friends,'' Joe said. "Keogh knows what he's looking for but he doesn't know who has it.'' However he progressed, he always came back to Eliot Keogh. The man got more and more interesting. The old pal long gone, who just happens to stumble into a fight—twice—with a man he's never seen before during a reunion weekend turns out to have a unique agenda, hunting for an old friend who suddenly got rich, over night, and then moved away. "Has he found anyone who fits what he's looking for yet?''

Dupoulis shook his head. "Mostly people think he's a little weird, a little obnoxious. Those who remember him seem glad enough to see him again. He hasn't made much of an impression one way or the other.''

"I guess I'll have to have another talk with Mr. Keogh,'' Joe said, wondering why he was repeatedly misled by this man. He turned to Ken. "I want you to track down the conductor on the 5:54 on Saturday. See if he remembers Mrs. Rabelard. Find out if anyone met her at North Station, if she got on another train, or the subway. She's made it out of state, it seems.''

"She could be in China by now," Ken said.

"Possibly," Joe said, "but I don't think so. I think she's still in North America, probably still in New England.''

"Why?" Ken asked, perfectly serious.

"No one ever thought she was anything but local in a broad sense, someone from this part of the world," Joe said. "No accent, no odd ways of doing things, of dressing or talking, no special foods or knowledge or other interests that would pinpoint another region. Things like that people notice. They remember. But she fit right in.''

For a moment, Dupoulis relaxed, his face lost its guarded, aloof expression. "That doesn't mean that she belonged here, only that she fit in, as you said.''

"That's right. She didn't belong here, I didn't mean that," Joe said, thinking too hard to notice the change in Ken. "But she chose this place to be in. And then she chose to leave it. After twenty years. There has to be a reason.''

RICHARD OSTELL LIVED on the outskirts of Mellingham, in an apartment over a garage. Silva was not at all certain he would find him at home late on Sunday morning; if he'd been a few minutes later, he would not have. Richard saw the chief drive into the large graveled courtyard and turn toward the garage. Although the house and grounds gave the appearance of being an estate still owned and maintained by a single family, the house had been divided into condos, the gatehouse sold with restrictions, and the garage turned into a storage facility with a single apartment above,

Richard's apartment. Residents parked unobtrusively in the back, except for Richard, who had negotiated the right to park outside the garage. He was unlocking his car door when Silva arrived.

Richard Ostell was one of the few men Silva knew who were taller than he was, but unlike some tall men Richard didn't seem to be defined by his ready physical dominance. He clutched at his keys, passing them back and forth between his hands, as Joe explained what he wanted.

"I was hoping to get to the office earlier than this," Richard said, "get as much done as I could before the barbecue this afternoon." There was no geniality in the man's description of his plans, and Joe was not inclined immediately to think he was the cause of Richard's somber mood. The chief followed the other man up to his apartment without comment.

"I saw Vic yesterday afternoon, in the hospital," Richard said, waving Joe to a seat. The other man's movements were jerky and awkward. The long, open room, combining living, dining, and kitchen area in a single sweep of space, was heated by the sun soaking in through a half-dozen windows along the south side; the room was sparsely furnished but the few pieces that filled the space were good ones—a leather and chrome armchair, a leather sofa, a cherry table with four chairs, all handmade. Metal shelving along one wall held a jumble of books, records, tapes, and a small television. A pile of magazines leaned out from behind the sofa. "The doctors still don't know what's the matter with him."

Joe offered his sympathies. "He's lucky to have a partner, at least."

"Some luck," Richard said with a grim laugh. "This couldn't have happened at a worse time."

"How do you mean?"

Richard glanced warily at Joe. "Just the market is bad, that's all." Joe waited but the other man said no more.

"I read your short story," Joe said. Richard looked confused, then understanding dawned on him.

"Oh yeah, that," Richard said, his mood warming.

"I thought you wanted it back," Joe said, his hand moving to his bulging shirt pocket.

"Me? Nah." He smiled. "Oh, hey, let me take care of that. Gwen's a good sport but she didn't have to do that." He reached for his wallet in his pants pocket, but Joe stopped him with a wave of his hand.

"It was something else I wanted, about how the man actually dies."

"Pretty awful, isn't it?" Richard said, shaking his head. "My teacher had a lot more to say about it than what he wrote on the cover page." The recollection of the critique brought guffaws rather than complaints. "He actually told me that it wasn't a story at all, just a long description of how a man dies in a mill. And even that was bad. Too bloody. Impossible way of dying. No character development. Boring." He laughed, a man with no hard feelings for the death of an adolescent dream. "Old whatshisname wasn't open to any kind of popular fiction, so you can imagine what he thought of most of what us kids wrote."

"How exactly did your character die?" Joe asked. "I couldn't figure it out."

"Well, that's the part I thought was brilliant," Richard said, relaxing. "He gets poisoned by the slurry and as he's dying, just seconds from being dead, he reels off, passes out, and falls into a nip point, which just speeds things up a bit. It's a question of one more second and the slurry gets him or one short slip and the nip point gets him. The first is murder and the second is an accident. I thought I was being really clever.''

Joe nodded in appreciation of the creative mind at work; the murder method did exhibit a certain smattering of genius. Nevertheless, he forbore from pointing out that the accident was no accident, and the crime was still murder. "How did you come up with the idea?"

"I worked at Mr. Chase's mill the summer before my senior year. He got jobs for the three of us, me, Hugh, and Eliot." Richard grinned. "It ruined us for all time. We wouldn't do anything else after that." He laughed. "Now my boy's the same way. Worked there once and goes over there as much as he can. Loves the mill. Fills in whenever he can. It's in the blood, I guess. My writing teacher never got that."

"Did he, your teacher, I mean," Joe said, "understand all the technical stuff?"

"He said the story was inaccessible because I didn't explain the technical business, and if I did, it would make the story even more boring." Richard shook his head. "He wasn't a man who believed in the possibility of writing good stuff in formula fiction, as he called it. He sure put my light out."

"I hear schools have changed," Joe said, thinking of his own years at a school he would rather forget. "What is a slurry, anyway, for my own edification?"

"It's the watery mass of fibers that's fed into the Fourdrinier and actually becomes paper after the water is drained off," Richard explained, sounding enthusiastic for the first time. "Mills used to use a lot of chemicals in breaking down pulp to make the slurry and again in finishing and sizing different kinds of papers, but nowadays the slurry is pretty clean, just water and fibers. You couldn't kill a mouse with it in any mill that makes high end papers.''

"And nip point? What is that?''

"That is dangerous, deadly, and mills have signs posted at every nip point, just in case anyone gets careless,'' Richard said, growing serious. "The nip point is where paper goes between two rollers. Everything's rolling so fast you can't really see what's going on. If you get careless, get too close or something, you can lose a hand or worse.'' It was a different Richard Ostell who explained how the Fourdrinier worked—relaxed, animated, precise, answering each of Joe's questions with interest and detail.

"I can't agree with your teacher,'' Joe said at the end of Richard's explanation. "I'd bet that readers would find all that interesting.'' Richard nodded, pleased with how carefully Joe had followed his apparent divagations.

"I'd forgotten all about that story,'' Richard said. "I thought it got thrown out after the divorce. Didn't know the school had a copy.''

"This looks like an original, typed on a typewriter,'' Joe said, pulling out the story. He flipped the pages open.

Richard chuckled. "When we wrote papers back then, it was work, typing with a carbon. One big mistake and you had to start all over again. And it took hours.''

"It sure reminds us how much things have changed,'' Joe said. He folded the story and put it back in his pocket. "None of the memorabilia seemed to surprise anyone except the award Mrs. Claflin never gave out,'' Joe said. Richard leaned away from the chief, tightening his shoulders and dropping his eyes as he did so. Bingo, thought Joe.

"I haven't opened the envelope,'' Richard said. "So I don't know what's in it.''

"I thought you were going to trade it for your story,'' Joe said, recalling last night's events.

"Did I say that?'' He tried to laugh. "The spirit of the moment got to me, I guess.''

"I thought it might help me,'' Joe said. "I have an idea that whatever's happened to Vic has to do with this reunion, with something that this weekend has brought back or reminded someone of. Do you mind if I take a look at the envelope?''

"I haven't got it,'' Richard said. "I must have left it on the bar.'' He looked toward the windows and checked his watch.

"Maybe the bartender will remember,'' Joe said. Richard started to stand up.

"Vic and Mindy had a twelfth anniversary coming up in a few months. Did you know that?'' Richard asked. Joe shook his head, leaned back in the sofa; Richard let the statement lie between them.

"How do you feel about Mrs. Rabelard?'' Joe asked. "Is she the type of woman to just pick up and go?'' The wary look returned to the other man's eyes.

"In a word, no.'' Richard seemed resigned to getting it out. "And she didn't much like me, either, but she kept it to herself. I'll give her that.''

"And you didn't keep it to yourself?''

"I wouldn't go that far,'' Richard said. "She rubbed me the wrong way, you could say, but I never made a point of talking against her.'' He threw his arm across the back of the sofa; his hand left a patch of sweat on the dark leather and squeaked as it slid across the back. He took a deep breath. "I guess she was okay but I always wondered if Vic was making the right choice. He fell for her so fast. I can understand that—he was a widower with two small girls—but he was obsessed with her, as soon as he met her; she was the only one for him."

"How do you mean obsessed?" Joe asked. The scenario of the jealous husband, briefly entertained and then dismissed, was stirring uncomfortably in the back of his mind.

"Before he met her he was a normal guy—dating a little here and there, no one special, as far as I knew. Mostly he was tied up with the girls. But after he met her? All he could talk about was Mindy, how beautiful she was, how brilliant, how loving. Man, he was gone on her."

"Would you call him excessively possessive?"

Richard mulled this over. "You mean like all these guys today who shoot their girlfriends?" He shook his head. "No, I don't mean obsessed in that sense. I guess I mean absorbed. He was totally absorbed in her, talked about her all the time. Adored her."

"And that made you uncomfortable," Joe said.

"He went overboard." Richard slapped the sofa once, then again. "It made me uneasy. It wasn't normal."

"Did you talk to him about it?"

Richard nodded. "He cut me off, wouldn't hear a word against her. So I kept my mouth shut."

"Then you weren't surprised when she disappeared," Joe said.

"No, I had a feeling right from the start that something like this might happen, but I figured it was all in my head. After a few years she still didn't like me, but I figured things were working out for them.'' He looked across at Joe. ''I have to tell you everything now, I suppose, having gone this far, even if it does sound foolish.''

''It would certainly help me,'' Joe said. Richard clasped his hands in front of him and leaned forward. The muscles in his legs strained against the heavy denim jeans he wore; he pulled his shoulders tight, drawing in his elbows.

''I always thought Vic was a conservative, play-it-safe kind of guy, and I still do,'' Richard said. ''When I was trying to talk him into letting me buy into Laspac, his family's company, the business was having a rocky time, and I kept telling him that I was willing to take all the risk. It would be all on my shoulders, every bit of it. If the mills said no dice, we don't like this man— he's a stranger, no one we know—then I'd walk away and he could keep half my stake.''

''How much?'' Joe asked. Richard told him. Joe whistled softly.

''I must have worked on him for weeks, then one day, after I started giving him the line again about how I was willing to take all the risk, he just turned away like he was listening to something outside the office. Then he said, out of the blue, 'Would you be willing to trade a whole life for ten or twenty years of happiness now?' It was queer the way he said it, like he wasn't really talking to me about the business.''

''What do you think he meant by that, ten or twenty years now?'' Joe asked.

Richard shook his head. ''He wouldn't say any more and I never asked him again what he meant, but when

I heard Friday night that Mindy was gone, I thought, 'That's what he meant. He and Mindy had some kind of understanding. The time is up.'" He paused, twisting his hands, as though by kneading finger against finger he could work out of his body the pain of his old friend lying in the hospital, more dead than alive.

"What do you really think?"

Richard glanced up, surprised at the bluntness of the question. "What do I really think? I think he made a pact with the devil and came to regret it."

SEVEN

Sunday Afternoon

THERE IS A MOMENT in every investigation—into murder, into the identity of a hitherto anonymous author of a lyrical poem, into the provenance of a valuable artifact—when the conscious mind knows that order is about to emerge from chaos, that the body of disparate information contains its own pattern and will fall into it under the merest tug of gravity. Pieces of information fill a room, blocking all that was previously known, clocks seem to keep imperfect time, the mind gropes in a darkness recognized only because blindness has passed and sight emerged. Joe's shoulder brushed the doorjamb into his office, and he knew he was on the verge of understanding what had happened to Vic Rabelard and his wife, Mindy.

Dupoulis had located the conductor who worked the 5:54 train on Friday night, and left a scribbled note on Joe's desk. Even Ken's handwriting was shrinking and growing cramped, Joe thought. The message was simple and direct: the trainman remembered any woman as pretty as Mindy Rabelard was, and no, she met no one. She walked out of North Station like she was on her way to collect her lottery winnings. There were quotes around the last phrase, but nothing more. Brief though it was, the message reinforced what Joe suspected, that Mindy Stoler Rabelard had walked away from one life to take up another, and what happened to her husband was a separate matter.

It was to confirm this that Joe was waiting on the telephone shortly after noon, listening to the unrecognizable, unmemorable music that filled telephone lines. When he finally reached his party, he was leaning back in his chair watching a teenager in a rigged skiff fending off dorries that seemed to maliciously thrust their sterns at him. Joe dropped his feet to the floor and pulled himself to his desk.

"No change," the doctor said in answer to Joe's question. "And I don't expect there to be."

"That sounds like you've found something out," Joe said. He had waited patiently for a report for over twenty-four hours.

"His partner was in here yesterday," the doctor said. "But there was nothing I could tell him."

"What do you know now?"

"We did all the regular tests," the doctor began. "Whenever someone comes in and we don't know what's wrong, we test for the usual things—drugs, poisons, pollution. It's a standard set of tests."

"What did you find?" Joe asked, wondering why doctors always seemed to turn into frustrated teachers whenever he wanted a quick, short answer from them.

"Nothing."

Joe groaned. He knew the man had found something.

"So we ran a test of his acetylcholinesterase level," the doctor said, warming to his topic. Joe resigned himself to a lesson in chemistry. "If it's low, it suggests neurotoxins might be involved."

"And was it low?"

"Way down," the doctor replied after Joe verbally balked at the figure he was offered. "Anyone with a depressed level of acetylcholinesterase was probably showing signs of dizziness, slurred speech, perhaps numbness in the extremities."

"He seemed disoriented," Joe said, thinking back to Friday night, "but the general consensus was that he was upset about a family situation."

"Hmm. Well, the signs can be deceptive," the doctor agreed. "Anyway, once we got those results, we ran a full set of screens on his blood." He paused as though Joe were supposed to know what the lab had done.

"Were you right? It's a neurotoxin?"

"What we got on the gems—"

"Gems?" Joe said, interrupting him.

"Gems is the gas chromatograph mass spectrometer," the doctor explained. "And what we got," he said, slowing down as he reevaluated the report, "was a monomer, acrylamide."

Joe started writing. "That's definite?"

"We ran the samples through gems twice," the doctor said. "Was he in some kind of industrial accident?"

"I don't think so," Joe said. "Why do you ask?"

"It's an industrial chemical and it seemed kind of strange to find it in anyone's blood," the doctor said, "but it came up in a skin sample too."

"He was in a fight on Friday afternoon," Joe said.

"He looks it," the doctor commented. "He had some flaking and scaling on his hands and neck so we ran tests on samples and got the same reading."

"So what does that mean? Did he swallow it? Fall in it? What?"

"I don't know how Mr. Rabelard got it into his system, but this particular monomer will go transdermal."

"It's absorbed through the skin," Joe repeated, to be sure, as he made notes. "Are those all the symptoms?"

The doctor hummed while he thought. "Dizziness, numbness in the lower extremities, sweaty palms and feet, poor reflexes, peeling and redness of skin, signs of anemia in blood." He paused. "This is unusual stuff. Do you have any idea how he got it into his system?"

"I have an idea," Joe said, afraid to go any further. "What's your prognosis for Mr. Rabelard?" Joe could almost see the doctor writhing in his chair.

"I told his partner it'd be a while before we knew anything," the doctor said.

"I'll have someone break the news to the girls," Joe said. "What can they expect?"

"This is a neurotoxin we're talking about," the doctor said. "Anything could happen."

"Could he get up on Monday and walk away?"

"No." The doctor was definite; there was no prevarication here.

"Tuesday?"

The doctor paused. "No one can say for sure at this point, but the only cases I've known about don't have happy endings."

"How bad?"

"If he lives—and he might not—he won't be able to go back to his old life."

"Brain damage?"

The doctor sighed. "Massive, in all likelihood."

Joe thanked him for the information.

"It was an accident, wasn't it?" the doctor asked just as Joe was about to hang up.

"I doubt it," Joe said.

Not now, he thought, not now that I know what is in his system.

Joe continued to make notes, long detailed descriptions of what each suspect had or had not done, as he now imagined. There were gaps, there were questions, there were errors (yes, a few), but the story of events his unconscious had promised was now pouring forth. His last question, the one he had not yet posed to anyone, the one question that might matter more than any other, still had to find a place. And the answer to that one meant the difference between a charge for murder, attempted murder, or manslaughter and mayhem.

Rather than make a premature decision, Joe placed one more phone call, this one out of state.

THE CLASS OF 1969, in the person of Polly Jarman, had selected one of Mellingham's public parks for its final event, a barbecue-picnic for alumnae, friends, and families. Polly and her local classmates held this event every year, so it required minimal planning while producing maximum participation at no cost to Polly. Whenever she toted up the figures for this event (number of participants, etc.) she knew the joy of success. The parking lot was filling up by early afternoon, and alumnae were spreading out picnic blankets and setting up barbecues on the grass overlooking the small beach on the outer harbor. Polly walked among them in her crisp white pants and blue and white sailor's blouse, a nautical delight moving among her schools of followers.

Joe cast his eye over the alumnae, noting who was

present and who was not. A number of men and women were putting together a volleyball game deeper into the grassy lot for parking while gas grills heated up and small children made their break for freedom. He expected to see Becka and Hugh Chase and did; Richard Ostell was sharing a picnic table with them. The three chatted like longtime friends, which they were, not like a romantic triangle, which they also might have been. Joe wondered if the three maintained their friendship because of the size of the town; if the same three in a city would give vent to jealousies and resentments that would drive them apart forever. The friendship between the men was the older one, and Joe imagined that Becka had learned early on to respect that. None of this showed, however, as the three tended hamburgers on a grill and poked through a picnic basket while they waited for lunch to be ready.

The one part of the scene Joe could not imagine was where Vic and Mindy Rabelard would have fit in. With her black hair and porcelain skin, Mindy Rabelard must have stood out among her husband's friends like a professional actor on a stage with high school thespians. For twelve years Richard had swallowed his reservations, and Becka had ignored obvious signals. When Hugh crossed the grass to a large cooler stocked with soda, compliments of the town tradespeople, Joe realized that was the man he knew the least about.

Joe was growing impatient and beginning to think he had miscalculated. It was already almost two o'clock. He looked up the road and relaxed. A light blue Volvo was creeping down the road, slowing, then rolling forward, then slowing again. Joe stepped onto the grassy shoulder as Eliot Keogh drove by, both hands on the steering wheel as he peered over its rim

through the windshield. He passed Joe without a sign
of recognition, his attention focused on finding a parking space. Suddenly the rear brake lights burned red
and the Volvo bucked to a stop. Eliot turned into the
sandy parking lot and bucked and rocked his way to a
stop at the far end of the last line of cars, taking two
full spaces for his own.

Eliot emerged from the car in slacks and a white
shirt. He opened the trunk, rummaged in it for a few
minutes, picking up and discarding several magazines
before he finally shoved one into a canvas bag, which
he pulled from the trunk before slamming and locking
it. He made his way to the picnic area, stopping to
speak to the first person he encountered. Polly pointed
to the Chases' picnic table, then put her arm through
his as they walked over together.

It was just the arrangement Joe wanted. He felt a
new affection for Polly Jarman.

THE FOUR OLD CLASSMATES at first looked like any
other group of friends sharing a picnic table, but as
they leaned forward and back, in to hear the punch line
of a joke or back to let their chests swell with laughter,
they formed a separate universe. People moved around
them without stopping to speak, and the four friends
took no notice of anyone else. Gradually, Becka moved
to the end of the bench, pressed by the centrifugal force
from the friendship among the three men.

Joe passed the time of day with a few unattached
beach-goers, until he decided he had given sufficient
rein to his compassion. Eliot Keogh, Hugh Chase, and
Richard Ostell had had ample time to reconnect, as
people now said, and one of them would just have to
face what was coming. Joe moved through the pic-

nickers as unobtrusively as a chief of police can do in his uniform on a Sunday afternoon in a public park.

"Hey, Chief Silva," Becka called out as Joe drew near the table. "Come join us." Joe waved his acceptance, attributing her enthusiastic welcome to the boredom that must be settling in from listening to her male companions.

"Ah, yeah," Richard said. He was the first to notice Becka's offer, and his effort to appear agreeable and welcoming was commendable if unconvincing. The paper plates and condiments were shoved to the side and Hugh was on his way to the grill before Joe could stop him. The occupants of the table were as nervous as anyone expecting bad news.

"Not for me," Joe said when Becka produced a can of beer from a cooler. He waved away a hamburger on a roll. Silence fell, then the three other men began to speak at once. Laughter.

"I called the hospital before I came over here," Richard said. "The doctor said he'd just spoken to you." Eliot looked bored, and Hugh put down the jar of mustard he'd been trying to open.

"You didn't tell us that," Becka said. She had on a white canvas hat with a narrow brim peaked over her eyes, and she sat up to look across at him without tipping her head back to see clearly.

"He wouldn't tell me much, except that Vic was still out cold." Richard put his forearms on the table and leaned forward. "But he told you a lot."

"Don't get belligerent, Rich," Becka said.

"Every time I asked him something, he'd mumble and tell me I should talk to you, Chief." Richard spoke as evenly as possible, making it clear he was keeping his anger under control.

"If you want to talk to Rich," Hugh said, starting to clamber off the bench.

"I don't have anything I can't say to all of you," Joe said. Hugh sat down again, somewhat reluctantly, to Joe's eyes.

"You know what happened," Becka declared, leaning forward. "Well, we're his friends. We have a right to know too."

"We don't have a right to know, Becka," Hugh said.

"I want to know," Becka said. Hugh shrugged, and looked at the chief. "What did the doctor say?"

Joe was not at all surprised that Becka had taken the lead, become the most aggressive, the most on edge. "The doctor said they've identified the reason for Vic's collapse."

"Which is?" Becka prompted him.

"A monomer called acrylamide," Joe said. Becka frowned.

"It sounds like something you put in latex paint," she said. "What is it?"

"A neurotoxin, from a medical perspective," Joe said. "It attacks the nervous system. That's why Mr. Rabelard was stumbling and seemed disoriented on Friday night."

"But what is it?" Becka insisted.

"It's an industrial chemical," Hugh said, watching Joe. "It's an off-white powder, used in electrophoresis."

"You lost me," Richard said.

"It's common in biochemistry labs," Hugh explained. "You use it with other chemicals to make gels for doing electrophoresis. What you do is, you pour the mixture between two glass plates. While it's still liquid, you put a comb in it. When the liquid hardens to a gel, you take out the comb and you have a row of wells. When you want to test something like blood, you pour the samples into the wells and run an electric charge across them, with plus or minus on each end. Proteins have charges, and they move to the top or bottom, depending on whether their charge is plus or minus, and they move fast or slow through the gel depending on whether they're small or large. The smaller the protein, the faster it moves through the gel. So you have long, positive proteins at the top and slower ones next down, until the bottom, where you have short, negative proteins.''

Becka looked at her husband as though he had three heads. "Is that what you used to do? No wonder you got into sales."

"It's used for DNA sequencing now," Hugh added.

"How did Vic ever get hold of something like that?" Becka asked.

"That's one of the things I haven't figured out yet," Joe said. He turned back to Hugh. "What else is it used for?"

"Hard to say," Hugh began. "That's about all I know about it. Some mills use it for sizing paper. Some use it to accelerate the drainage of water in the Fourdrinier. That's all I know." He took a deep breath. "If that's what Vic took, I suppose we should think about how we're going to tell the girls. Except for that one call," he said, nodding to his wife, "no one seems to have heard from Mindy."

"What about your mill, Mr. Chase?" Joe asked. "Does it use this chemical?"

"Tveshter Mill?" Hugh shook his head. "And even if we did, it wouldn't be possible for anyone to get hold of it.'' He cleared his throat. ''We don't keep chemicals around the way you think we do. If we were using acrylamide in any step in the papermaking process, we'd never see it. The chemicals are delivered into a tank from a tanker truck, the same way heating oil is delivered to your home. It goes into a storage tank and then it's pumped to wherever it's needed—the head box or wherever.''

''But you said you don't use it anyway,'' Richard said.

''Right. We use caustics, different kinds of bleaches, with the pulp, and that's it,'' Hugh said. ''But even if we did have it, no one could get at it.''

''I see,'' Joe said, and he did.

''And it's also a hazardous substance,'' Hugh added.

''What does that mean?'' Joe asked.

''There are safeguards for chemicals like that,'' Richard said. ''No one can walk in off the street and buy it in a jar. The buyer has to have a tax ID number and the company has to keep records about who they sell it to.''

''You know,'' Becka broke in. She had been listening to the discussion with suppressed excitement, and now raised her hand and jabbed her finger at Richard. ''Some of those guys who drive those trucks. They are just that far away from being street dealers.'' She measured a bare inch between thumb and forefinger. ''You remember the one who refused to deliver a load from out on Route 495? Remember? He called you? He said he wanted one percent more because of the snowstorm?''

''Becka, babe, that was years ago,'' Richard said. ''And he was a gypsy driver. It was a freak.''

''It was extortion,'' Becka said to Joe. ''You wait.

It'll turn out to be one of them. One of them wants revenge and he's been biding his time. You wait. I'll bet you any amount of money.''

EVERY GOOD HOSTESS tends to each one of her guests individually, and Polly Jarman was no exception. She moved among the picnickers as though she had personally invited each one to a private affair. With each one she engaged in light banter, the length of each stop depending on Polly's view of their rank in society, which in turn was determined by how well they took up her game. The most astonishing changes hung on a word. When she got to the table where Joe was sitting, she was diverted momentarily by a waving classmate, and thus gained time to circle the table. She had grown wary of this group.

"We're having trouble getting up our volleyball game," Polly announced before the conversation could veer off into unknown territory. This group of old friends had become a dangerously unknown quantity since Friday night. "I'm sure some of you want to join." She forced a smile.

Becka shook her head. "We're just not up to it."

That was probably the wrong comment to offer Polly; it reflected on her ability to keep her guests happy. She rose to the challenge. "Now, Eliot, you used to be our star player," Polly said, circling the table once again until she arrived at his side. Eliot flushed and protested, but Polly would not be put off; she pulled him from his seat and marched him off to the improvised court. Joe estimated Eliot would survive the first round, just barely, if he was lucky and stayed out of the way.

JOE TURNED HIS ATTENTIONS back to the picnic table; he knew Becka, Hugh, and Richard were willing him to leave, to follow Eliot across the grass, but Joe had no intention of complying.

"I've never attended a reunion," Joe began, ignoring the hunched shoulders and averted eyes that would have sent a more sensitive man on his way. "I guess I don't have any very close friends from high school or college that I want to see again." He waited. Becka was the first to capitulate.

"We live here, so I suppose it would be odd if we didn't attend," she said. "I mean, we're right here. It'd be hard to avoid the reunion even if we wanted to." Hugh looked up at his wife suddenly, and Joe wondered if she'd given him a kick under the table.

"You and Eliot get along as though he'd never left," Joe said, addressing the entire group. Again, he waited. It would become clear to all three eventually, he told himself, that he was not going to leave without having the conversation he wanted.

"It's easy to slip back to how we were," Richard said. "We had a lot of fun together." He looked to Hugh for support. Around them picnickers were finishing up their lunches, cleaning off gas grills, and repacking coolers and canvas bags. Those who were only married to alumnae devoted their energies to children and cleaning up, leaving spouses—male and female— to enjoy the company of classmates. The sun sprinkled light on the tops of trees, which hoarded it there; small waves sputtered up the narrow beach, and Joe refused to let the ripples of well-being permeate the group.

"Comes back as though it were yesterday," Hugh said.

"When was it exactly?" Joe asked. All three took a few moments to absorb his question.

"When did we last see Eliot?" Hugh asked Richard.

"Well, we had that party for him," Richard said. "Just before he left."

"That was it," Hugh said to Joe.

"And you never heard from him again," Joe said.

"Sure we did," Becka said. "I mean we were all friends. He wrote us about his new school and what it was like up there." She narrated what she remembered to Hugh and Richard, as though waiting for them to correct her.

"He was way up in New Hampshire, almost by the Canadian border," Hugh explained. "He missed the ocean."

It was a familiar lament, and perhaps the most common any shore-dwelling person made after a move inland. Moving inland meant losing a sense of boundaries, of living without a primal source of energy and life, without the comfort of the essential. Joe could well understand how Eliot might feel.

"But they never came back for a visit?" Joe said.

The other three glanced at each other. "There was some trouble back then. I suppose you should know, but no one talks about it anymore. I mean, it hardly matters. Something happened back then."

"Eliot took it hard," Richard said, taking up the story. "He was so proud of his dad. Remember when Mickey made that joke about it?" Richard said to Hugh, then turned to Joe. "Eliot exploded. Went after him. I thought he was going to strangle Mickey. It was in the middle of some game and all of a sudden we were all riveted to this brawl in the bleachers. Eliot was wild! Sorry, Chief, you probably don't know what it was about. Eliot's father was charged with embezzling company funds, or something like that.''

"Eliot mentioned that,'' Joe said. All three relaxed at once. Richard let out a long sigh.

"He told you? Jesus, I thought he was still touchy about it. It was a long time ago,'' Richard said. "I'm glad he's put it behind him.''

But you haven't, thought Joe. Aloud, he said, "Was Mr. Keogh convicted?'' All three nodded. "And that's when Eliot dropped out of your lives.'' They nodded again.

"No,'' Becka said, "actually it was something else.'' The men protested. "It was his mother.''

"Aw, come on, Becka,'' Richard said.

"I remember. We were still married then, and you got a letter from him with the obituary for his mother,'' Becka said. She turned to Joe. "She died right after Mr. Keogh was convicted. It literally killed her.''

Hugh dropped his hands to his thighs, and nodded in agreement. "She's right. That was the last time I heard from him too.'' He looked at Richard. "It came just before I was discharged.''

"When was that?'' Joe asked.

"When I was discharged, in November 1974.'' Hugh looked across the grass creeping down to the revetment. "A week before Thanksgiving I got out. I never heard from him again, did you?'' Both Becka and Richard shook their heads.

"Why does this matter to you?'' Richard asked.

"I'm not sure it does,'' Joe replied. "But it might explain why he's spending this visit asking about people who used to live here when he did.'' It is always a shock for a man or woman to discover that someone they know well is in fact a man of secrets, a stranger.

Becka frowned; she evidently found the idea peculiar and the picture of Eliot searching the streets of Mellingham for old pals absurd. Richard and Hugh took the idea more seriously.

"You mean that after all these years, he's still looking for—" Hugh stopped in mid-sentence.

"He's looking for someone who came into a lot of money back then and moved away," Joe explained.

"What? He thinks someone made money off of his father's getting caught?" Becka said, jumping to the obvious conclusion. "Eliot always was a dreamer." She shook her head in disbelief and disdain; Hugh and Richard watched her in silence.

ELIOT KEOGH HOVERED on the edge of a large group of men and women in shorts and shirts listening with various degrees of attention to Polly Jarman. Every time he moved a step farther away, one or another woman would turn and motion him to move in closer. Beads of sweat popped out of the creases in his neck, making a transparent necklace until, nervously, he ran his hand down his face and throat, then gently fingered his thin layer of hair lying across his bald spot. Joe decided it was time to rescue him from his misery.

"Where are you parked, Mr. Keogh?" Joe asked.

"Eliot," he quickly corrected the chief, then winced. He couldn't decide all at once what was the proper protocol between a chief of police and a man he had twice questioned. Joe drew him away from the group still taking in Polly's elaborate rules for the game, which would be followed for all of ten seconds. The two men walked down the rutted road toward another part of the park. Joe knew he was by now enough of a fixture of the landscape of Mellingham to not evoke comment merely by his presence. Eliot, however, did not know this, and as a result was feeling even more self-conscious, and now sweating profusely.

"This weekend probably hasn't been what you expected," Joe said. The volleyball game had taken form with shouts of encouragement from children and spouses and friends sitting on the sidelines. For a little while longer two dozen adults would forget the worries that made them grind their teeth at night, hire a lawyer for their teenager, or watch the executive parking lot furtively on a Friday afternoon for unidentified limousines.

"I'm not sure what I expected anymore," Eliot said. "But it must have been too much." He avoided the eyes of a couple jogging eagerly toward the volleyball game. "My wife tried to warn me that people would be different now." Joe nodded. "Twenty-five years is a long time," Eliot said, as though just realizing that.

"That's a long time not to come back to a place where you say you were the happiest you'd ever been," Joe said. They reached a curve in the landscape, where the harbor gave way to mud flats and marsh. Eliot moved closer to the boulders spaced along the road as it veered to the cliff falling down to the marsh.

"What is it you want to know, Chief Silva?" Eliot turned to Joe as he spoke, his arms hanging at his sides, a look of weariness on his face. "You've questioned me twice. I know you still think I have something to do with that man's condition." Eliot sat down on the nearest boulder.

"Maybe, maybe not," Joe said, taking a seat on another boulder. "I was hoping you could help me find out something about acrylamide, since it's used in the paper industry and you're in the business."

Eliot looked skeptical, but he relented. "My mill doesn't use it. We do high-end papers but nothing that calls for that chemical in sizing or finishing."

"But you know what it is?" Joe persisted.

"Sure." Eliot studied him, unable to capture the drift of the questions.

"What's it look like?"

"It comes in different grades," Eliot said. He spoke now like a man resigned to talking to someone who didn't care about the answers. "The biochemistry labs would want a fine powder, sort of like Nestle's cocoa mix, and a mill would use a rougher grade, like soap flakes. Only, Hugh was right about how the mill receives and stores it; no one there has access to it."

Joe listened as though every word counted, as indeed it did, but not in the way Eliot imagined. The salesman listed bulk chemical supply companies, lab supply companies, and testing labs without demur. He added a reference book for the hundreds of others, for good measure. Joe wrote it all down.

"I'm sorry to have to take up your afternoon with this," Joe said. Eliot brushed it off. Joe put his notebook away and drew out an envelope. "Do you mind taking one more look at the picture of Mrs. Rabelard?"

Eliot shrugged and Joe handed him the envelope. In the narrow channel that cut deep into the marsh, a small gaff-rigged dory was tacking to a dock, its pilings set at what Joe guessed was probably the low-water mark. The dock itself was no more than the end of a long walkway of weathered planks two boards wide. The little boat veered to starboard, its sail falling to leeward. Eliot held the two photos in his right palm. Mindy Rabelard's enigmatic smile seemed to be directed to Joe.

"If I'd ever seen a woman like that, I'm sure I'd remember," Eliot said. "But I never came back here."

"You said she was the woman in the white pickup Friday afternoon," Joe said. "Driving with her husband."

Eliot nodded. "I've wondered about that." He drew aside Patricia Syzycky's photo of Mindy, and looked at the one Joe had found in the Rabelard home. He leaned over it, studying the faces of the Rabelard daughters.

"Who is this?" Eliot asked, pointing to one face.

"Vicky Rabelard."

Eliot stared at her. "It doesn't seem possible."

Joe waited. The little boat bumped gently against one of the pilings, then turned and nudged alongside the ladder on one side of the dock. The sailor released the boom and dropped the sail; the end of the boom dipped into the water and the foot of the sail followed it. The sailor made the boat fast to the dock. Eliot looked over at Joe with glazed eyes.

"She could be her mother all over again," Eliot said, returning his gaze to the picture. "Younger, but that's her, all right."

"They're stepdaughters," Joe said automatically.

"Really?" Eliot looked surprised. "Look at the hair, the expression on her face."

"You mean you recognize Vicky?"

Eliot nodded, absorbed in his own recollections. "I'd forgotten all about them. Whaddya know? I don't remember her name but it'd be easy enough to find it out. Her boyfriend was found guilty just after my dad was. I remember it because—" He stopped and let the photograph rest in his open palm.

"Maybe if you tell me where all this happened," Joe said.

"Sorry," Eliot said, straightening up on his boulder. "You're still trying to figure out what happened down here. All right, let me think. My father worked in sales for a New Hampshire mill, the same one I work for now. He was covering the mid-Atlantic seaboard when he was charged with selling the mill's industrial secrets. We moved up there when Dad first learned he was under suspicion. It took four years to bring it to trial but they did it. During the trial we—my mother, my brother, and I—we were supposed to sit behind Dad and look like the perfect American family. And we did. At least in the beginning."

"What happened?"

"I found it very hard to be there day after day, especially when sometimes nothing was going on but the lawyers arguing with each other," Eliot said. "So I'd go around the courthouse, looking in on the other trials."

"And Mindy Rabelard was there?" Joe asked.

Eliot nodded. "She was doing what we were doing. That's what I thought at first."

"Who was on trial?"

"Her boyfriend. He was charged with a long list of things from a crime spree he went on with another man. They never got the other guy," Eliot added. "Someone died and an older woman was badly hurt, I think. I kept thinking nothing could happen to my dad—he hadn't hurt anyone. It was all a mistake—not like this guy who killed someone."

"What happened to him?"

"He was convicted." Eliot rubbed his fingers along the edge of the photo. "We were all there that day waiting for Dad to be sentenced. It was supposed to be probation and restitution but it turned out to be six years and then another six for probation. Juries up there feel very strongly about anyone who does anything that might affect their jobs. It was a real shock.''

''How much did the other man get in the other courtroom?''

''That's why I remember it,'' Eliot said. ''When the judge announced my dad's sentence, my mother collapsed. She started babbling about needing wood for the fireplace this winter. She died two days later.''

''I'm sorry. And the other man?'' Joe asked.

''That was before. He was convicted a few days earlier and he was being sentenced too. I was in the courtroom waiting for our case to come up down the hall. I wanted to see the end of this case, the one with the wild man and the beautiful girl,'' Eliot explained. ''I used to go there so much that all the guards knew me. I sat up front and compared everything the lawyers did with my dad's lawyer. That man's crimes were so much worse than anything my old man did. I was convinced Dad would get off because this other man was so despicable.'' He sighed. ''I was young.''

''What did he get?'' Joe asked.

''Just what he expected. Before the jury came in, he turned around to—Mindy, is it?—and told her that he wouldn't get more than twenty years or less than nineteen. And not to count on time for good behavior. She just nodded like he was ordering a coke and a burger. 'Be back when I get out.' That was all he said to her. He got nineteen years and four months.''

And she kept her word, Joe said to himself.

''That was the last day I thought about anything except my own family for a long, long time," Eliot continued, slipping the photos back into the envelope.

"And yet you never came back to Mellingham until Friday," Joe said. "Why now?"

"I ran out of leads in the mill," he replied bitterly. "First I told myself that I didn't come back because of shame. It was too hard to face everyone back here. Then it was time—too much time had passed. Everything would be different; there was no point. Then not enough time had passed. I wasn't successful enough. Mellingham was the land of perfection and I wanted to come back a roaring success. In the end, the invitation for the reunion gave me the opportunity to carry on what I'd been doing all along—looking for the man who destroyed my family. Someone turned him in. He was a good man but someone must have had it in for him because the mill went after him like he was some kind of psychopath. It destroyed my family, and nearly destroyed me. So I swore I'd find out what happened. I couldn't let it rest. I had to find out who it was. I figured if there was no mention in any of the files in the mill, there had to be some information down here. I was desperate."

"And money seemed the most logical thing to look for," Joe said. "A reward from the mill. Some kind of unexplained windfall?"

Eliot opened his mouth, then closed it, and turned away. Across the marsh, the sailor had hauled in his sail, secured the boom, and was now tossing battens and sail bag onto the dock. His afternoon pleasure was at an end.

"I wanted to know who started it all," Eliot said. "I have a right to know."

Joe stood up, signaling the end of the interview. "I'd

like you to stay in Mellingham one more day,'' he said to the other man's surprise.

"I gotta get back on the road,'' Eliot protested.

"Tomorrow afternoon,'' Joe said. "Not before.''

EIGHT

Sunday Evening

TONY OSTELL KNEW the worldwide importance of recycling from his college courses on environmentalism and global economics, but it had little more than intellectual meaning for him and no emotional reality. He gathered the scattered newspapers on Sunday evening and tied them into neat bundles, dropping them on top of the clear and brown bottles and tin cans left from the previous two weeks. His family was careful about what ended up in the tasteful blue, rectangular plastic bucket that was collected every Monday morning, ensuring that at least this end of Basker Court was unlittered by rejected cat food tins (unwashed), glass soda bottles (returnable), or piles of glossy magazines (tied with torn nylon stockings).

The bucket sounded like a snowplow on dry pavement as he dragged it along behind him down to the sidewalk. He never carried it because it was the last task he undertook before going off to meet his friends and he didn't want to get his clothes dirty. He thought of it as his last task for the week, whereas his mother thought of it as the first of the week. He shoved the bucket into its place. This week it sat alone at the end of Basker Court. Tony shrugged. It couldn't be helped.

The bucket was right where Chief Silva expected to find it when he arrived at seven-thirty, less than half an hour after Tony had left, and he picked it up and carried it to the side of the house. In the three hours since he'd left the alumnae picnic, Joe had been busy on the telephone, tracking down anyone who could be tracked down on a Sunday afternoon, learning as much as he could. It wasn't everything but it was enough.

Joe nudged the bucket out of sight and went to the front door. Hugh Chase answered his knock; he did not seem surprised to see the chief or the three other police officers standing in the driveway. Since Friday evening, Hugh Chase had been the blank page in the story, and even now Joe wasn't sure he had filled in the details correctly. Hugh gazed at Joe with the mild expression he always wore. Neither anxious nor surprised, neither hopeful nor resigned. He was a hard man to read.

Neither Becka nor Hugh had changed their clothes since returning from the picnic, and Joe knew he had interrupted a casual evening devoted to recovering from a tiring weekend. He put his question to Hugh, and prayed he had not miscalculated.

"I don't get it," Becka said. "Can you search without a search warrant?"

"He's asking us to let him search tonight," Hugh explained. "Otherwise, he'll be back in the morning with a warrant."

Becka struggled to grasp the implications of Joe's request. Her genial nature was ready to say yes, sure, go right ahead, as though the chief were asking for no more than the right to inspect the sink before he took a drink of water. Her long years of marriage made her think first of her husband's opinion, and when he seemed willing, she was ready to concur. Still, she wanted to hold out, to say no, this is my home.

"I don't know, Hugh," she finally said, turning away so she spoke into his shoulder, his shirtsleeve muffling her words. "I mean, what's he looking for?"

She had put it baldly, almost too baldly; Joe could sense Hugh's inclination to cooperate weakening. From a distance Joe had noted over the years the nature of the individual residents of Mellingham. Hugh stood out for his irenic mood, his ability to distance himself from an argument. It had seemed to Joe a strength at first; now he wondered if it was a weakness, a way to avoid conflict, to co-opt debate and sidestep challenge. Did he have an inner strength or did he have no stomach for a fight? Or was it wisdom? A man acting in the only way to control his temper? A drawn look came into his eyes; Becka tugged at him with her indecision.

"I don't know," Becka mumbled into his shoulder. "I mean, we are talking about the police here."

"That's right, Becka," Hugh said. "Our neighbor is in a coma and we should be willing to help in any way we can."

His firmness startled his wife. "Well, sure, but—" Becka said. "Shouldn't we go through all the steps?" she pleaded as Hugh moved away from her. Joe produced the required form and Hugh signed it, then held out the pen to his wife. The two were standing by a table set against the wall in the hallway where daily she lay out the mail. Diffidently, she took the pen from her husband's outstretched hand and approached the table. Hugh later took her into the living room, and they chatted about a story an old classmate had told him. It occurred to Becka that he was carrying on a formal dinner conversation, as though she were a guest to be treated graciously, carefully. She reached across the sofa and squeezed his thigh as he told her about the man who longed to lead treks across Nepal but couldn't free himself from his father's bakery. When his father died and the son was sixty-one, he sold the business and invested in a company that made hiking equipment. But by then it was too late. He took one trip to Nepal, broke his leg, and spent the rest of his working life designing equipment he would never use.

JOE POCKETED the form and returned to his men outside.

"I want photographs and drawings of both yards," Joe explained. "Especially across the Rabelard's yard facing the Chase's garage." He sent off the first team, Maxwell and Daley, and motioned Dupoulis to follow him to the recycling bucket. Joe removed the piles of newspapers and with a pen poked among the tin cans and glass bottles.

"That one, I think," Joe said, pointing to a small amber bottle about the size of a vitamin jar. Dupoulis removed it and placed it in a plastic bag. "That's all. Get it back out on the sidewalk now." The sergeant nodded and took the jar to the cruiser and the bucket to the sidewalk. Joe went back to the garage. In the distance he could see Maxwell and Daley working their way across the Rabelards' lawn in a blade-by-blade search.

"The most logical place for us to begin," Joe said to Dupoulis when the younger man reappeared at his side, "is the garage." Ken nodded readily and moved to open the garage door for the chief. When Joe had explained his plans earlier in the day to the three officers, the change in Ken's attitude had been almost too much not to comment on. The sergeant inched his way closer and Joe noticed his jaw grow slack, his cheeks relax, his waist expand, as though the strength of will that held him upright and taut also prevented him from absorbing crucial, desired information. Joe held his tongue and looked away from the sagging midriff that was strikingly similar to the old Dupoulis torso. Joe pushed aside a bamboo wind chime as he entered the garage.

"I'll take that side," Joe said, nodding to the work-bench running along one wall.

"Right. I'll tackle this stuff," Ken said, surveying piles of magazines, boxes of odds and ends, and stacks of lawn and garden equipment.

The workbench ran the full length of the wall; a double hung sash window missing three panes from the top sash looked out onto the Rabelard back yard. The bench was littered with rusting cans, half-empty jars of shellac, broken clay pots, straight pins, boxes of plant food and moth flakes, and broken screwdrivers and other tools. Something white had spilled on the ground. Joe tried to contain his disgust. He believed in taking care of one's tools and keeping a work area clean and tidy.

He made his way among bags of mulch, loosely rolled mosquito netting, a box of odd-sized pieces of wood left over from a home-building project, taking samples wherever seemed necessary. Nearby Sergeant Dupoulis worked methodically in silence, moving from pile to pile. Through the yew trees Joe could see Maxwell moving in front of the cobblestone barbecue; one missing pane was level with Joe's chin. He turned his attention again to the workbench. A few grains of what looked like salt were sprinkled across the rutted planks of the workbench. Farther along, past the window, was a bamboo tube, the smallest chime from the set hanging just outside the garage door. Joe reached for it but then thought better of it, drawing it away from a tin can by his pen. He maneuvered the bamboo into a plastic bag.

"This sounds like that story you were telling us about," Dupoulis said, standing up with a manuscript in his hand. Joe pulled down a corner of the page, scanning it for familiar phrases.

"Looks like it," he agreed. "Where'd you find it?"

"In this box of papers and yearbooks." Ken nodded to the old cardboard box at his feet. "The yearbooks are from the sixties."

"Okay. Take the story."

Dupoulis bagged the story and took the chief's finds out to the cruiser. Joe followed him as far as the door. He had found the essentials but not the most important item, and it made him uneasy. He was a methodical man; he liked all the pieces to be there and to fit, and an important one was missing. There might be another way of getting at it, but as yet he hadn't figured it out. Tomorrow he could follow the usual channels and hope for the best.

Joe heard the car door slam. Beyond, children's voices took on the disembodied quality evening gave them; they sounded tinkly and light, like the pink and purple splotches from the sunset nudging the trees behind Basker Court. Even farther away a car honked its horn. Now all the sound was outside, distant. It was one of those moments when, finally, you eavesdrop on the world. Inside the only sound was a squirrel scraping its claws as it landed on the workbench, thinking the large invaders had gone. A tiny sparkling yellow circle above signaled the hole large enough for a squirrel to slip through. The squirrel in question huddled behind a box of moth crystals, its rapid heartbeat and flicking tail reminding Joe of the early black and white cartoons in which two-dimensional creatures leapt jerkily from one action to the next. The squirrel blinked. So did Joe. Only once.

Dupoulis reentered the garage, slamming the door against the jamb. The squirrel bolted. The blue and white box rocked back and forth.

"Right here, I think," Joe said to the uncomprehending Dupoulis. The two men moved along the workbench until Joe pointed to a small white smear and a few grains of a powder. On the ground below were more tiny grains. Joe moved to the blue and white box at the end of the bench. The corner of the box was open. Joe lifted the box, shook it, and felt the weight at the bottom. He waved the open corner beneath his nose, and thought of his uncle.

"Now your average squirrel," his uncle said every fall, "is stupid. He not know. He smell. He stupid.

"You watch him all spring and summer. You see what he do with his food, put it here, put it there. Anyone see. Stupid animal. He survive because we stupider.

"But you got to get smart, get rid of them. Stupid, yes; safe, no. Now what you do, you do this. This is what you do. You take a little crystal for the cloth and you toss it here and you toss it there. Make the attic white. Make the cellar white. And another one stand outside and watch and the squirrel come right out through the secret hole. Wherever it is, this no secret no more. A stupid animal, you see. Afraid of smell."

Joe waved the box under his nose again. Not a hint of naphthalene reached him.

BECKA AND HUGH CHASE had presumed that at some
point the police would move into the house and continue their search there. Becka especially had been
struggling with the apparent thoughtfulness of the police in beginning outside so that she and Hugh might
gradually become comfortable with the search of the
interior that now seemed inevitable. Edgy, reluctant,
growing fearful though she counseled herself that it
was unnecessary, she had agreed to Hugh's suggestion
that they move out back while the police search the
house. Hugh launched into a story about Polly Jarman's
husband and a hobby collectors' meeting he attended
every year. Like many quiet people, Hugh was quite
the raconteur when he wanted to be. Becka sat cross-
legged on the bench, chin in hand, elbow on table.

Joe watched them for a moment from the corner of
the house. Neither he nor any of his men had found
anything inside and he was almost ready to leave. The
late-setting sun glinted on Becka's light brown curls,
and Joe was struck by the beauty of her middle age.
He wondered how aware she was of it. Becka's life as
a wife and part-time cafeteria supervisor seemed too
plain for her looks, but then her looks seemed too de-
pendent on her current happiness to last. Joe felt suddenly cruel.

Hugh stopped in mid-sentence as the chief approached. "All done?" he asked. Becka looked quickly
at his hands; they were empty.

"I guess that was okay," she said, straightening out
her legs and clasping her hands in front of her. She
had the brightness of someone who was trying too
hard. Hugh kept his eye on the chief.

"I don't think we'll need to come back," Joe said,
"unless I have some more questions."

"Haven't you asked everything you can think of?" Becka said.

"I'm sure it must seem that way, Mrs. Chase," Joe said. "It's all just to help me get a sense of what happened Friday night."

"I know it is," she said. "It's hard for all of us. He was fine one minute, then gone the next. I mean, it makes you suspect life." She threw open her hands as she spoke.

"That's the hard part," Joe said. "Finding out exactly what happened when." Every officer is trained in the art of interrogation, in prying or bullying or wheedling information loose from someone who doesn't want to tell you the time of day. The training operates on the premise that the only loquacious species on the planet is suddenly the most taciturn. It wasn't true. Nine times out of ten in Joe's opinion a person would tell you all you wanted to know and more if you stepped back to listen. The human being needs to talk. "I have no idea of his state of mind before he got to the Loblolly Bar later in the evening," Joe explained as he stood at the end of the table looking over the yard. Becka's garden had already degenerated into graying tulips, leggy pansies, and burned out crocuses.

"He was normal, wasn't he?" Becka said first to Joe, then to her husband. "Except that business at work." Joe looked at Hugh expectantly.

"Last week he did something," Hugh began. "We had a large back inventory of some tech paper at the mill—something I'd told him about a while back. I probably shouldn't have. That kind of thing we keep in-house—mostly by default. Most of the people at Tveshter don't have a lot of close friends in the business or anyone who'd know what it meant."

"What're you leading up to, Mr. Chase?" Joe asked.

"I'd started negotiating with a company I thought was finally going to take it off our hands, very quiet," Hugh said. "Only Vic bought it. It arrived at Laspac on Saturday."

"And?"

"And he didn't tell his partner, Richard, anything about it—that he was buying it or who he was selling it to. Now that he's out of commission, Richard has to find out if he had a buyer, who it was, and how much the deal was for. Or, if there's no buyer, who he can find to take it." Hugh leaned forward. "It's a real headache for him. He stands to lose a lot of money."

"You sound like you knew nothing about this," Joe said.

"He didn't tell you?" Becka asked.

Hugh shook his head. "He said something about balancing the books. I can guess what he meant. I helped him out in the early eighties when he was having trouble. He must have thought now was the time to repay the favor."

"But he didn't tell you he was doing that," Joe said.

"No." He had large strong hands, clean, muscular, but light in color, like those of a man who rarely if ever performed manual labor. "He called in the order the day after I congratulated him on his upcoming anniversary."

"You never told me about this," Becka said.

"I wasn't sure what to make of it," Hugh said. "Besides, I have to figure out what to tell my people."

"Did he say anything about his anniversary?" Joe asked. If Vic believed his wife was going to leave him soon, it might explain his erratic behavior.

"No. But he got kind of agitated and kept saying

that he hadn't forgotten how I'd helped him out,"
Hugh said. "It was kind of embarrassing." His mouth
curled into a taut line of disgust.

"You were embarrassed by it?" Becka repeated.

"He was overreacting," Hugh said. "At least I
thought he was. He didn't owe me for that. Anyway,
Richard is still trying to cope with the delivery. He
hasn't got much time to get it on the road. This could
cost him big bucks."

"Gee, and he seemed so normal," Becka said. "Except for the business—" Joe turned to her. "Friday
night he came over while we were eating out here.
He'd been in a fight, Vic, I mean. He had cuts and
bruises all over him but he said it was nothing." She
had started to describe his earlier visit, his unexpected
appearance in her kitchen, but veered away from it.

"I offered him some first aid cream," Becka explained. Hugh interrupted to offer the chief a cool
drink. "But he turned it down. Until the bugs started
to get to him." Joe only half heard her through Hugh's
solicitation. He asked her to repeat what she had said.

"What happened to it?" Joe asked. "There was
nothing like that in the dining room or the kitchen
when we arrived."

"It was there on the floor," Becka explained. "I just
took it. I didn't think anything about it. It was mine,
after all." She was suddenly on the defensive.

"Have you used it since?" Joe asked.

"Well, no. Mosquitoes don't seem to bother me the
way they bother Vic."

"I'd like to see it," Joe said. Becka nodded slowly,
looking over at her husband for some sign that what
she was doing was all right. He had a half-smile on his
face she couldn't interpret. She walked to the door, and

Joe held it open for her; behind him Hugh sat at the table, leaning on his elbows, hands over his face. In her closet she retrieved a pair of khaki shorts hanging on a peg and reached into one pocket, then the other. She drew out a small tube with red lettering and handed it to the chief.

"We use it all the time. I have gobs of it," she said. Joe studied the tube and its lettering, turning it over in his hands. He took out his notebook and gave her a receipt.

"Did you see him use it?" he asked.

She nodded, looking from him to the tube, back and forth, as though her eyes could trace in the atmosphere the clues that were producing the thoughts and conclusions in his mind.

"Oh!" Becka gazed in wonder at the tube as Joe slid it into a tiny plastic bag. "You don't think—"

"Think what, Mrs. Chase?"

"Well, you hear about how big bakery companies put sawdust in their bread and dairy companies put the ingredients of lighter fluid in their ice cream. You don't think there's something in there that he had an allergic reaction to, do you?" She gazed at him, her mouth slightly open, her brown eyes searching his face.

"It's possible," Joe said. Deathly allergic reactions, corporate trickery, the accidental and cruel hand of fate were all tolerable, plausible prospects to the late twentieth-century sensibility. But not malice in someone we know.

JOE TIDIED UP the boxes he had been searching through in the Rabelard cellar and headed upstairs to the back door. He had left Becka in the house and Hugh out in the back yard. When he descended the back steps of the Rabelard house, Becka was crossing the grass with an envelope in her hand. Hugh took it between thumb and forefinger and held it. When Becka stood waiting to see what he was going to do with it, he thanked her; she gave him a quizzical smile, waved to the chief, and returned to the house. Hugh held the envelope until Joe crossed the lawn to where he was sitting.

"When I was a kid I used to agonize about making the right decision," Hugh said. "I don't agonize anymore but I still don't know why I do what I do." He took a sheet of paper out of his pocket and held it so that Joe could read it. On office stationery for the Tveshter Paper Company were listed six items for one of the labs; at the bottom was listed acrylamide, in a one-ounce jar. Beneath that were the initials HC. The price of the jar came perilously close to the initials.

Hugh watched Joe's face, and when he was satisfied, he slipped the order form into the envelope, then placed the envelope on the edge of the picnic table. A light breeze lifted the edge of the envelope; neither man made any effort to hold it in place. It rose and fell like the edge of a little boy's T-shirt.

Hugh stared at his hands clasped in front of him. From inside the house Joe could hear Becka moving around in the kitchen, opening and closing cupboard doors. She was even singing to herself.

"She's making an ice cream sundae, with chocolate," Hugh said. "She's convinced that you believe that Vic had a bad reaction to the medication. That's why he's in a coma." He rubbed a tiny ink stain on his thumb. "It's her way of celebrating." The envelope slewed sideways a few inches across the table. Hugh looked at it. "That's just to help you figure out tonight what you could learn officially tomorrow."

"You haven't spoken to your wife, then?" Joe said.

Hugh shook his head. The tall, taut body seemed to be shrinking right in front of Joe, losing its power and life, thinning like his blond hair.

"She won't stay with me after this," Hugh said. "When Becka and I were first married, I used to think about the marriage vows—the pairs, in this or in that, for this or for that. When we had a very bad year, I'd think, can she put up with this? Is this the hardship that will kill it? I kept wondering about the breaking point. Where was it? When would she reach it? When would I reach it? Then I stopped thinking about it." He opened his hands and studied them. They were pink from his rubbing them, sweaty though the sun was almost gone and the two men had to rely on the lights from the kitchen windows to see each other. Joe slipped the envelope into a plastic bag and labeled it.

JOE SILVA was a man of faith—in the inherent goodness of most people most of the time, in the rightness of doing what is hard, and in taking obvious precautions. Officer Maxwell was in place at the street end of Basker Court before Joe drove back to the station house.

Sergeant Dupoulis was waiting for him, the various bags they had filled earlier in the evening spread out on the chief's desk for a final look before being taken off to the lab. Joe went over them one by one and then added the envelope supplied by Hugh Chase.

"What's in it?" Dupoulis asked.

"An order form listing acrylamide, among other things," Joe said. "Mr. Chase gave it to me, in that envelope." Dupoulis looked quickly at the plastic bag.

"He's confessed?"

"No, he wanted me to find what he knew there'd be a search warrant for anyway." It was easy to look upon the offer of this single piece of evidence as the act of a good citizen, or as an act of desperation, or perhaps even as an act borne of ignorance.

"Maxwell is watching the house," Joe added, "just in case." Ken nodded, relieved.

"I didn't figure Hugh Chase for this one," Ken said.

"He's trying to be a good citizen, and he wants us to know that." Certainly, Hugh Chase's contribution to the evidence had been unexpected at first light, but on reflection, Joe realized he should have anticipated it. It wasn't exactly part of a pattern, but his act this evening had a precedent. He went over the collection of bags, satisfied, and had them sent off. "The order form is a bonus. It's the envelope he thought would be the most important for us right now."

Dupoulis cocked his right eyebrow. "Are we looking for a matching set, perhaps?"

"Exactly, Sergeant, exactly." Joe grinned. He liked working with Ken.

"Got it," Ken said, and carried the box out to the cruiser to send it on its way. Joe turned to the newspaper he had found in the Rabelard cellar, spreading it out on his now empty desk.

The newspaper was dated Friday, November 8, 1974, soon after Mrs. Keogh had collapsed in the courthouse and died. *The Marion County Clarion* was a regional weekly, full of reports of town committee meetings, school lunch menus for the coming week, summaries of national news, and essays by local residents. It was, in short, doing its best to be all things to all people. Joe leafed through the paper, or rather he lifted one page and turned it over, laying it down as gently as he could, reading headlines, first paragraphs, until he came to the item he was looking for. Under the simple headline "Killer Sentenced" was a succinct three-paragraph report:

A Canadian convicted of aggravated assault, manslaughter, attempted robbery, and robbery in a three-week crime spree in which one person was killed and fourteen people injured was sentenced yesterday to prison. Pierre J. Lereon was sentenced to nineteen years and four months without possibility of parole for his role in a crime spree that covered much of northern New Hampshire, Vermont, and New York.

Lereon was identified by several witnesses in three states, several of whom traveled long distances to testify at his trial. He was said to have been accompanied during this period by a young man who was never identified, and is still at large. In Vermont one witness testified that he had been accompanied by a woman, but police could find no corroboration for this.

Lereon began his crime spree in the smallest county in the state and soon traveled over three states before returning to New Hampshire. During his arraignment his attorney attempted to offer an insanity defense, but Lereon repeatedly interrupted him to insist on pleading not guilty. During his trial he did not take the stand, and several times tried to interrupt the proceedings. The trial attracted a great deal of publicity because of the number of victims and the wide swath of his travels.

Joe looked back up at the date: 1974. It explained far more than he had expected. It was no wonder Vic Rabelard had panicked Friday afternoon. He had spent the last several years believing he had won, had persuaded his wife to stay, to break her promise to leave him when her twenty years were up, only to confront the possibility that he had miscalculated, that she could be found and carried off.

Joe reread the news report. Eliot Keogh's story, as absurd as it had seemed each time he had told it, no matter how persuasive his apparent honesty, now made complete sense. Driving along the outer stretches of Pickering Street, Vic Rabelard and Mindy had passed by the Preserve and Eliot Keogh's light-blue Volvo, with its Canadian license plate. That and her upcoming twentieth anniversary in Mellingham were enough to trigger her memory of a man long out of her life, to remind her of another promise she could not ignore. The timing of the Volvo's appearance, and perhaps the face of a man who seemed vaguely familiar though she could not place him, a remnant of her days in the courtroom, must have seemed an omen that her time was up. Whatever she said to her husband then must have undermined every confidence he had ever had that he could make her change her mind and remain with him always. Eliot Keogh became the enemy. It was no wonder Vic Rabelard went half-crazy with rage, chasing down and attacking the stranger supposedly from Canada.

The greater irony, it seemed to Joe, was that Vic Rabelard lay now in a coma completely unaware of what had happened to him or to his wife. And if the doctors' predictions were accurate, he never would know, not even if he recovered consciousness and enough strength of body and mind to ever leave the hospital. And that was something his wife might never know.

NINE

Monday Morning

A WARM SUMMER SUN on the patches of sweat on the driveway always seemed portentous to Hugh Chase, partly because he associated them with airports in subtropical climes, which is where he first became aware of them, and partly because the world was still quiet at that hour when he looked out on his driveway and saw the steam rising. But mostly this morning felt portentous because it was. He knew Joe Silva would be back, that in fact the police had never really left the night before.

Hugh stood on the back steps with a mug of coffee and felt the damp rising off the grass. It would be humid today. It was not yet six o'clock and already the sweat was spreading across his chest. It was even too early to complain about it to anyone; he could hear no one else in the neighborhood. Becka and Tony were probably still asleep, he told himself as he settled into a lawn chair in the back yard. He wanted to sit here and wait, be ready when the moment came, watch it unfold. This consciousness of choosing to watch made him feel less passive. During the past several hours, he had lain in bed in the dark and gone over repeatedly what he would and would not say. There wasn't much in either category. The difference between immaturity and maturity, he had concluded, was the difference between doing the right thing by accident and doing the right thing by choice, consciously, when it had to be done, without explanations or excuses. He wouldn't say that, of course; he would think it and remember it when he needed to.

The early morning wore on slowly while he waited. When the first sign of what was about to happen appeared, it was the one contingency Hugh had not planned for. Richard Ostell pulled into the driveway and parked halfway on the narrow verge behind Tony's car. Richard climbed out and then Eliot Keogh climbed out on the passenger's side. When they saw Hugh out back, the two men walked down the driveway toward him.

"Great idea, this," Eliot said as he approached. Hugh glanced at Richard, who shrugged his shoulders. "I'm glad I ran into Chief Silva. I was beginning to think I was going to have nothing but bad memories every time I saw him—or any policeman." Eliot sat down on the bench of the picnic table and slapped his hands down on his thighs. "Nice place," he said, looking around.

"How 'bout some coffee?" Hugh asked, still looking at Richard for an explanation.

"Don't bother. I'll get it," Eliot said, jumping up. "In the pot, right?" Hugh nodded and mentioned the other breakfast foods he had left out on the counter. Eliot hurried into the house. At least that hadn't changed, Hugh mused; Eliot had spent his first sixteen years living as much in his friends' homes as his own. When he had disappeared beyond a slamming screen door, Hugh turned to Richard.

"All right," Hugh said, "what happened?" Richard fell into a chair and stretched out his legs.

"Chief Silva called me this morning at five-thirty—five-thirty—and told me I should come over here for an early breakfast," Richard said looking around, "and I should bring Eliot with me. He ran into Silva at the Agawam this morning so he was ready when I arrived." Richard paused. "How do you run into someone at five-thirty in the morning?" He hung his thumbs on his belt, crossed his legs at the ankles, and stared at the sky. After a moment of silence, he turned to Hugh and said, "Why?"

Hugh had been trying to think of something to say to fend off the inevitable question but then decided against it. It was probably only a matter of minutes before every detail was made plain to everyone—at least that was his hope. In a way, it would be a relief to face it all. Perhaps then he could get on with a future, a real one this time instead of a construct that gave the illusion that all was well. He had once read that people with psychological problems who finally decide to face them and go into therapy often found their fastidious, meticulous grooming undergoing a change. The obsessive concern with appearance gives way to an ease with one's dress and manner. Hair is allowed to fall into disarray by a gust of wind or a nervous hand; designer slacks give way to clean but unpressed denims; a casual jacket becomes a well-worn security blanket. The patient grows healthier and sloppier. A real person emerges. Hugh wondered if his life was going to be like that, if his house would become run down or his job uncertain. He had visions of shingles flying off his roof during a rainstorm, lying uncollected, ignored, on the lawn until he mowed right over them; or newspapers rising in stacks like sky-scrapers across the kitchen floor. Eliot came out the back door carrying a tray.

"Got some for you too, Rich," Eliot said, depositing the tray on the picnic table. "Hope you don't mind how I poked around in your kitchen?" Eliot set out coffee and plates with rolls and glasses of juice as he spoke, paying little attention to the replies that didn't come. The weekend had been a rough one for him. Richard and Hugh joined him at the table, talking desultorily as they ate. Hugh kept one eye on the back door and the other on the street, wondering if Becka or Silva would be the next to appear.

HUGH COULD SEE Becka moving about in the kitchen just as a second cruiser arrived. She must have heard it too because she paused at the sink and turned back toward the front of the house. Hugh put down his mug. He should go in, and he should take Richard with him, warning him what was about to happen to all of them. It seemed to him that Richard was the one of the three of them who had aged the least. All of them had had their losses, but Richard remained young, living his life of independence, making jokes about everything, including a disastrous loss at work or a girlfriend who walked out of his life. Hugh was idly wondering what it must be like when Becka threw open the screen door. Her eyes were wild with confusion and fear; her bathrobe had fallen open, revealing creamy breasts that would begin to sag in a few years. Eliot and Richard moved at once to her side. Hugh got up to follow, wondering why he moved so slowly, as though his body were different from theirs, of different stuff that had a harder time pushing through the atmosphere.

"You said it was nothing," she said to her husband. "We were just helping the police out." She began to shake, gripping the railing with a fierceness he had never seen in her before.

Richard and Eliot began asking her what was wrong.

"They're taking him, our son," she said to Richard. "They say he poisoned Vic." Hugh never remembered exactly what happened after that. Becka flew into his arms, propelled by Tony crashing through the back door, shoving her aside, and running to his car. He managed to get it started, careered around the front of his father's car before running his front wheel onto the stone steps, the fender crashing against the iron railing. He braked and tried to extricate himself but a police car pulled across his path. In a series of rigorous and fluid movements, Sergeant Dupoulis pulled open the door, grabbed Tony's hands, and hauled out the young man from his dented, scraped red car.

"I'd better begin again from the beginning," Dupoulis said when he had Tony standing upright against the car while another officer stood nearby. "You have the right—"

"What is this?" Richard demanded of Joe as the two men drew close to the car. Becka was right behind them, insisting they couldn't do this, that there had to be a mistake. She was still arguing when the cruiser drove away with her son in the back. Richard put his arm around Becka and pulled her along. A police officer emerged from the front of the house carrying a bag.

"What's he doing?" Richard asked.

"He had a warrant," Becka said, sobbing. "I'm getting a lawyer." She repeated this all the way inside, until they were finally out of sight of the neighbors, who were beginning to gather on the sidewalk to speculate on the bizarre car accident at the Chase house.

"I've arrested your son for the attempted murder of Vic Rabelard," Joe said to Richard.

"Not possible," Richard replied, exhibiting the proverbial stiff upper lip to the surprise of his friends. They didn't at first understand that he was rigid with shock.

"Let's go in here," Joe said, ushering them into the living room. "I want to tell you everything I can."

"You'd better," Richard said; he half rose and half sat as he spoke, caught between curiosity about what was going on and an impulse to fight for his son. Joe attended to the comfort of Becka and Hugh, hoping everyone would settle down; they were a volatile group, and every one of them, except Eliot Keogh, had reason to attack him. This would be the hardest day of their lives, Joe thought.

"You know that I've been treating Mr. Rabelard's collapse as a suspicious matter," Joe began with the accompaniment of Becka's weeping. "He had behaved suspiciously on Friday, twice getting into a fight with a stranger, and appearing unsteady on Friday night, when he was sent home in a taxi."

"He was all right," Becka said, catching her breath. "He was perfectly fine when he left."

"That was how it looked," Joe agreed. "When you found him, he was collapsed on the dining room floor, where he seems to have fallen the night before. He had a sandwich and a glass of iced tea, both of which were tested. We also found a pair of men's glasses, which weren't his." Joe paused. "I thought at first they might help me identify someone who visited him before he collapsed, but I later concluded that no one had seen

Mr. Rabelard after the taxi driver left him at his door. What I didn't find there was the tube of antiseptic cream that you picked up, Mrs. Chase.''

''You said he had an allergic reaction,'' Becka said, still casting around in her mind for some explanation that would bring back her son.

''His collapse wasn't an accident,'' Joe said, ''caused by an allergic reaction. I'm sorry, Mrs. Chase, but Vic Rabelard was poisoned by acrylamide, which he unwittingly administered to himself in a skin cream that your son prepared and gave him.''

''You're making this up,'' Becka said. Her voice rose in fear. ''That was my cream. That's what I use all the time. It was my idea to give it to him.'' Becka looked to Hugh for support. He pushed himself up straight in his chair.

''That's right,'' Hugh said. ''Every year.'' He watched himself take the role his wife had cast him in, wondering how long it would take before she would accuse him of hypocrisy.

''You think my son would tamper with something that I might use?'' Becka asked. ''That's an outrage. You don't even know him.''

''No, ma'am,'' Joe said. ''I don't think your son had any intention of hurting you. The cream was meant for Mr. Rabelard. He borrowed it or something like it from you every year. It was a habit of his, and this year Tony was ready for the opportunity.''

''Why would he do something like that? The Rabelards are like family,'' Becka said. ''Besides, it was the same tube I get every year. There was nothing wrong with it.''

''There was nothing wrong with it when you bought it,'' Joe said. ''Tony opened the end of the tube, removed the cream, mixed the powdered form of acrylamide with it, and refilled the tube. Then he closed it up. Pinching the end with a pair of narrow-tipped pliers.'' Joe waited for them to absorb this.

''And then he just forced it on his neighbor,'' Richard said, growing angry.

''No, sir. He made sure Mr. Rabelard would ask for it while he, Tony, was around by making him uncomfortable; Mr. Rabelard thought he was being bitten by mosquitoes so he asked for the cream.''

''Nonsense,'' Becka said, growing bolder. ''How can you make someone think they're being eaten by mosquitoes?''

''Tony shot straight pins at Mr. Rabelard's neck through a peashooter he made from one of the tubes from the bamboo wind chimes,'' Joe said. ''It was very clever.''

''A pea-shooter? Pins? That's absurd,'' Richard said. ''You're making this up.'' His protestations came at every point in Joe's narrative, like a lawyer objecting to questions in a courtroom, but they had begun to lack conviction.

''I know it's hard to believe, but all the evidence points to Tony,'' Joe said. The young man's father was now sitting on the edge of the sofa; his ex-wife was curled into a ball at the other end, her hands clasped between her thighs as she tried to keep herself from trembling. Hugh sat quietly, meditatively in an armchair near his wife. Eliot sat beside him on a wooden chair, too absorbed in the drama to realize how uncomfortable he was. ''We found several straight pins near where Mr. Rabelard stood while he tended his grill. Branches of the yew bushes had been broken and pulled aside near the garage window to give a clear view of the barbecue from inside the garage.'' The care with which the preparations had been made seemed to surprise everyone.

Richard dropped his head into his hands. "I once told him he'd make a good industrial designer because he was so inventive."

"You can't listen to him, Rich," Becka said. "Tony wouldn't do that, he just wouldn't. Don't I know him? Don't I?" She stretched her hand out to him.

"He shot the pins at Vic's neck, making him think the mosquitoes were bad that night, and then he supplied the cream to ease the itching," Joe said. "We have the jar in which the powder came with Tony's fingerprints on it, the tools he used to fix the tube, the peashooter, the pins, the powder he attempted to hide in a box of moth crystals in the garage, also with his fingerprints on it, and the clothes he wore on Friday, which we think will show traces of the powder. He spilled some while he was mixing it with the cream."

Quietly Becka went on crying, mumbling about getting a lawyer, reaching out to hold Hugh's hand. The neighbors had drifted away, only one police car remained, and the day was advancing into ordinary time.

"He wouldn't do that," Becka said, gathering courage for a final assault against the accuser of her only child. "Why would he? He's just at the start of his life. And how could he get a poison like acro-whatever it is? He's just a kid. He works in a bookstore."

"He also works at a paper company sometimes, filling in for other people, and he's free to come and go there at will. That's where he got the toxin," Joe said. He had spent the better part of the night with an old friend, a fellow officer now working in a lab, poring over the small invoice, noting inconsistencies as well as fingerprints. "We have the altered order form with his fingerprints on it."

Richard looked up and studied Joe standing across the room; then he looked at his old friend, Hugh. Becka stopped crying; the stains of her tears down her cheeks turned crusty. Out of the chrysalis of her tears emerged a different view of Hugh and herself.

"You?" she said barely in a whisper. Hugh met her gaze. "You? You did it again? You did it to your own family? What is wrong with you? With all of you? The three of you?" She looked from Hugh to Richard, back and forth. "I'm family. Don't we matter, not to either one of you? Is your precious friendship so important that you'd throw us both away, both me and Tony?" Richard was only beginning to take in her words, but Hugh was wincing at every syllable. "I was never really married to either one of you, was I? Your friendship always came first. I never really mattered. Tony never mattered. You threw us away."

She stared at Hugh. There was nothing to hear in the room, in the house, perhaps even in the neighborhood if she could stretch her mind to such a compass. The way of life she had been living seemed a mere mote of dust on a sunburned path to her future. She turned to Joe. "I have to see my son. He needs me. I'm all he has." She rose and left the room. Moments later she went out the front door. Richard never looked at her. He pushed his right fist into the palm of his left hand, as though trying to determine which one was the stronger.

IT WAS ALMOST NOON before Richard hung up the telephone for the last time. Hugh had spent the hour right after Chief Silva left calling up lawyers until he found one who seemed willing to take the case. Richard had gone through his own list of names and come to the same name in the end. The man was hired, as long as Tony agreed. At this point his father wasn't prepared to guess what his son would or would not agree to. He hung up the telephone after talking to Tony in the police station, reassuring him and promising to visit later in the afternoon with the lawyer.

"Becka's still there," Richard said when Hugh returned to the living room. "She's afraid to leave him alone. I don't know what she expects—rubber hoses, storm troopers, maybe. In Mellingham, yet." He fell into an armchair. "She doesn't want me down there, insists Tony doesn't want me. He'll be better tomorrow, ready to talk. We can start helping him then. We'll get him off, get right on it." He went on a few minutes more in this vein, comforting himself with his plans to rescue his son. "Oh, by the way, Hugh, Becka asked me to tell you that she's not coming back. She'll send someone by to pick up her clothes."

Hugh leaned forward in his chair. The message was not unexpected. He would in fact have been surprised if she had come back at all. No mother could live with a man who had turned her son over to the authorities, no matter how egregious the crime. In this instance, the victim was still alive. Hugh rubbed his hands over his face; he could see Eliot's shoes out of the corner of his eye and realized Eliot had been sitting there in total silence almost the entire morning.

"Where did Chief Silva get the invoice?" Richard asked, breaking into Hugh's thoughts. Hugh lowered his hands and gazed at his old friend. "Where did he get it?" His voice grew lower, gravelly, almost as though he were growling out the words with the last vibrations of his throat before it stilled forever. Hugh went on gazing. In another second Richard lunged at Hugh, who jumped to his feet and fended off his blows with raised arms. Eliot managed to get between them, push them apart, get Richard into his chair. Hugh fell back.

"I'm sorry, Rich," Hugh said. "I didn't have the guts to tell you first. I found it on Saturday morning when I was looking for the forms on Vic's purchase of that paper. I had no idea Tony had ordered something." He sighed and eased himself into his chair.

"Couldn't you have gotten rid of it?" Richard asked in a whisper.

"Even if I'd destroyed the form, the police could have gotten the same information out of the computer."

"You could have cleaned it up," Richard said.

"He ordered the stuff from a place I didn't even know carried it," Hugh explained. "He must have called them. They'd remember. It's a hazardous material. He left a trail, Rich. It was only a matter of time." The three men sank into their own private worlds, each struggling to make in a matter of minutes adjustments that realistically would take years.

"I've been thinking about Vic," Hugh said.

"I think I found a buyer for that truckload," Richard said. "I can hold on until he's better."

"Richard," Hugh said, "he's not going to get better. Not the way you think. He may regain consciousness, if he lives, but he's not going to be Vic again." The atmosphere in the room changed again. "You had to know that."

"Vic once asked me if I'd risk the rest of my life for ten or twenty years of happiness now," Richard said. "I guess that means Mindy isn't coming back and he knew it Friday when she left."

Hugh shook his head. "I don't know what to do about her. I can't believe she just up and left her girls."

"Well, she did, and that leaves just us," Richard continued.

"Just us," Hugh agreed. The living room was large but it was filled with overstuffed furniture in flowery prints, small tables with knickknacks on them, and pictures of pleasant country scenes. It was a very feminine room. It seemed to Hugh that at that moment he was living in someone else's house, a companion observation to his earlier sense of living an untrue life.

"Okay," Richard said. "What's done is done. If it's just us, this is what we'll do." He made the leap to the next step that was the signal feature of his character. "I'll keep the business going, and when Vic gets out of the hospital, he can stay with me." He went on to detail what the insurance would and would not pay for, how he would manage with an invalid at home. "You'll have to take the girls. They have no other relatives that I've ever heard of."

"None," Hugh agreed. "We better talk to them and see how they feel about all this."

"They'll agree," Richard said. "Vic once told me they think of you like another father." The two men glanced at each other, rage flared in their eyes, muscles tensed, and the moment passed. "We'll have to sell their house. Maybe it won't be too hard on them. They're pretty tough."

"You know, I always thought tragedy changed everything," Hugh said, standing up. "Like the death of a major figure in your life. I had this idea as a kid that you lurched from one way of life to another depending

on the tragedies in your life. It isn't true. Life goes on
pretty much as it always has after a disaster. It gets a
little harder or it gets a little easier. But it's the same
life.''

"Shut up and get us a beer," Richard said. "You're
beginning to sound like somebody's mother.''

AN HOUR LATER the kitchen table was littered with
plates and empty beer bottles. Richard and Hugh had
avoided any more talk about the obvious. Their deci-
sions made, they had moved on to baseball, computer
software, the industry. Eliot had the least to say, concentrating on his sandwich, and then on his beer. They
were almost the way he remembered them twenty-six
years ago.

"What did your wife mean?" Eliot asked. "'You
did it again, only this time it was your own family.'''
The question sounded so innocuous that Richard and
Hugh were slow to grasp what was happening.

"Did she say that?" Hugh asked. Eliot nodded,
waiting.

"Must have been a reference to an old argument we
had,'' Hugh said. "Becka never forgets anything. She
holds me accountable for mistakes I made from even
before we were married.'' He tried to laugh.

"So what did it mean?" Eliot asked. All three knew
that Eliot meant to strip away the last layer of deception but the instincts of two of them were, understandably, to ride smoothly over the rough patch. Eliot had
no intention of letting that happen. He wanted to know
exactly how it was, every jolt and bump and creak. He
had come this far and he didn't want to wonder anymore. This time he could know for sure and he would.

"Tell him," Richard said. Hugh cast him an exasperated look. "All right. If you won't, I will. At the end of your junior year," Richard began, turning to his old friend, "your father bought a new car with cash. That was 1968. It was four thousand dollars—a lot of money back then. You told me because you were very impressed that your old man was doing so well. So was I. I told Hugh. Tell him, Hugh. It's time to get it all out."

"All right, all right. I was impressed too." Hugh looked at Eliot. "I told my father. He wasn't impressed. He quizzed me, then told me not to mention it to anyone else, and not to talk about it with you or Rich." He was not ready to say the rest; he would never be ready. He had spent too many years avoiding the truth. Even now, with a will and a desire to move his past into the open, he realized he didn't know how; he had no practice to fall back on.

"It was right after that your father got into trouble," Richard said, stepping in. "Mr. Chase told the IRS. That was the beginning of it."

"That's what that citizenship award was all about, wasn't it?" Eliot asked. Neither man could look at him. "Somehow Mrs. Claflin heard about it and thought you'd acted intentionally. Why was the award never given?"

"My father persuaded Mrs. Claflin that it would upset the investigation," Hugh said. "So she agreed to hold the award."

"Must have given both of them a bad moment there," Eliot said in a tone of voice his friends had never heard before. "Her being so big on good citizenship and your father so proud of you."

"I don't know why we didn't tell you years ago,"

Hugh said. Now that the truth was out, the consequences didn't seem as terrible as he'd expected.

"I came back here this weekend thinking I'd find out who turned in my father," Eliot finally said. The truth surrounded him like a trap, but he was not a stupid animal. He would not rip his leg off in a desperate attempt to free himself. "I even started going door to door, looking for someone who had come into a lot of money." He turned and sneered at the memory of his own behavior. "I was sure someone did it for money, for a reward. The mill was working on a new paper for government work. It had to be that. At least that's how I thought about it for all those years." He shuddered once. "I came to get even. I didn't know how I was going to do it, but that was all I thought about. Finding who did it. Nailing him." Both Richard and Hugh shifted uncomfortably in their chairs.

"Yeah," Richard said. "Don't blame you for that."

"No?" Eliot responded. "I've built my life around finding the man who ruined my family. My mother died within days after my father's sentencing. Dad got out of prison eventually but there was nothing left for him; no one wanted anything to do with him, so he killed himself when he couldn't get a decent job. My older brother took off, never to be seen again. My one goal in life was getting even." He started to sound angry. "As though that would prove my father didn't do anything. It sounds like a bad soap opera." He pushed his chair away from the table. "So here I am. I did what I said I'd do. I found the enemy, chased him down after twenty-five years, and confronted him. And the enemy turns out to be my two oldest friends. And my own big mouth. What a bitch!"

TEN

Monday Afternoon

BECKA CHASE SAT with her knees pressed together, her left leg pushing against the old iron bar of the Mellingham jail, concerned only with her son. By comforting him she hoped to comfort herself, so she had listened to everything he had to say at least ten times over, but she found no comfort in any of it. Still, she would go on listening until she understood intricacies of life beyond everything her prosaic mind had ever shown her. He patted her hand gripping a cast-iron bar when he stopped pacing.

"You don't get it, Mom, do you?" Tony asked her. She shook her head.

Becka had once visited a friend in Philadelphia who lived near an old nineteenth-century prison, a monument to the modern ideas of penal reform along Quakers principles that nevertheless looked like something out of Dickens, with its massive stone walls and windowless expanse. She couldn't understand how her friend managed living so close to it, to the gray bulk looming forever on the edge of her neighborhood, and then she saw that her friend and her neighbors simply ignored the prison. And now her own life was going to be like that. Her son would be convicted of attempted murder and put someplace like that. She would move from Mellingham to be as close to her son as possible, but no one would know her, no one would acknowledge her because she would not ignore the prison. She would focus her attentions on the wrong side of the street and so she would cease to exist.

"I don't understand what happened, Tony?" Becka whispered. "He was our neighbor, our friend. You've known him all your life."

Tony cocked his head and looked at her and smiled. "You don't have to talk like that to me, Mom. I know what he was."

"What're you talking about? He was our friend. He's your father's business partner."

"He was a piece of shit, Mom. I know what he did to you. I know you left Dad for him." Becka gasped. "You used to drop me off at Larry's house and I watched you drive away. But sometimes Larry wasn't home from school yet because he walked and I took the bus. So I'd walk around town until he got back and sometimes I saw you heading over to that cottage behind the town warehouse—you and Vic. I even heard you once. I was just a kid, I didn't know what was going on, but I knew you were there so one day when Larry and I had a fight and I wanted to go home, I just walked on over to the cottage and there you were." He dropped his eyes and blushed. "Yeah, well, I knew how you felt about Vic."

"Oh, Tony." Becka struggled against her sobs.

"So then he made you leave Dad and he didn't marry you." He slammed his fists together. "He was a real shit, Mom, a real shit."

"That was over a dozen years ago."

"Last week wasn't," Tony said.

"What are you talking about?"

"I saw him, I saw him trying to get to you again. I knew what he was up to. I knew he was having trouble with Mindy so he was going off again, looking for someone to make him feel better. He wrecked our home with Dad, and he was going to wreck our home with Hugh. Maybe Hugh isn't all that Dad is, but you love him and I figure he's okay. We were happy there. But Vic didn't care about that, not him."

"Tony, you can't mean it."

"Why can't I? I know how Hugh felt about you having an affair. I knew what he'd do. He's that kind of guy, real strict. But Vic didn't care. He'd push you any way he wanted to get what he wanted. That was my home too, you know."

"Tony, no one kills—"

"I saw how he treated you," Tony hissed, and Becka was suddenly afraid of her own son. "I saw him on Friday, and if I were big enough I'd have done something there and then, but I couldn't. Don't try to put me off; I know what he was like. He's come at you before. I've seen him. And he acts like nothing's wrong. He pats me on the head like I'm some ten-year-old, too stupid to know what's going on. He can't do to me what he did to you. He was a shit."

"You mustn't talk like that, Tony," Becka said, shushing him in case any of the police officers could hear him, wondering when her son took on the role of taking care of her.

AS A GENERAL RULE Joe Silva did not initiate long conversations in the second office on the main floor, where Sergeant Dupoulis was at that moment typing on a computer keyboard and whistling between his teeth, a habit Joe had learned to live with. He moved over to the sergeant's desk and sat down next to it. Dupoulis stopped typing, looked expectantly at the chief, and then flushed. He was caught and he knew it.

"I'd figured you'd get cranky while you were dieting," Joe began, "but I was kind of surprised when you got so stiff."

"Yes sir."

"You didn't have anything to say to anyone," Joe went on.

"No sir."

"You really had me worried there."

"Yes sir."

"You must have been downright miserable."

"Yes sir." He paused. "It cut into my back something awful."

Joe nodded. "Kind of ironic. Women take them off and men put them on."

"Yes sir."

"Never liked a woman in a girdle," Joe said, "It isn't natural."

"Yes sir." Dupoulis waited, then collapsed. "I tried, sir. I really did. You don't know what it was like. I was starving myself. I did everything they told me to do at the diet place—writing down every single thing I ate, reading every package before I ate anything, even weighing some of my food. It was the most miserable six months of my life. It's unnatural living like that. For me, anyway. I just wasn't meant to be thin."

"Maybe not," Joe agreed. "Anyway, after the way you handled yourself today, catching Tony Ostell, I don't think the selectmen are going to worry too much about weight interfering with the performance of your duties. I'll put in a word."

"Thank you, sir." Dupoulis leaned back in his chair, a familiar figure once again.

"Is that why you didn't wear it this morning?" Joe asked. "Had an idea you might have to go after someone?"

"Not exactly, sir," the sergeant said. "I just wanted to be comfortable for what I thought would be a difficult job."

"Good decision, Ken," Joe said, standing up. He was about to touch him when he realized he couldn't, that in the culture that dominated in Mellingham, one man didn't embrace another. Proud to think himself free of an Anglo standard he personally deplored, he found himself trapped by another. "Good work," Joe said again and left the room. It was indeed a strange world.

ELIOT KEOGH looked different to Joe Silva the minute he saw him standing in the doorway to his office. The paper salesman was wearing the same clothes he'd had on earlier in the day, but that was all that was the same. Joe motioned Eliot to a chair and waited to hear what he'd already surmised.

"I think the pair of glasses you found might be mine," Eliot began after sitting down.

"And why do you think that?" Joe asked.

"I lost them during that fight with Mr. Rabelard out at the Pickering Preserve," Eliot said. "And when I went back out to look for them, they weren't there."

"Can you describe them?" Joe asked. Eliot did so; satisfied, Joe opened a desk drawer and removed a manila envelope, opened it, and slid out the glasses.

"How did you know they were mine?" Eliot asked.

"I watched you drive on Sunday," Joe said, "and

you avoided driving around Mellingham on Saturday. You were searching your car for them at the Inn on Saturday before we talked. Am I right?'' Eliot nodded. ''I also watched Vic Rabelard identify someone in a crowd in the Loblolly Bar he would not have been able to see if he'd needed to wear these.''

''I was beginning to worry about getting the car back to the airport without them.'' Elliot put the glasses in his shirt pocket.

''If you hadn't come for them, you wouldn't have gotten out of town,'' Joe said. ''Not the way you drive.''

''That's why you wanted me there this morning?''

''Partly,'' Joe agreed.

''Partly?'' Eliot paused.

''You've been looking for someone,'' Joe said, ''and I thought you should find him before you left.'' Eliot stiffened.

''How did you know I was looking for anyone?''

''Mr. Keogh, you lived in this town long enough to know the answer to that,'' Joe said.

''I guess so,'' Eliot conceded, relaxing a little. ''So you knew Hugh Chase was the person I was looking for?''

''I put it together,'' Joe said, deciding not to relate his Sunday telephone call to Mrs. Claflin.

''Good guess,'' Eliot commented. He thought about the two men he had left in silence on Basker Court, of how he had congratulated himself for keeping his temper, for controlling his rage. It was a new experience, taking pride in his emotional control. ''I finally got the whole story.'' Eliot told Joe about his father's purchase of a flashy car with cash, and the path of the news, all the way to the IRS and back to the mill. ''I have built my life around tracing the person who did this to me, to my family, cursing the man—or woman—who took me away from the best friends, the best life a guy could ever have.'' He sighed, but his breath caught in his chest, trembled there, and sank down, like his anger earlier in the day. He took a deep breath, and continued.

"Here," Joe said, pushing a glass of ice water toward him.

"Thanks." Eliot drank. "I have lived my life trying to correct my father's life, going to work for the same company, proving how honest I am day after day, year after year. I never bought anything big with cash, nothing more than twenty or thirty dollars. And all so I could face down the man who started it all, the man who was so mean that he could turn in my old man. As though that would make him innocent.'' He reached for the glass of water again.

"And you found him," Joe said.

"Yup." He gulped down the water. Upstairs he could hear a chair moving across the wooden floor, voices.

"At least you faced it," Joe said.

"Yeah." He set the glass down, lifting it on its edge to see if it left a ring on the desk. "At least I faced it, faced knowing that my father cheated his company, cheated the government, lied to his family, and risked everything for a few thousand dollars,'' Eliot said, still looking at the glass. "I've been operating on the hope, the delusion, really, that if I found the person who turned him in I'd also find a reason to believe my father was innocent. It was a hope hidden so deep I don't think I realized I had it. It was the one part of my childhood I never grew out of. And it was a lie. He was guilty of everything he was convicted of." Eliot paused. "It's like finding out he really was a stranger."

"What are you going to do now?" Joe asked.

"Now, I'm going to learn to live without the lie." He took out his handkerchief and wiped the beads of sweat from his forehead and chin.

"It's over now," Joe agreed.

"You know what really surprises me?" Eliot continued, "I might never have known if Vic Rabelard hadn't singled me out. He got us all stirred up this weekend. If it weren't for Vic, I probably would have left Rich and Hugh alone in their grief or left early— frustrated and angry. And never found out. Where is she now—Mindy?"

"Somewhere in Canada," Joe said. "We think she crossed the border on Sunday. The authorities will try to locate her and tell her what's happened to Vic, but I'm not optimistic."

"She won't come back, will she?"

Joe shook his head. "I got the feeling she was never really here."

Eliot would leave and get over the open wounds of his childhood, but for the others, the wounds were fresh. As hard as it might be to believe, Mindy had left her stepdaughters and husband, and they would have to live with that forever. For years to come people would be shocked at the story, exaggerate it into a legend, yet still be amazed when they heard the same story from another town, read about another case in the newspaper.

"Rich and Hugh have already worked out how they're going to take care of Vic and the girls," Eliot said.

The memory of that conversation in Hugh Chase's

living room stayed with him the longest. By the time he was on the road to Logan Airport in the late afternoon he had forgotten his embarrassment at having doors slammed in his face for his impertinent questions; he had forgotten the scabs and bruises on his face, neck, and hands, so that he failed to notice the surprised looks from the young woman at the car rental desk and the man at the airlines check-in; he had forgotten the wonderful feeling of frothy, fey foolishness on Friday night, even forgetting to tell his wife. Instead, he remembered the morning in Hugh Chase's living room when he and Richard divvied up the work of caring for Vic and raising his daughters. At first Eliot was outraged and bitterly resentful that the two men who had been the cause of the long years of misery and loss his family had suffered could pretend to show such compassion for another; then he was jealous that they had never done as much for him while his family was falling apart. In the end, he loved them for who they were and who they had been, he admired them for the way they stepped in to help, and he was proud to remember them as friends because he believed that, ultimately, given the opportunity, they would have done the same for him.

IN AND OUT

A DON PACKHAM AND FRANK MITCHELL MYSTERY

Mat Coward

Whether he's miserably depressed or buoyantly cheerful, a day with the delightfully unpredictable Detective Inspector Don Packham is never dull for his partner, DC Frank Mitchell. When the body of Yvonne "Chalkie" Wood, a member of the Hollow Head Pub's darts team, is found bludgeoned, Packham and Mitchell accept an unspoken challenge from a clever killer.

Her untimely murder puts the detectives on a case of money, sex and secrets that requires luck, skill—and an excellent aim—to solve.

Available May 2003
at your favorite retail outlet.

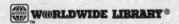

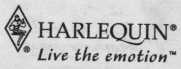

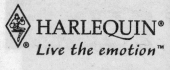